"What is it,

She didn't exactly know. She only knew that something had happened to that magic moment they'd shared. Suddenly she felt curiously awkward and unsure of herself. "Jay..."

"You don't have to apologize. You never have to apologize to me. Remember that, will you?" They sat, side by side, on the edge of her bed. "I feel like I've broken into a dormitory at a select girls' school." He flashed a devilish grin at her.

"Yes, it looks like that, doesn't it," Hilary agreed, appraising her room. "I should do something about it."

"On the contrary, maybe you should leave it exactly as is. It's a study in pale pink and white and girlishness." He glanced down at the bed. "You must have had many romantic dreams in this, Hilary. How many handsome young princes came here to court your favors?"

Dear Reader,

Spellbinders! That's what we're striving for. The editors at Silhouette are determined to capture your imagination and win your heart with every single book we publish. Each month, six Special Editions are chosen with *you* in mind.

Our authors are our inspiration. Writers such as Nora Roberts, Tracy Sinclair, Kathleen Eagle, Carole Halston and Linda Howard—to name but a few—are masters at creating endearing characters and heartrending love stories. Their characters are everyday people—just like you and me—whose lives have been touched by love, whose dreams and desires suddenly come true!

So find a cozy, quiet place to read, and create your own special moment with a Silhouette Special Edition.

Sincerely,

The Editors
SILHOUETTE BOOKS

MAGGI CHARLES
The Star Seeker

Silhouette Special Edition

Published by Silhouette Books New York

America's Publisher of Contemporary Romance

For Rives...
our friendly neighborhood banker

SILHOUETTE BOOKS
300 East 42nd St., New York, N.Y. 10017

Copyright © 1987 by Koehler Associates, Ltd

ISBN: 0-373-09381-0

First Silhouette Books printing May 1987

America's Publisher of Contemporary Romance

Printed in the U.S.A.

Books by Maggi Charles

Silhouette Romance

Magic Crescendo #134

Silhouette Intimate Moments

My Enemy, My Love #90

Silhouette Special Edition

Love's Golden Shadow #23
Love's Tender Trial #45
The Mirror Image #158
That Special Sunday #258
Autumn Reckoning #269
Focus on Love #305
Yesterday's Tomorrow #336
Shadow on the Sun #362
The Star Seeker #381

MAGGI CHARLES

is a confirmed traveler who readily admits that "people and places fascinate me." A prolific author, who is also known to her romance fans as Meg Hudson, Ms. Charles states that if she hadn't become a writer she would have been a musician, having studied the piano and harp. A native New Yorker, she is the mother of two sons and currently resides in Cape Cod, Massachusetts, with her husband.

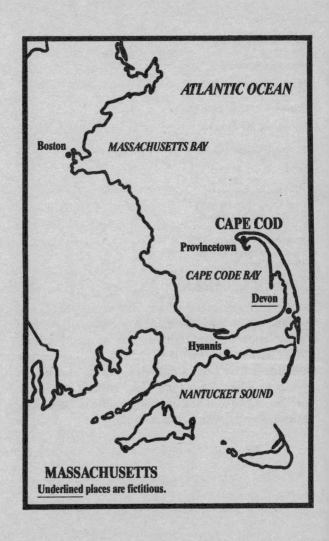

ATLANTIC OCEAN

Boston   *MASSACHUSETTS BAY*

CAPE COD

Provincetown

CAPE CODE BAY

Devon

Hyannis

NANTUCKET SOUND

MASSACHUSETTS
Underlined places are fictitious.

Chapter One

The huge community hall had been transformed into a carnival midway for this special occasion. The fortune-teller's booth was in the far left corner, set up to symbolize a nomadic tent pitched among the remote dunes of the sultry Sahara.

Soon rumors began circulating that the fortune-teller—billed as Madame Zola, Palmist Extraordinaire—was good. Very good. So good that Hilary had no desire to consult her and was relieved when George Delacorte suggested they bypass the tent and get something to eat.

"I'm starving," George explained, and Hilary smiled. George, thin as the proverbial bean pole, was always hungry.

As they stood in line at the concession stand, Ed and Helen Bentley joined them. Ed, looking perplexed, exclaimed, "Boy, that Madame Zola's scary! Was she ever right on. She told me things..." He paused, shaking his head in wonder. "You should go for it, Hilary," he advised.

Helen sputtered, "Men! It was all I could do to push you in there!" She scowled at her husband. Then, mellowing, she admitted, "Madame Zola *is* good, Hilary. Uncanny, really. She looked at my palm and—" Helen shivered. "It was kind of scary."

Hilary forced a laugh. "Probing the future can be frightening," she told Helen. "I don't think I want to know what the stars have in store for me."

"That's a chicken philosophy, Hilary," George Delacorte scoffed. "Come on, let's skip the hot dog and consult Madame Zola." He added suggestively, "Maybe she'll tell you there's a tall, blond, exciting man in your life. Someone who looks exactly like me!"

Hilary smiled. George was tall and blond, but far from exciting. He was a beloved friend, comfortable as an old sweater.

George's tone changed. He peered down at Hilary and said, "Seriously, why not see what Madame Zola has to say? You could do with a psychological shot in the arm." He tugged Hilary out of line as he spoke. She tried to draw back, but his grip was firm. Not wanting to make a scene, she shrugged and accepted his lead, daunted by his perception. She hadn't realized her unhappiness was so obvious.

Still, as they neared the fortune-teller's tent, Hilary made one last attempt to divert George. "There's a line a mile long," she pointed out. "We'll be here all night...."

"You stand in line and keep our place, and I'll go back and get the hot dogs. Then we'll have the best of both worlds," George temporized.

Munching her hot dog as they slowly edged forward, Hilary chided herself for taking this small happening so seriously. But she really didn't want to have her fortune told. She didn't want to look beyond the next minute. When they were close enough to the tent for her to read the sign stating that Madame Zola charged ten dollars per person, she took the opportunity to balk.

"That's ridiculous!" she protested. "George, where's your sense of Yankee thrift?"

George was already fishing a twenty-dollar bill from his wallet. "It's for a good cause," he told Hilary calmly.

It was, of course. The carnival was the brainchild of the Cape Codders Club. The Saturday night proceeds were going to the families of four fishermen who had been lost at sea off Provincetown shortly before Christmas.

Defeated, Hilary insisted, "You first."

"Okay," George agreed, "if it'll make you happier." At the tent opening, he turned to tell her he'd wait for her by the cotton-candy booth.

Hilary nodded, preoccupied. There was no use telling herself that she was paranoid for feeling nervous about having her fortune told. She *was* nervous.

She was just getting over the past. She had no desire to probe into the future. Probably Madame Zola was a rank amateur who'd struck it lucky with Ed and Helen. Probably the "palmist extraordinaire" was the wife of a member of the Cape Codders Club—a business-oriented organization—or a member herself. It was stupid to be so apprehensive.

Time went by. Hilary passed the minutes by tilting mental swords at memories she wanted to keep at bay. Finally, George emerged from the tent…and he wasn't smiling. He looked as if he'd just been given a shock.

Scrutinizing him, Hilary decided he *was* in shock. He glanced at her abstractedly, focused and managed to say, "You're up next." Then he turned and vanished into the crowd.

Hilary hesitated, yearning to flee. Behind her, a woman said, "It's your turn, dear." The woman's irritation fil-

tered through her surface politeness. Trapped, Hilary lifted
the tent flap and went inside.

She found herself in a fantasy midnight world. The tent
walls were deep blue, sprinkled with gold stars. The dim
lights were also blue, except for a single red globe next to the
fortune-teller's table.

The table was small and round, draped with a fringed red
cloth that brushed the floor. The floor was covered with a
vivid, multipatterned Oriental rug, and incense burned. It
was a musky, seductive scent, sandalwood or patchouli.

Madame Zola sat behind the table in a wide chair pad-
ded with bright-colored satin pillows. In contrast, the chair
in front of the table was a plain wooden one.

Hilary became aware of a hand waving her toward the
wooden chair. A melodious voice commanded, "Sit down,
please."

Hilary sat, hoping someone had told Madame Zola there
was a long line waiting outside. Then maybe the fortune-
teller might be motivated to hurry with this interview.

The palmist's smooth, caressing voice intoned, "You need
not be afraid, mademoiselle. There is no need to fear the
future. Knowledge is power."

Why should such an old cliché sound so profound? It
went to prove that putting a point across depended mainly
on the way it was delivered. Next, the woman would be
saying, "It is written in the stars," or something equally
trite, Hilary muttered silently, trying to find safety in scoff-
ing.

As if on cue, the fortune-teller stated solemnly, "What is
written in the stars is for our guidance. To steer our way to
celestial heights." Amazingly, these ridiculous statements
did not sound trite at all. "So, mademoiselle," the palmist
went on, "move your chair closer to the table, if you
please?"

Hilary edged forward.

"Now," came the command, "give me your hand. The right one."

Responding like an obedient child, Hilary stretched out her hand. It was at once enveloped by a hand considerably larger than hers, a hand encased in a silky pink glove. Mesmerized by the touch of the palmist's glove, Hilary glanced up wonderingly into Madame Zola's face, only to find it was impossible to see very much.

The fortune-teller was wearing a high turban fashioned of gold metallic cloth. A black lace veil stretched above her nose, hiding most of her face from view. Only her eyes were visible...and she had gorgeous eyes. Dark as midnight, large black velvet orbs fringed by luxurious silken lashes. Hypnotic eyes.

Hilary felt the full force of their power and wasn't ready for it. She was actually becoming giddy from the effect of the palmist's intense midnight gaze. Heavens, this woman was a witch!

Madame Zola said gently, "You are troubled. Very troubled."

Hilary was unable to move, unable to divert her concentration away from those spellbinding eyes. Was it her imagination, or were Madame Zola's eyes actually growing larger with every passing moment?

"I see no ring on your finger," the seer intoned, "nor a lighter circle where a ring might have been. You have not been committed then..."

Hilary twitched tensely, and was sure Madame Zola caught the instinctive movement. With a slight, affirmative nod the palmist droned on, "You have not been committed *legally*. But there has been a relationship. Ah, yes, *cherie*, you have given yourself totally to a man, and he has rejected you...."

Hearing this, it was impossible for Hilary to remain still. She wiggled, and now there was a note of triumph in Madame Zola's voice as she continued, "Two men. Yes. Because of the second man, the first man rejected you. Yes." Madame Zola paused, her attention fully upon Hilary's palm. "I see tragedy, despair," the sonorous voice chimed, a fateful clock tolling dreaded hours. "Death!" Madame Zola intoned, and Hilary flinched.

"I am right, am I not?" The palmist's voice became velvet soft again. "Yes," Madame Zola nodded, "there are lingering shadows beneath your eyes. Such lovely eyes, too. So light, so clear. Like arctic ice, with just a hint of blue reflection from the winter sky. One wonders what will happen when that ice thaws, *cherie*!"

There was a suggestive purr to the fortune-teller's voice, and Hilary sat up straighter. If Madame Zola came on like this to another woman, how must she come on to a man? No wonder George had looked so shaken as he emerged from the tent.

"This man you loved...he was cruel to you," Madame Zola stated suddenly, speaking in a monotone. "He cast you aside, you became a discarded garment. You fell into the gutter of your own disillusionment—"

"Please!" Hilary protested.

Madame Zola's dark eyelashes fluttered. She pressed a pink-gloved hand across her forehead and moaned slightly, as if she were emerging from a trance. "What?" she asked vaguely.

"You said I fell into the gutter of my own disillusionment," Hilary quoted. "I did *not* fall into a gutter, either actually or...or metaphorically. I was hurt, yes. Bruised and shaken. But I did not stoop to the gutter, Madame Zola."

"Ah," the fortune-teller breathed. "So sometimes my words do not express exactly what I wish to say, mademoiselle. My English, it is not perfect."

Hilary was already aware that Madame Zola spoke with a slight accent. But just now she could have sworn the accent had oddly intensified.

"I will find the right words," Madame Zola decided, her accent definitely more pronounced. "This first man, he did cast you aside, did he not, *cherie*?"

"Yes," Hilary admitted. "Yes, he did."

"And it was because of the second man?"

"I suppose that's true."

"The second man. He was older?"

"Yes, he was older. He was my uncle."

"Of course. Family duty was forced upon you, and your sense of loyalty caused you to renounce your lover. Yes, I can see that here, written in your palm. A very strong loyalty line. Nearly as strong as your heart line, which is very strong indeed."

The fortune-teller was scanning Hilary's palm as she spoke. Temporarily, Hilary gained a reprieve from the emotional force of those astonishing dark eyes. Then Madame Zola glanced up, and the impact was stronger than ever.

"You should, perhaps, not have left your lover," she said.

"I *had* to leave him," Hilary blurted desperately. "But it was only temporary; Roy knew that. Uncle Chad was so terribly ill. Despite the fight he was putting up, we knew his days were numbered. I had to go to him and stay with him. He'd done that for me when my parents died. He'd given up so much for me. Maybe if it hadn't been for having a twelve-year-old girl thrust into his care, he would have married. Maybe everything would have been different for him."

It was all Hilary could do to keep from putting her head down on the table in front of her and crying her eyes out.

Memories swirled, and this was exactly what she didn't want. She'd come back to Devon a week ago, determined to repair some badly shattered life pieces and start looking forward, not backward. She was more than ready to turn a new page. A whole book of new pages . . .

So much had happened during the past eight months since she'd last been on the Cape, very little of it good. Her Uncle Chad, her only surviving relative, had become ill. Very ill. There had been surgery and the later verdict everyone had dreaded—cancer.

Long weeks of chemotherapy followed for Chad Forsythe. He was incredibly brave throughout this miserable time and remarkably cheerful. Hilary stayed with him, moving to his Back Bay town house, going with him to the hospital for the treatments, trying to prepare food that might tempt his flagging appetite, determined just to *be* there for as long as he needed her.

He was very, very dear to her. After the death of her parents, her bachelor uncle had become both surrogate mother and father to her.

Her devotion to Chad, though, had provoked a disastrous side effect. Her relationship with Roy LeClair suffered irreparably. Until she moved in with her uncle, Hilary and Roy had been sharing their lives and Roy's apartment on Boston's Beacon Hill. Neither of them wanted marriage right away. Instead, they enjoyed the best of two worlds. They had the freedom of being independent while still being deeply committed to each other. Or so Hilary had thought.

During the months of Chad's illness, Roy had resented being put in second place. Hilary tried to make this up to him whenever they were together, but those were snatched times, woefully incomplete. She always needed to return to her uncle too soon, at least from Roy's point of view. Problems began to surface, and there was never a chance to work at solving them.

Still, the subject of ending their relationship never arose. Despite their temporary difficulties, Hilary felt secure about Roy and thought he felt equally secure about her. So, the morning after her uncle's funeral this past January—a funeral Roy hadn't attended—she packed her suitcase and trudged back over to Beacon Hill. Tired, grieving and battered by the erosive emotions of the last few months, she wanted Roy as she'd never wanted anyone before.

Her key was buried deep in her handbag and, rather than dig through everything, she knocked on the apartment door. There was no response, though Roy was usually home painting at that time of day.

Thinking that perhaps Roy couldn't hear her, Hilary rang the bell. No one answered its summons. Only then did she put down her suitcase, fumble for her key and insert the key in the lock. But nothing happened. The key wouldn't turn, the lock wouldn't work.

It took Hilary a long, shocked moment to realize that Roy had actually changed the lock and shut her out....

The memory of it all swept over her now in a sickening wave. She never should've entered this tent to have her fortune told. She started to get up, intending to bring this bizarre session to an end, but Madame Zola waved her back to her seat with an imperious hand.

There was an odd expression in the fortune-teller's eyes. Sympathy and concern? Or was it anger? Somehow those disparate elements managed to merge, as Madame Zola stated firmly, "If your lover abandoned you because you felt you had to go to your uncle in his need, then he is not a man worthy of your love." Staring deeply into Hilary's eyes, she added portentously, "I see a love cast away... but another love emerging."

"Please," Hilary protested. "I don't want another love."

"You cannot alter destiny," Madame Zola said loftily. "There will be another love in your life. A lover so magnificent he will brush the past from your memory. He will transport you to uncharted regions. Together you will seek the stars, and they will shower upon you riches and a passion you cannot imagine.''

Madame Zola drew a long breath and continued, more calmly, ''You came to this town only recently?''

''Yes.''

''But your ties are old ones?''

''Yes. My grandmother was born in Devon. She married a Bostonian but then inherited her family's homestead here. It was left to Uncle Chad, and now it's mine. Before long, I have to make some decisions....''

''It is a valuable piece of property?''

''Yes, although I've never really thought much about what it's worth. It's more a question of whether I want the responsibility of maintaining it. Having such a large house at this stage of my life might be more of a burden than a luxury.''

''You are indeed fortunate,'' Madame Zola murmured. ''A wealthy young woman...and so beautiful, too. The stars showered you with their favors, *cherie*, though just now you may doubt that. But soon the moon will shine upon you with silver radiance. I see this written in the fate lines that cross your palm.''

''I wouldn't call myself wealthy,'' Hilary protested. ''Uncle Chad did safeguard the money my parents left me, and I am his sole survivor, but—''

What was she doing, discussing both her intimate personal affairs and her finances with this...this charlatan?

But was Madame Zola a charlatan? Despite the woman's outlandish costume, despite the phoniness of her blue tent and her dim lights and her curiously accented mumbo jumbo, there was something not only mysterious but almost uncanny about the fortune-teller. Those amazing eyes and that hypnotic voice added up to a potent combination, a magical charm. Also, she possessed a certain sincerity. Even Hilary, despite her suspicions, had to admit that.

The fortune-teller said softly, "So, you are alone in the world. You must think for yourself, make decisions for yourself." Madame Zola paused meditatively, then continued, "Your hand, *cherie*, shows me how temporary this present unhappy condition is in your life. Your name," the fortune-teller digressed, "I . . . I see an H?"

"Yes."

"Helen?"

"No. Hilary."

"Hilary. It is a musical name. Rhythmic, like yourself," Madame Zola went on, somewhat obliquely. "Ah, my Hilary, you may look like an ice maiden. But you sit before a descendant of the ancient pharaohs of Egypt. From my ancestors, the great gift of divination was passed to me in a direct line."

Was it imagination, or was Madame Zola's accent—presumably French, possibly Egyptian—strong in some words and entirely missing from others?

"It is in my power to see beyond the curtain that conceals the future," the fortune-teller intoned. "To look beyond, to unveil the deepest secrets and shine light into the darkest corners of tomorrow. As I look beyond your curtain, Hilary, I see the darkness drifting away. I see your aura, and within it you are bathed in light, in the radiance of love. A radiance that is pure silver and gold, made molten by passion. You will experience a passion that will consume you, and from its flames will emerge a complete and even more wonderful person. . . ." Madame Zola paused and, reaching for a nearby glass of water, took a long sip.

It occurred to Hilary that maybe the clear liquid wasn't water at all. Perhaps it was straight vodka or some Near Eastern concoction she'd never seen. Whatever it was, Madame Zola seemed to be enjoying it.

"One's throat grows dry," the fortune-teller explained, setting the glass down again. "The concentration . . . it is soul-sapping. In each life upon which I touch, I go beyond myself, I live outside myself. Do you understand?"

"I'm not sure I do."

"For this small interval in time, I share your life and your future. Holding your hand—this becomes a vital communication between us. You feel that, do you not? Much of your fate is written in your palm, but not all of it. The rest is made clear to me because of my powers. A great gift. A gift I share with you."

Madame Zola's voice became deeper, her eyes even more hypnotic. "I see before me a beautiful young woman of...twenty-six?"

"Twenty-eight," Hilary corrected.

"I see a woman upon whom nature has looked favorably. A lovely figure. Such gentle curves. Your bosom rises and falls with suppressed emotion as you listen to me.

"To the world, you may seem an ice maiden, until one comes to know you very well." Madame Zola nodded. "You present such a cool exterior. That lovely pale blond hair, which you wear so attractively on the top of your head, in a style distinctively your own. Ah, how the men in your life must long to see that gold-silver hair tumbling about your shoulders...."

Hilary shifted uncomfortably.

"Those eyes, crystal clear in the light of the midnight sun," Madame Zola went on. "A silken skin and features fine as a precious cameo..."

Hilary felt herself flushing. This kind of analysis was embarrassing. Also, she could see no point to it. "I don't think we need to go any further," she stated, then tried to disengage her hand from Madame Zola's pink-gloved clasp.

The clasp tightened. "Ah, but we have only begun," Madame Zola protested. "I must tell you of this lover soon to cross your horizon. Tall and dark and handsome, he will lay siege to your heart. And he will conquer you, *cherie*, as you have never been conquered before. He will—"

"Please!" Hilary said firmly. "I really do think that's enough!"

Again, she tried to release her hand. But the clasp held firm. Desperately, Hilary summoned her reserve strength and tugged. Her hand slid out of Madame Zola's grip, the pink glove coming with it.

Hilary found herself staring down at a large square hand sprinkled with dark hair. There was a ruggedness to the wide knuckles, echoed in long, blunt-nailed fingers. And there wasn't even the slightest trace of polish on the nails!

Hilary gasped aloud. Still unable to believe her suspicions, she sprang to her feet and quickly stretched her arm across the table. Before Madame Zola realized what was happening, Hilary had clutched the gold turban and wrenched it off the fortune-teller's head. The face veil came with it.

Hilary froze, her eyes widening. "You're a man!" she accused.

Madame Zola's laugh was low and rich and rang out freely. "So I am," the palmist agreed. And added wickedly, "At least I was, the last time I checked."

Furious, Hilary glared at this imposter. "You're a fraud!" she choked. "And a consummate con artist," she added bitterly, remembering the information she'd actually volunteered to this charlatan.

She turned. "I'm going out there and tell everyone in this place what you're doing," she threatened.

She started for the tent entrance, but the palmist was quicker than she was. Madame Zola rose from the table, crossed the Oriental rug with one stride, then shot out a long arm and grasped Hilary firmly just above her elbow.

"Dammit!" the palmist complained. "Don't you have any sense of humor?"

"What does a sense of humor have to do with this?" Hilary sputtered, spinning around to face him.

"This is a charity benefit, remember? The fortune-telling bit is supposed to be fun, as well as raise money. I was roped into doing it. But once I said I would, I decided to go for it and give people all the mileage I could."

"By conning them?"

"By letting them answer a few of their own questions. You, for example. You couldn't wait to let the words spill out."

"You forced them out of me!"

"The hell I did," the bogus Madame Zola denied. "Everyone wants a shoulder to cry on occasionally, Hilary. Sometimes, an anonymous shoulder. There's nothing wrong with that. You gave in to your needs. It was a human thing to do."

"I did not give in to any needs," Hilary denied frostily.

Madame Zola chuckled. "Forever the ice maiden, eh?" he observed.

Something in his tone arrested Hilary. She'd felt so indignant she hadn't really looked at him. Now she did. And discovered that even in this dim light he was quite something to look at. He was tall, almost six foot two, dark and handsome, just like the lover he'd verbally painted, the lover about to enter her life. His hair was also dark and thick as velvet.

Rather like Roy's hair, Hilary realized, annoyed with herself for making that connection. Still, Roy did have beautiful hair. One of the things she'd enjoyed most was running her fingers through his dark mane.

Hilary set her lips tightly and blocked off the channels along which her thoughts were beginning to race. Certainly, this was not a dark head she would ever run her fingers through. She would never see this man after this miserable night. She didn't want to. It was galling enough to know there'd now be someone in Devon who knew much too much about her.

She saw his dark eyebrows arch as he urged, "Look, I'm appealing to the better side of your nature. A lot of people have been venting a lot of things, here in this tent. I admit, I'm amazed by that. But whatever they've said, whatever those who follow say, it stops right here. Do you understand?"

"Are you asking me to put my faith in you?" Hilary scoffed.

"Yes. I consider what you've said in here as inviolate as what you might tell a priest in a confessional. I mean that."

Strangely, she believed him. But before she could say so, she saw "Madame Zola" shake his head. He said, regretfully, "Perhaps you really are an ice maiden, after all."

The glint that crept into his eyes didn't register quickly enough. And by the time Hilary's alarm system started functioning, "Madame Zola" was drawing her into his arms.

He was wearing a ridiculous costume. A long, bright green skirt and a loose orange peasant blouse, tied at the waist with a purple sash. Strings of gold chains and multicolored beads encircled his neck. But as he pulled her closer, Hilary had no doubt that beneath the outrageous clothing there was a disciplined, muscled, downright lethal masculine body.

His mouth claimed hers, and Hilary would have sworn there was a privately-wired electric current running through his lips. Its voltage jolted her. Not only did she feel the kiss clear to her heels, but on its way to her heels it did sneaky, sexy things to her body.

The pseudo fortune-teller drew back long enough to murmur appreciatively, "God, you're lovely." Then his lips quickly shut off any possible reply.

Hilary could feel her bones beginning to soften, and a warm sensuality infused her, making her pliant from head to toe. It was a terrific feeling, so terrific she instinctively yearned to prolong it. Reactions like this fell into a very rare, very special category.

She tried warning herself that it was insane to be behaving in such a fashion with a female impersonator who was also a charlatan. But her warning bells malfunctioned.

She answered "Madame Zola's" second kiss with an electric invitation of her own. Her arms encircled his neck, then her fingers moved up to test, just briefly, the rich softness of his hair.

Together, they swayed passionately, lost somewhere among the stars this impossible man had been talking about. Until abruptly the ticket taker moved the tent flap just enough to hiss through the opening, "Hey, there's an awfully long line out here. Could you speed it up a little?"

With that, the spell was broken.

Chapter Two

Monday morning, Hilary backed the old Chrysler convertible she'd inherited from her uncle out of the garage and drove uptown to the Devon branch of the Commonwealth Bank and Trust Company.

She needed some fresh air and a change of scene. She needed to talk to someone, to seek advice from a knowledgeable person who would be interested in helping her. She'd spent all day Sunday wrestling with her problems, only to have her attention diverted again and again to the memory of Saturday night.

The carnival had turned into such a fiasco! Hilary had fled the fortune-teller's tent to find George Delacorte waiting patiently for her by the cotton-candy stand. She practically flung the pink fluff George held out to her into his face, then demanded he take her home.

Understandably, George was perplexed. The evening was still young. Hurt at first, then annoyed, George stiffly acceded to Hilary's wishes.

George's annoyance faded, though. He called Sunday morning to suggest they drive out to Provincetown for lunch. The weather cast a gray, beginning-of-March day, and it looked as if it might snow before nightfall. Hilary, feeling frustrated and lonely, was tempted to toss the papers she'd been studying into oblivion and play hooky with George.

Still, she didn't want to falsely encourage him. She cherished George as a friend; but since she'd come back to Devon, he'd been trying to cross a few of her personal borderlines. She declined his invitation, knowing that, once again, he was miffed.

Hilary stayed by herself for the next twenty-four hours, subsisting on toast, white wine, and two cans of soup. By Monday morning, feeling slightly hung over, she knew she needed to talk to a local financial expert before she made any firm decisions. The logical choice was Horace Mayo, who had been the manager of Commonwealth's Devon branch for as long as Hilary could remember and had been a good friend of her Uncle Chad's.

The scene in the fortune-teller's tent was still intruding upon Hilary's thoughts as she parked in front of the bank. She doubted very much that she'd ever forget Madame Zola. The fake fortune-teller had been even more disturbing as a man than he'd been as an allegedly female clairvoyant.

The snow had yet to materialize. The wintry March air was very cold, the sky an oyster gray. A strong wind was blowing, putting the chill factor well below zero. Shivering as she scurried up the walk to the bank, Hilary asked herself why she hadn't opted for an exotic vacation and postponed her return to Devon until May. Better yet, until June. It could be chilly here in May, too.

A middle-aged woman with beautiful silvery hair and a custom-made smile was presiding at the receptionist's desk. When Hilary asked to see Horace Mayo, the smile faded.

"You haven't heard?" the woman asked.

Hilary restrained her natural impatience and fought the onslaught of an awful premonition at the same time. "What should I have heard?" she queried cautiously.

"Mr. Mayo suffered a severe heart attack shortly before Thanksgiving," she was told.

She shuddered. "Oh God, that's terrible," she murmured. She'd liked Horace Mayo very much. "Is Mrs. Mayo still in town? I should call on her...."

"My dear," the receptionist interrupted, "Mr. Mayo didn't *die*. As a matter of fact, he made a remarkable recovery. He and Mrs. Mayo are on a Caribbean cruise. But on the advice of his doctors, he retired from the bank."

"Oh? Well...overall, that's good news, I guess."

The receptionist brightened. "Mr. Mahoney has taken his place," she said. "Shall I see if he's free?"

Hilary hesitated. She ran the name Mahoney around in her mind, but it didn't mean anything to her. Still, she needed to speak to someone familiar with local affairs. If Mr. Mahoney was considered competent enough by Commonwealth to succeed Mr. Mayo as manager of its Devon branch, he must be fairly conversant with the town's business climate.

"All right," Hilary decided reluctantly. "I'll see Mr. Mahoney."

Mr. Mahoney, as it happened, was not free at that precise moment. "He's on the phone, long-distance," the receptionist reported. "But he should be through shortly. If you'll just take a seat..."

Hilary sat down on a prim, overstuffed chair. The upholstery was scratchy, especially through the wool slacks she was wearing. After a time, she glanced at her wristwatch. Mr. Mahoney had been on the phone for eight minutes. The time stretched to ten minutes, then twelve. After fifteen minutes, Hilary stood up, prepared to have the receptionist tell the bank manager not to bother. Right on cue, a desk buzzer sounded.

The woman looked up sweetly. "Mr. Mahoney will see you now," she said, as if she were conferring a very special favor.

Hilary gritted her teeth and walked down the short corridor to the manager's office. She knew the way. She'd been this route before, tagging along with her Uncle Chad in earlier times at his request. He'd always insisted she be well informed about his affairs.

She knocked and, in answer to a welcoming "Come in," pushed open the heavy wooden door—then promptly froze at the sight of the man seated behind the desk. She'd seen his face only in the dim light of a fortune-teller's tent, but she would have known it anywhere. Even more, his eyes were unforgettable. She felt herself doing a slow but steady burn as they swept over her, eloquent, magnetic as ever, incredibly sensual.

The thought of her last encounter with this man swamped her. In retrospect, she found it totally humiliating.

He pushed back his chair, evidently about to rise. Instead, he stayed seated and surveyed her, his lips curving into a tantalizing smile.

"Well," he said softly. "Hello."

Hilary forced herself to look away. She concentrated on the brass nameplate on his desk, hoping there might be some mistake. Maybe the new manager had preferred to occupy a different office.

The nameplate read J. A. Mahoney, Manager.

She groaned silently. Then, out of the corner of her eye, she saw he was standing up. She tried not to look at him, but this became impossible.

Once again, he made an impact. He was the last person in the world Hilary would've expected to be a banker. Yet in his perfectly tailored three-piece gray suit, pale gray shirt and striped gray and blue tie, he not only looked like a fashion plate, he also projected the quintessential banker's image.

Charlatan! Hilary thought bitterly.

He was watching her with the kind of grave yet courteous expression she'd long thought must be instilled in potential executives while they were still in business school. Only the devilish gleam in his dark eyes gave him away.

He asked politely, "Won't you sit down, Miss Forsythe?"

Hilary started, wondering how he could know her last name. Then she remembered that the receptionist had announced her over the intercom.

She sat down because trying to beat a hasty retreat would not only symbolize personal defeat, it would also be very undignified. Quickly, she made up her mind to reflect his attitude, to be as cool and nonpersonal as he was.

She saw him glance at a fat file folder on his desk. He said quietly, "I thought you must be Hilary Forsythe."

"Oh?"

"I don't imagine there are that many Hilarys around Devon," he observed. "Especially Hilarys fitting the description I'd heard—a young, beautiful heiress, come back to the Cape to decide what to do with the property she's inherited."

Hilary bristled. "Might I ask where you heard that?"

"You might ask," he replied calmly, "but I won't answer." With a smile that would have melted an iceberg, he added, "I do respect confidentiality, Miss Forsythe. It's essential wherever one does business but most especially in a small town. Now, how may I help you?"

The subject switch was so abrupt that Hilary blinked. Discovering this man in this office had thrown her completely off base. She was far from ready to get down to facts with him. The memory of their first encounter still distracted her. As she thought about "Madame Zola," something surfaced.

"So," Hilary blurted, half to herself, "that's how you knew so much about everybody."

J. A. Mahoney had taken some papers out of the folder and was scanning them. He looked up, frowning slightly. "What do you mean?"

"Saturday night, when you were playing palmist, everyone was saying you were hitting the nail right on the head," Hilary informed him. "They couldn't figure out how you knew so much about them...past and present. So, that made your predictions for the future especially valuable. Actually, you'd merely done some homework using your bank's files, hadn't you, Mr. Mahoney?"

The gleam in his eyes vanished. They became mirthless and surprisingly cold, like chips of Carrara marble. Certain chips could be cutting and, thinking this, Hilary flinched. If this man was as devastating in his anger as he was in his passionate advances, she didn't want any part of him.

"I suppose that's a natural conclusion for you to draw," he admitted, a chill to his voice. "And...it is partly true. So what are you going to do? Call the local papers so they can run a front-page story about the local banker who's violated confidential files?"

"Should I?" Hilary queried, feigning innocence.

J. A. Mahoney leaned back in his chair, his handsome face inscrutable. After a moment, he said wearily, "Of course you shouldn't. Anymore than you should get so bent out of shape because I happened to have a little fun with you the other night."

A little fun?

He sat forward. "Look," he said reasonably, "I told you I was talked into playing palmist. Once I knew I was going to do it, I got into the act, okay? And, it was enjoyable. But

I didn't delve into the bank files and ferret out all sorts of dark secrets about people, which is what you're thinking. As it happens..."

He hesitated and, after a moment, Hilary encouraged, "Yes?"

"I have a...weird memory," J. A. Mahoney confessed. "I suppose you could say I was born with it. I remember things, in detail. Extraneous things. I always have. It's not what you'd call a photographic memory, exactly. It's just that I unconsciously assimilate a considerable amount of what might be called superficial knowledge.

"On the other hand," he continued, flashing his disarming smile in Hilary's direction, "I'm apt to totally forget things like my own telephone number, or a dinner date I have next Tuesday, or what it was I intended to stop for and pick up in the supermarket on the way home."

"You prefer to limit your information to other people's business, is that it?" Hilary suggested.

He shook his head. "That's a nasty crack," he reproved. "No, I don't prefer to limit what I remember to anything specific. I usually don't *try* to store up facts. It just happens."

He sighed. "I see a lot of people in a day's work," he said. "They tell me a lot of things. A large portion of what they say—the really confidential things—never finds its way onto paper, never gets in the bank's files. Still, the data remains up here," he confessed, tapping his temple with a finger. "In my memory vault. Next time I see the person in question, I remember what they've said previously. Usually, it's an asset."

"I'd say you're a walking red flag, Mr. Mahoney," Hilary decided.

"And what's that supposed to mean?"

"You're dangerous. You could be a singularly successful blackmailer if you decided to turn to a career in crime. I, for one, would certainly hate to have you know very much about me...."

"But I already know quite a bit about you, Miss Forsythe," he pointed out maddeningly.

Hilary presumed he was referring to their session in the blue tent Saturday night. A personal heat wave stirred as she remembered the way she'd succumbed to him. Chagrined, she wished she could melt entirely and simply dissolve out of sight.

The former Madame Zola said, perceptively, "I wasn't thinking about Saturday."

More embarrassed than she could ever remember being, Hilary answered tartly, "So, you're a mind reader as well as a phony palmist."

"No," J. A. Mahoney contradicted, still smiling. "You have a very expressive face, that's all. Look, as I said before, you shouldn't be so bent out of shape about Saturday. I told you everything that went on in the tent is confidential. I meant that. I wouldn't spill other people's secrets for the world."

He concluded, "Again... what Madame Zola discovered about you the other night will remain between us. I would never tell anyone about your relationship with Roy... what was his last name? Come to think of it, I don't think you ever mentioned it."

Hilary stared at him, aghast. "Oh my God," she murmured weakly.

He grinned. "Stop worrying," he advised. "Seriously, you have nothing to fear from me."

Hilary wanted to tell him this was the understatement of the century. Any woman in her right mind would have a great deal to fear from J. A. Mahoney! Just being in the same room with him was enough to stir up her female hormones in a most disturbing way. She, who had always prided herself on being logical, was behaving like a distracted butterfly.

"When I said I know a fair bit about you, I was referring to the contents of *this*," J. A. Mahoney said now, his smile fading as he tapped the folder on his desk. He spoke gravely. "Horace Mayo, my predecessor, accumulated a fairly substantial file on your late uncle over the years," Hilary was informed. "Mr. Forsythe gave all of his business involving his Cape Cod interests to this bank, and over the years those interests were both diverse and extensive. He bought and sold quite a lot of property, and financed at least two successful business enterprises through us. Eventually, your uncle sold his interests in the businesses and most of his real-estate holdings as well—at considerable profit. But you probably know all that."

"Yes." Hilary tried to pretend this was Horace Mayo sitting across from her, tried to pretend she was gazing into Horace's watery, pale blue eyes instead of "Madame Zola's" hypnotic midnight ones. "Yes," she repeated, "I know that."

"At present," J. A. Mahoney continued, "you are down to—if it can be put that way—a summer cottage out in Wellfleet and the old Forsythe homestead on Sea Street, here in Devon."

Hilary nodded, "That's right."

"If I seem to know more about you than perhaps you think I should, it's because the bank clips media information about important clients and adds it to their files. There was a fair bit about you in the material dealing with the summers you spent here with Mr. Forsythe. And, of course, there are the obituaries..."

The word was enough to send a cold chill coursing through Hilary.

J. A. Mahoney was indeed perceptive. Very perceptive. Hilary appreciated this when he said quickly, genuine sympathy in his rich, mellow voice, "I'm sorry. It hasn't been long, I know."

"Almost exactly two months," Hilary told him. "Uncle Chad died right after New Year's."

"And you were very close, weren't you?"

Hilary looked at J. A. Mahoney suspiciously. Was he being "Madame Zola" again?

He caught the look and said wryly, "I'm afraid I'm never going to live down Saturday night with you, am I? Look, Miss Forsythe, believe me, I'm not trying to play palmist. I gather from your reactions that you and your uncle were close, that's all. It makes your loss that much harder."

For a moment, his handsome face was curiously bleak. As was his voice when he said, "Time does help. It will get better..."

He let the rest of this statement trail off, and Hilary at once became curious. She was somehow certain he was speaking from experience. She reminded herself that everyone lost people dear to them. That was an inescapable fact of life. But she had a gut feeling that J. A. Mahoney, just now, had been referring to someone very special.

She slanted a glance at his hands. No wedding rings. Not that the absence of a wedding ring was necessarily significant. Anyway, wedding ring or no wedding ring, Hilary would have bet that J. A. Mahoney's comment dealt with a woman in his life. Someone who had been very important to him. His mother, maybe? Hilary didn't think it was his mother.

J. A. Mahoney was again studying the papers in front of him. He asked abruptly, "Do you intend to sell your Cape properties?"

She hadn't expected the question and was not prepared to answer it. She'd spent all of Sunday trying to deal with this exact subject and hadn't gotten very far. "No," she said after a moment, "I haven't made a firm decision about selling. In fact . . . some alternatives have been suggested to me. Whether they're viable or not, I don't know." Shrugging, Hilary temporarily ran out of words.

She was aware that J. A. Mahoney was watching her patiently, his dark eyebrows slightly upraised. She tried to regroup, tried to say something that would reflect the intelligent woman she really was. But there was so much to think about, so much to remember.

Briefly, Hilary wished that J. A. Mahoney could share a portion of his unusual memory with her. She wanted to get her facts and priorities in order, then keep them in order. But to do that she needed to distill calm from her present mental chaos. With his arresting eyes fixed upon her, that wasn't easy.

She couldn't totally blame her confusion on him, of course, though he was certainly adding fuel to the emotional pyre. One problem was that the thought of Roy and his defection still stung badly. Another was the aching sorrow she continued to feel for her uncle.

Cautiously, she said, "I...I'd like to keep the cottage for summer use. I could always rent it if I didn't want to stay there myself. Uncle Chad often rented it. He considered it primarily an investment and preferred staying in the old Forsythe house himself."

J. A. Mahoney nodded. "Renting the cottage should be no problem," he agreed. "I believe your uncle used the Trevor Andrews real-estate agency. They're good people. I'd advise you to continue doing business with them."

"I will...if I rent the cottage," Hilary replied dryly. "Possibly I may just keep it for close friends to use. It's the house here that really concerns me."

"Yes?"

"That area of Sea Street used to be all residential," Hilary said. "Over the past few years, a number of businesses have edged in. I'm not saying they're objectionable. But they have changed the character of that part of town."

"Yes, that's true," J. A. Mahoney concurred. "That area was zoned for limited business at least ten years ago," he told her. "That means there are restrictions, many of them aesthetic. No one can put up a gas station, for instance. On the other hand, a variety of businesses and selected shops do have the legal right to be your neighbors."

"I realize that," Hilary told him. "As a matter of fact, I've been thinking of joining the club."

He frowned. "I'm not quite sure I know what you mean."

"I've been thinking of starting a business myself."

"You?"

"Why not?" she demanded, his amusement nettling her.

"Have you ever run a business, Miss Forsythe?"

"My, my," Hilary taunted. "Are you saying there's something you don't know about me?"

"Perhaps," he conceded.

"Well, for your information, I ran a business of my own in Boston. All the time I was..."

He grinned. "Living with Roy?"

Hilary had a sudden urge to strangle him. "I was running a shop on Charles Street when my uncle became ill," she said frostily. "I closed only because he needed me."

"What kind of business?" J. A. Mahoney asked briskly, his question cutting across sad memories.

"My shop was called Nostalgia," Hilary told him, "and that's essentially what it was. Not an antique shop, really, although I did acquire some nice old things from time to time. I dealt more in current collectibles, like jewelry dating back to the thirties and forties, including lots of rhinestones. Rhinestones have become hot items again. I also had vintage clothes—satin ball gowns, velvet dresses, things like that. And Deco lamp shades and vases, prints, ashtrays..."

J. A. Mahoney didn't exactly interrupt Hilary, but he did edge his way into what she was saying. "I'm aware of the nostalgia kick," he said. "It's understandable. Sometimes our computer age gets to people, and despite its wonders, they want to revert to something more sentimental. So they gather objects they can associate with a world that was supposed to be a lot simpler. A time loaded with serendipity." He paused, looked as if he didn't believe in either nostalgia or serendipity, and shot another quick question at Hilary. "Was your shop successful?" he demanded.

"Yes," she snapped, feeling that he was putting her on the defensive.

"Are you suggesting you open Nostalgia II here on the Cape?" J. A. Mahoney asked skeptically.

"I've been considering it, yes."

"Well, I'd have to advise against it," he said bluntly. "There are a number of excellent shops around here that specialize in exactly the kind of thing you're talking about."

"I know that," Hilary told him impatiently. "I've spent every summer in Devon since I was twelve years old, including last summer. I canvased the shops you're talking about and bought quite a few things for my store in Boston. So I know what you're saying."

"Then would you mind telling me how your shop would be different?"

"So you can file my idea in your memory vault, as you call it," she suggested.

J. A. Mahoney winced, visibly irked. The gleam in his dark eyes was gone as he said, seriously, "I wish we could start all over again. It appears I'm going to have to work hard to develop your faith in me. Incidentally, can you carry a tune?"

Again taken off guard, she said crossly, "Of course."

"'Of course' is the wrong answer," J. A. Mahoney stated. "You can carry a tune because you have the gift of a musical ear. I don't. When I try, I go completely off-key, and it drives everyone around me crazy."

"Fine, but what does that have to do with..."

"Also, my sense of rhythm is atrocious," J. A. Mahoney continued. "If they're playing a waltz, I keep time to a rumba. If they're playing a tango, I keep time to a waltz. Which makes me an especially lousy dancer.

"So," he added, while Hilary was digesting this, "because I know a few things about you, I want you to know this about me. As I've said, I have what I, at least, call a weird memory. It came with me. I never tried to acquire it. It would be as hard for me to forget facts as it would be for you to sing off-key. But let me assure you I've sometimes wished I could suddenly develop amnesia. Do you understand what I'm saying?"

"Yes," Hilary admitted after a moment, her voice small because he was making her feel small. "Yes...at least I think I do." She dared to glance at him, and found he was consulting his thin gold wristwatch.

He said, with no discernible note of apology, "You'll have to excuse me. I have a luncheon engagement, and I'm already late. We'll have to defer our discussion about your business venture, but I suggest we get back to it as soon as possible."

J. A. Mahoney was suddenly *all* business.

"Shall I come back tomorrow morning?" Hilary asked quickly.

"Why don't I come over to your place tomorrow morning instead?" he suggested. "If you wouldn't mind my making it early, that is. I should be at the bank by ten at the latest."

"Come for coffee at eight, if you like."

"Fine. If you're planning to start a business in your old family home, it makes sense to show me what you intend to do while we're right on the premises."

"I agree."

"Until tomorrow, then?" J. A. Mahoney asked, flashing a devastating smile.

"Until tomorrow," Hilary echoed, and was so blinded by the man that she nearly stumbled into the door on her way out of his office.

Chapter Three

Knowing that J. A. Mahoney was going to loom up at her doorstep by eight o'clock, Hilary couldn't concentrate on anything else the next morning.

She was suddenly aware of the dustiness and mustiness of the old summer house, which was what her uncle Chad had always called the Devon homestead. A century ago, Forsythes had been born, had lived and died in this house. Later, Boston became the family focal point, and the Devon property was kept for seasonal use only.

In the earlier years, Devon had been a small seaside hamlet. The street running in front of the summer house had been a sandy lane heading to the beach. Within the last twenty years, Sea Street was both paved and widened. More recently, private residences had begun to yield to business pressure, as Hilary had explained to J. A. Mahoney, and she was being nudged by a variety of enterprising neighbors.

As she raced around the house with cleaning rag and spray polish in hand, Hilary bemoaned the way she'd spent the past ten days. On the sunny days, she'd driven aimlessly around the Cape, sometimes going as far as Sandwich to indulge in a solitary lunch at an old inn, sometimes winding up at a cinema in the Cape Cod Mall in Hyannis. Once, she drove out to Provincetown and wandered along Commercial Street. A lot of the shops were closed for the season, a lot of the zaniness absent from the scene. But Provincetown, with or without its summer overlay, was always fascinating.

On chilly March days, with snow flurrying and an icy wind blowing in from the east, Hilary had curled up in front of the television set and let her mind grow lazy as she sampled the daytime video menu. Nights, she'd gone to bed early, except for an occasional dinner date with George Delacorte. And she'd kept those dates to a minimum, for George's sake, not hers. George would gladly have taken a vacation from his accounting business, fed her three meals a day and kept her company. But to let him do that just because she was lonely would be ladling out false hope.

Now, she gave her house a quick going-over, put a pan of frozen croissants in the oven, and brewed a pot of coffee. The coffee finished perking at exactly the same instant J. A. Mahoney rang the doorbell.

Hilary was wearing faded blue jeans, an old gray sweater and well-worn lavender running shoes. She darted a frantic look in the gilt-edged hall mirror before opening the front door, and didn't like what she saw. A face too pale, hair that needed brushing, lips requiring lipstick. In short, she looked a mess. But it was too late to do anything about that.

J. A. Mahoney, on the other hand, was dressed for work, and dressed very well. At Hilary's invitation, he divested himself of his handsome wool overcoat to emerge resplendent in another three-piece suit, this one a dark navy that dramatically enhanced his already dramatic coloring.

He was a far cry from the gold-turbaned Madame Zola!

"Cold out," he commented, rubbing his hands together.

Hilary was sure it must be frigid out, but just looking at J. A. Mahoney was enough to start her personal mercury on a rising trend. For his sake, and because the old house was cold, she was glad she'd thought to get a fire going in the living room. She led him to the hearth, excused herself and hurried to the kitchen.

Her hands were trembling as she picked up the large silver tray laden with coffee and croissants. The tray was heavy, and would have been enough to manage even if she weren't so shaky. As it was, carrying it was a challenge. It would be just her luck, Hilary thought grimly, to slip and dump the whole thing right into J. A. Mahoney's well-tailored lap!

The thought of this happening inspired mirth. Especially since he'd labeled her an ice maiden. Ice maidens were supposed to be in control at all times, weren't they? Hilary chortled silently, because just the sight of this man was enough to start her spinning erratically. The problem was she couldn't look at him without remembering their passionate kiss in the fortune-teller's tent. Fortunately, he was totally unaware of this, she assured herself. But her inner laughter subsided as she also warned herself she must be careful to keep him in ignorance, and that might not be easy.

In the bank yesterday she'd tried to muster and maintain a merited level of righteous indignation toward J. A. Mahoney. Unfortunately, it had been overridden by her awareness of him as a very sexy, highly desirable man. If the rest of his lovemaking lived up to his kissing—

Hilary slammed the lid down on her treacherous thoughts, took the last couple of steps to the coffee table in front of the fireplace and set down the tray just in time.

J. A. Mahoney, she discovered, took his coffee black. She also discovered that croissants were his favorite breakfast pastry. She thought of many other things she'd like to discover about him but slammed her mental lid again.

She watched him sip his coffee, watched him survey the room, memorizing—she was sure—every last detail of its design and decor. Finally he said, "Too bad you can't go for your nostalgia theme here. This house is so classically Victorian. When was it built? About the 1880s?"

"About then, I'd say." Hilary nodded. "And it's probably more classical now, at least on the exterior, than it was for many years. By World War I, my family was using this house primarily as a summer place. One Forsythe—my great-grandfather, I think—built a wide veranda all the way around the first floor. I have some old photos of oversized wicker rocking chairs lined up in a row out there. Later, a privacy-lover Forsythe ordered the porches stripped off the front and sides, so now there's just a big back veranda that overlooks the so-called garden. It's been a long time since anyone's paid much attention to the garden. I wasn't born with much of a green thumb, but if I decide to stay here and start a business I might try to grow a few things."

"If you've wisely decided to dispense with the nostalgia theme, do you have any other ideas about the kind of a business you'd like to start?" J. A. Mahoney inquired, his tone so blandly polite that it made Hilary suspicious. Every inch and ounce of him was projecting the image of a proper banker. Yet she couldn't believe there wasn't some of Madame Zola lurking beneath his impeccable facade.

Determined to be as suave as he was, Hilary said, "Yes, I know exactly the kind of business I'd like to start."

"Have you defined your plans sufficiently to talk about them?" he asked, reaching for his third croissant.

Hilary nearly forgot his question because she was noticing that while he evidently had a healthy appetite, he cer-

tainly didn't have a weight problem. He was perfectly
proportioned. If she were drawing up a master plan of him
she wouldn't change a single detail!

She brought herself up short and forced herself to concentrate on her business plans. Leaning forward, the fire-
light in this rather dark room turning her hair to an alluring
sheath of white gold, she said, "I've traveled a fair bit over
the years, mostly with my uncle. Every place I've gone, I've
looked for souvenirs. Something that would bring back
memories, that would really represent the place I visited.
More often than not, what I've found has turned out to be
a disappointment. I remember buying an Indian doll out in
Colorado. When I examined it later I discovered a small la-
bel saying Made in Hong Kong. I bought some coral beads
in Aruba, then found out that the coral, at least that kind of
coral, didn't come from anywhere around there. Do you see
what I'm driving at?"

J. A. Mahoney smiled faintly. "I'm not sure."

"I've always wanted something *special.* Something, as I
just said, relating directly to the place I've been to," Hilary
explained. "Look at the majority of Cape Cod souvenirs
offered for sale. They were definitely not made on Cape
Cod. Well, I'd like to open a shop dealing entirely with local products.

"I'd have nothing on display or for sale that wasn't made
on Cape Cod by talented artists and craftsmen," she elab-
orated. "Sometimes you find the kind of thing I'm thinking of in summer, at the better arts and crafts shows. You
find *some* good local items in shops, but they're often lost
among the other merchandise. I think there's a market for
the local products only. I'd be willing to sell everything from
beach plum jelly to Steve Hudson's beautiful photographs
of the Cape... provided everything was all made *here.*"

Hilary was deliberately working up her enthusiasm as she
spoke. She was acutely aware that she had a long way to go

and a lot to think about before she could translate her concept into a practical work plan. But she felt she was on her way.

She was daunted when J. A. Mahoney said casually, "Your idea might be feasible, but I'm not sure. You'd want to check out the competition very thoroughly. In fact, I'd say you should do an in-depth market survey to make certain the tourists are as interested in purely local crafts as you are. People might actually prefer a little wooden dinghy made in Korea to one made in Barnstable, if only because the import would undoubtedly be cheaper."

He paused. "I'm not trying to discourage you, Miss Forsythe," he said. "You could be on the right track. But even if you are, where does the Commonwealth Bank and Trust Company come into this?"

Hilary felt as if he'd flung a damp rag in her face. A rag that had just been used to scrub the kitchen floor. She worked her way from instant defeatism to defiance, running through several different emotions en route. She knew she undoubtedly looked like an ice maiden at that moment. She always looked like an ice maiden when she was irritated. Paradoxically, inner flares of temper always sparked an outwardly frigid mien for her.

She said coldly, "I must remind you, Mr. Mahoney, that I went to the bank yesterday expecting to find Mr. Mayo there. Mr. Mayo's a longtime friend of the family. This is something I could have discussed with him. He would have understood what I have in mind. As it is . . . well, there's no point in taking up any more of your time."

J. A. Mahoney stared at her blankly, his magnificent dark eyes inscrutable. Then, to her surprise, he smiled slowly, displaying beautifully even white teeth.

"Whew!" he whistled, forcibly expelling his breath. "Once again, something tells me we should start over. Do you suppose I could have another cup of coffee?"

Somewhat ungraciously, Hilary filled his coffee cup. As she handed the cup back to him, their hands brushed. Small patches of the ice maiden's skin melted on contact.

J. A. Mahoney rose. Coffee cup in hand, he asked politely, "Do you suppose you could show me around the house? And give me an idea of how you'd handle converting this," he added, gesturing with his free hand at the walls around him, "into the kind of shop you're talking about?"

Hilary hadn't seriously considered the specifics of converting living quarters to commercial space. Nevertheless, she quickly decided she'd rise to his challenge.

She led him through the downstairs rooms, trying to conjure up some coherent, though impromptu, plans as they went.

The house, as J. A. Mahoney had observed, was Victorian in design. In contrast to older Cape Cod houses, the rooms were quite large and the ceilings high, giving a feeling of lofty spaciousness.

They wandered through the library, the dining room, the pantry and the kitchen, then peered through the kitchen door at the last remaining veranda, where dried autumn leaves had spent the winter in protected corners. Retracing their steps, Hilary tried to execute a series of verbal sketches. Finally, they reached the foot of the winding staircase that led to the second floor.

J. A. Mahoney waited for Hilary to lead the way up the stairs, but she drew back. Suddenly she remembered that her bed was unmade and her clothes were strewn in places where they shouldn't be at all. The bathroom was also a mess, littered with bottles and jars of moisturizing cream and hand lotion and hairstyling mousse and a variety of other objects, some of them too intimate to come under his probing gaze.

She said quickly, "I intend to reserve the upstairs for my... apartment. So there's no need to go up there."

J. A. Mahoney looked at her quizzically. For a moment, Hilary thought he was going to disagree with her. Instead, he said, "Okay." Then he added, "Could we take another look at that back porch?"

"The veranda?" Hilary corrected.

He grinned. "That's right, the veranda."

The veranda needed painting, Hilary noted, as they studied it again. The whole house needed painting and wallpapering, she realized dismally. And if the kitchen equipment was outdated, the bathrooms could be declared obsolete!

She began to feel boggled by the thought of so much renovation. It occurred to her that maybe she was an idiot not to unload the house on someone looking for quaint Cape Cod charm, then take the pieces of her life back to Boston and put them together there.

J. A. Mahoney said suddenly, "You know, Hilary, that veranda could be given a lot of character. You could operate a small tearoom there. It could easily be glassed in for all-weather use. You could give up the idea of experimenting with the green thumb you say you don't have, scrap the remnants of the garden and turn it into lawn. Then you could have tables out there, too. Perhaps some of the local women could cook their specialties for you. The old New England goodies like strawberry-rhubarb pie and grapenut custard pudding. Maybe homemade clam chowder or Portuguese soup."

He paused. "I'll be getting hungry if I keep pursuing this line of thought."

Hilary looked past the veranda and gazed at the tangled remains of the abandoned garden seared by winter frost. She marveled that she could actually envision the whole thing just as J. A. Mahoney pictured it.

"That's a *great* idea," she applauded. She was about to call him by his first name—after all, he'd just called her Hilary—then realized she didn't know his first name.

"James?" she queried. "Or is it John?"

"What?" he asked, puzzled.

"Your first name."

"Oh." He grinned again and Hilary's pulse leapt around frantically for a few seconds before it settled back into a steady rhythm. He drawled, "Well, most people call me J. A. An alternative is Jay."

"Is Jay your first name?"

"Not exactly."

He drew a long breath. "Are you ready for this?" he asked. "The *J* stands for Joaquim. The *A* stands for Alvaro. My full name is Joaquim Alvaro Mahoney."

Hilary's tongue-tied stare provoked a hearty laugh.

"I don't blame you for looking so confused," he said. "You see . . . my mother was Portuguese, and she wanted to preserve her heritage. My father, obviously, was Irish. They were close to middle-age when they married. My mother made my father promise that if they ever had a child, the child would be named Joaquim or Serafina." J. A. Mahoney paused. "I'm really glad I didn't turn out to be Serafina!" he admitted.

Matching his contagious smile, Hilary said, "Am I to conclude that you detest your name, so you don't want anyone to call you Joaquim?" Though she'd listened to his pronunciation, which sounded vaguely like "Joe-ah-queem," she still stumbled over the word.

"You see," he said triumphantly. "And at that you pronounced it better than nine people out of ten. Most people can't say the word at all. So it's not that I detest it . . ."

"All right," Hilary decided. "I'll call you Jay."

"Agreed." J. A. Mahoney nodded. He glanced at his watch, and added reluctantly, "I can't believe it's almost ten, and we still have a long way to go. You haven't told me where Commonwealth Bank and Trust fits into the picture. In fact, there are all sorts of things you haven't told me." A familiar gleam crept into his dark eyes. "All sorts of things," he repeated. "We must get into them, Hilary."

"Yes," Hilary responded vaguely. "Yes, of course."

Jay headed for the front door. On the threshold, he said, "I have to go to Boston for a bank meeting tomorrow. But how about lunch the next day? Or maybe dinner?"

"I may have to go to Boston myself," Hilary hedged.

"I'll check back with you then," he promised. Lingering, he added, "Thanks for the coffee and croissants. And thanks for sharing your plans with me. I hope I can be of some help."

He held out his hand and Hilary took it. She initiated the beginning of a handshake, then stopped short. The pressure of Jay Mahoney's palm against hers was absolutely erotic. She wouldn't have believed that just entwining her fingers with someone else's, just touching someone else's flesh...

Jay's eyes held her in a vise as strong as the magnetic force he'd exerted when he'd been Madame Zola. Hilary tried to convince herself that she was far too contemporary a woman to swoon. But it was hard to remain standing upright, because her legs were wobbly.

It was a short, sensually-loaded interval. Finally Jay turned abruptly, opened the door, then stepped outside, closing the door behind him.

Hilary was still trying to recover from this emotional severance when a knock echoed through the stillness of the empty front hall. She opened the door to find Jay looking down at her sheepishly.

"My coat," he explained. "I remembered it when I got stabbed by an arctic blast."

Hilary had hung his coat in the hall closet. She handed it to him, and he slipped it on. Then, at the door once again, he suddenly changed course and turned toward her. He touched her chin lightly, and Hilary decided that he really *had* hypnotized her. There was no way she could have moved with three of his fingers pressing ever so lightly against her skin.

Jay bent and brushed her lips with a kiss that was fleeting, yet full of fire. "There's a lot more I could have told you about your fortune and your future," he teased, raising his voice slightly and speaking with Madame Zola's phony accent.

With that, he left.

Hilary spent the rest of that day and all of the next working on plans for her shop. She racked her brains trying, unsuccessfully, to think of a good name, something provocative. A name that would immediately conjure up the kind of merchandise she planned to offer.

If she added a tearoom, this further dimension should probably be included in the name. Possibly, though, the tearoom could simply be featured in the advertising.

Hilary knew nothing about the food business. If she entered that area she'd need to have a knowledgeable, dependable assistant. She found herself thinking that maybe Jay could put her in touch with the right person for the job.

In fact, she found herself thinking about Jay Mahoney during the course of most of her waking moments over the next forty-eight hours. His feather-light kiss had, in its way, branded her as much as his sultry embrace in the fortune-teller's tent.

In bed both nights, Hilary dreamed about Jay. They were in the middle of the Sahara together, in a dark, nomadic abode. Jay wasn't Madame Zola this time. Rather, he was an Arabian sheik who had kidnapped her from a jasmine-filled garden and carried her across the desert on his camel!

When she awakened on Thursday morning—the day Jay suggested they have lunch together—Hilary's first conscious thought was that he would be calling her. As she continued working on her plans, she listened for the sound of the telephone with such intensity that her ears were aching by ten o'clock. When, by noon, the perverse instrument was still silent, she dialed George's office and asked George to call her back so she'd be sure her phone was working properly.

George did, and promptly invited her to have dinner with him that night.

Hilary had made up her mind she was going to refuse George's next invitation because it just wasn't fair to keep encouraging him. Instead, entirely for her own selfish reasons, she accepted.

George took her to a new restaurant in town that was the "in" place to go. The setting was a Hollywood version of New England with the waiters and waitresses garbed like Pilgrims. Still, the atmosphere was very romantic. There was a wood fire burning in a magnificent stone hearth, and candles flickered on every table.

Hilary sighed, imagining what it would be like to be here with Jay Mahoney. Glancing at George, she felt like nothing less than a traitor, so she was especially nice to him.

All through dinner, though, Hilary kept wishing Jay Mahoney would walk in—preferably with some of his business friends—so he would see her with another man. She knew she was being hopelessly childish, but chastising herself about that didn't work. She still wished Jay Mahoney would walk in, because she wanted so much to see him.

She let George kiss her when he took her home, but there weren't any sparks ignited. She knew it, and George knew it.

As she undressed, Hilary wondered if maybe Jay had called while she was out. Maybe he'd been delayed in Boston. Maybe, maybe, maybe...

Hilary got into bed and pulled the blankets tightly around her, feeling cold and lonely. And as she stared into the darkness, she hoped that dreams of jasmine gardens and a handsome Arab sheik would transport her through the night.

Chapter Four

Hilary awakened to a world in which sounds were muffled, and the frost patterns on her bedroom windows were so thick she couldn't see beyond the glass panes.

She huddled in bed, hating the idea of the view she was sure she'd see once she got up, crossed the room and peered through the narrow gap at the base of the single window she'd opened the night before. She didn't consider herself a fresh-air fiend, but she'd never been able to sleep with all the windows entirely closed, regardless of the temperature.

Her worst fears were realized when she finally forced herself to slip out from under her warm bed covers—two wool blankets topped by a magnificent patchwork quilt made many years before by her grandmother. Sure enough, the outside world had turned totally white. Tree branches bent beneath a layer of snow, frosted as neatly as if they'd been brushed by a master pastry chef. Hilary couldn't esti-

mate how deep the snow on the ground might be. The fact
that this much snow was visible at all was traumatic enough.

She hated snow almost neurotically. She'd learned to deal
with flurries, but snow in any substantial amount brought
back dreadful memories of the most terrible time of her life.

She'd been twelve years old in Switzerland on a winter
holiday with her parents. A nagging head cold had kept her
confined to the Alpine lodge in which they were staying, a
huge old structure that looked like a many-turreted ginger-
bread house. But for that, she too would've been skiing on
that fateful morning when the deadly onrush of a massive
avalanche trapped her parents, killing them both.

Hilary shuddered, remembering the way news of the disaster had been brought to her by kindly people who had
gently explained what had happened. At first, her loss had
been too great to assimilate, either mentally or emotionally. For days, she'd lived in a state of shock. Then her
Uncle Chad had arrived on the scene, and a Swiss doctor
had instructed him to give her tranquilizers on the flight
back to the States. Mercifully, those hours in the air had
passed in a kind of limbo.

Chad Forsythe, bless him, had never truly realized how,
after that, the sight of snow affected his niece. On snowy
winter days in Boston, he'd accepted her pleas to stay
cooped up indoors, to the point of drawing the curtains in
her bedroom and burying her nose in a book, trying to escape the outside world.

Now Hilary wished that she'd confided in her uncle about
this fear of hers. He would've insisted she get professional
help—maybe a psychiatrist or a psychologist could have
done something for her then. At this late date, her hatred of
snow was too deeply entrenched to exorcise. Her only viable course of action was to try to live with it. But at moments like this, success didn't come easily.

She went downstairs, made coffee and tried to get her mind on something other than the weather. She found some notepaper and a felt-tip pen and began jotting down ideas for her shop. Fortunately, she had a good three months before she needed to finalize her act, although the time was bound to fly by.

She wanted an interesting mix of arts and crafts, something that would require a considerable amount of investigation on her part. She could advertise, and encourage local artisans to get in touch with her and show her what they had to offer. Or she could simply begin asking around. George, the Bentleys and several other people she knew in Devon might be able to suggest potential contacts. As could Jay Mahoney...

Hilary had been trying not to let Jay Mahoney's name creep into her mind. But now that it had, it was impossible to blank him out—for business reasons as well as personal ones, she told herself.

She was somewhat miffed that she hadn't heard from him, as he was already a day late with the call he'd promised to make. Perhaps he'd been detained in Boston. Otherwise, it seemed logical to think he might have phoned last night. But he hadn't. Nor had Hilary dreamed of the Arabian desert, or of a handsome, dark-haired sheik whisking her away on the back of his camel.

More's the pity, she thought wryly, as she poured herself a second cup of coffee and thought about fixing something for breakfast.

She put a cranberry muffin in the toaster oven and, while waiting for it to heat, wandered toward the back of the house. She was thinking about the way the veranda could be transformed into a tearoom, as Jay had suggested.

In her absorption with future plans, she briefly forgot about the snow. Then she saw that the veranda had been transformed into an arctic setting that might appear beautiful in another person's eyes, but was bleak and ghastly to her. That odd, choking fear clutched her, and she turned away abruptly, her eyes filling with tears even after all these years.

Memories could be so damned treacherous!

The phone rang, and its harsh jangle was music to her ears. Especially since her intuition was surging, telling her it would be Jay Mahoney at the other end of the line.

It wasn't. The woman who answered Hilary's eager "Hello" had a well-modulated voice that oozed charm and business training.

"Miss Forsythe?" she asked politely.

The three little letters in Hilary's "Yes," slid on a downward scale.

"Eleanor Roberts, Miss Forsythe," the woman announced briskly. "Mr. Mahoney's secretary. Mr. Mahoney asked me to get in touch with you."

"Oh?"

"Mr. Mahoney will be tied up in a bank conference all day," Joaquim Alvaro Mahoney's secretary said sweetly. "But he wondered if you might be free to have dinner with him this evening?"

Hilary froze. Then hot, indignant thoughts brushed across her mental horizon, sweeping a mounting irritation with them.

Just who the hell did J. A. Mahoney think he was?

That was the first question Hilary, tight-lipped, silently expelled. It was followed by a rash of others, none of them very complimentary to Devon's leading young banker.

Into the tense silence, Eleanor Roberts queried, "Miss Forsythe?"

"Yes?"

"I was afraid we'd been disconnected," Ms. Roberts murmured discreetly.

"Sorry," Hilary murmured back, her natural poise reasserting itself.

"Mr. Mahoney wondered if seven o'clock would be convenient?"

"I'm afraid not," Hilary retorted automatically. She was staring out the kitchen window, thinking not so much of J. A. Mahoney as of going out into the snow. "I'm sorry," she added, "but I won't be able to have dinner with Mr. Mahoney tonight."

The secretary issued polite, regretful phrases and rang off.

Hilary ate half her cranberry muffin, then threw the rest away. Even the world's best gourmet food would've tasted like cardboard to her at the moment, so she returned to her planning. It was a lonely business, though. She'd always been told she had an inventive mind and she never lacked for ideas, but now she wished she had company, someone to give her input. Preferably someone tall, dark and handsome with eyes that could melt the rime of ice gripping her heart.

Impatient with herself, she went upstairs, made her bed, straightened her room, then dressed in warm clothes. After that, she turned on the television and watched two soap operas. They only made her feel worse.

Still, time *did* pass. And Hilary was thinking about heating a can of soup for lunch when the doorbell rang. No intuitive vibes alerted her about whom she would encounter, so it was a decided shock to find Jay Mahoney standing on her doorstep.

He was wearing a thick wool parka and fur-covered boots that came almost up to his knees. He looked fantastic, like a Russian cossack about to mount his white horse and race across the frozen steppes, Hilary thought, a bit incoherently. A Latin cossack! she amended.

Jay looked very Latin at the moment, his handsome face mirroring annoyance mixed with more than a dash of temper. Scanning his face, Hilary spun slightly out of control. She decided he could easily play the lead in a revival of one of those classic Valentino movies she could remember her grandmother raving about.

There was, however, nothing very exotic about the way he snapped, "Dammit, Hilary! Do I have to stand out here and freeze, or are you going to invite me inside?"

"I'm sorry," she mumbled quickly, and nervously moved back.

He brushed past her, then nearly slammed the door behind him. "Why," he demanded irately, "can't you have dinner with me? Am I mistaken, or didn't we pretty much set this up the last time I talked to you?"

"I thought we had planned on yesterday, and I like my invitations issued on a somewhat more personal level," Hilary informed him.

"Do you, now?" His gaze raked her, and she got the distinct impression that at any moment he might turn her over his knee and give her a good old-fashioned whacking. "I only asked Eleanor to set up the time..."

"Oh?"

"Yes!" Jay Mahoney practically shouted. "I'm sorry I'm a day late, but my hands were tied. The president of the bank's here from Boston. We drove down together late last night. There's a lot in the wind, and I'm going to be in conference all day."

"So your secretary informed me," Hilary told him, a shade too politely.

She thought she could hear him grit his teeth. He gave her a long level look, then said tightly, "I'm supposed to be at a luncheon right at this moment. More of a command performance, really...which I'm not especially fond of."

"Then don't let me detain you."

"I'm not at the luncheon, am I, Hilary?" he asked sarcastically.

"Don't you know where you are, Jay?"

"Oh, come on," he protested. "Look, I'm sorry. If I'd known you'd resent having Eleanor call you, I would have somehow managed to do so myself, believe me."

An impish grin tugged at the corners of Hilary's mouth. "You could have said you had to go to the men's room," she suggested.

Jay Mahoney broke out laughing. It was wonderful laughter, and filled the rather staid front hall of the old Forsythe homestead with warmth. Hilary wished she could record the sound and keep it to be replayed when she was by herself.

"Next time I'll remember that," he decided, his dark eyes sparkling with amusement. "Whatever," he promised, "I can assure you that in the future I'll handle my phone calls to you personally."

Hilary relented. "I'm sorry," she said sincerely. "It was childish of me to react like that. I had a rather bad morning, that's all."

Jay frowned. "A bad morning? Why?"

"It just...was," she evaded. Her hatred of snow was something intensely private. She'd never confided in anyone about it—not her uncle, not Roy. Nor any of the several good friends she considered close enough to talk to about most things.

She didn't need to look at Jay to feel his dark eyes studying her face. And there was concern in his voice as he said, "I think it's something more than 'just was.' Can't you tell me, Hilary?"

Now, she didn't *want* to look at him. It would be too easy to give way completely and say too much if she met those dark eyes. "No," she answered, softly but firmly.

His fingers gripped her chin and tugged gently. He said, "For God's sake, Hilary, what is this?"

Hilary looked up. She wanted to throw herself into his arms. She yearned to cry her eyes out, then let him kiss away all her fears.

"This bad morning you've had...was it caused by something so private you can't discuss it with me?"

Carefully she said, "Well...it really doesn't concern anyone else but me, so I'd rather not talk about it."

His face was incredibly expressive. He telegraphed his disappointment with a mere flicker of his eyelids. "Okay," he said evenly. "I don't like people prying into my affairs, and I won't pry into yours. But I have to ask you one more question. Is the reason you can't have dinner with me because you have another...engagement?"

Was he inferring that maybe she didn't want to have dinner with him? Hilary laughed aloud. She couldn't imagine anything she wanted more.

"No, I don't have another engagement, Jay. And I want to get together with you. We need to discuss business."

"Business?"

"Yes. We need to talk about your...well, about your bank's potential role in my shop."

"We do indeed, don't we?" he agreed smoothly, and added, "That wasn't exactly what I had in mind for tonight, though. I'll admit I was more interested in the thought of our getting to know each other better personally when I suggested you have dinner with me. But," he concluded, a devilish smile curving his lips, "maybe we can manage to combine the two. Business and pleasure. Measures of both, okay?"

"Any other time I'd be delighted," Hilary responded, casting an anxious glance outside. She wondered how long it took snow to melt when it was this deep. She remembered an old-timer friend of her uncle Chad's saying that snow never lasted very long on Cape Cod because the narrow peninsula was surrounded by seawater, and the salty air would rapidly melt most accumulations. Hilary hoped there was some truth to this.

"Gorgeous, isn't it?" Jay queried, following her gaze.

"What?"

"The snow. We've had a bitter cold winter, but there hasn't been much snow. When I woke up this morning and saw this, it made me feel like a kid again. I wanted to get out there and have a snowball fight with someone. Or maybe make a giant snowman, or snow ice cream, or boil some maple syrup and make sugar on the snow. Ever do any of those things, Hilary?"

Aghast at the mere idea, her voice quavered as she said hastily, "No."

He looked at her curiously. "You sound as if the idea's abhorrent," he commented.

"I'm not crazy about snow, Jay."

"Well, I wouldn't like it around all the time," he agreed, "but I love it like this once in a while." A gleam appeared in his dark eyes. "Tell you what," he suggested, "I was going to snatch a hamburger on the way back to the bank, but I'll skip lunch. You put on some more clothes and some boots and let's go outside and make a snowman together."

Hilary wanted to do what he asked. She ached to do what he asked. She fervently wished she could match Jay's spirit and plunge outdoors with him. She could even imagine the kind of fun it might be. But she couldn't do it.

"Maybe another time," she deferred.

In the moment of silence that followed, Hilary felt as if Jay Mahoney could see right through her. He contemplated her thoughtfully, then said affably, "Okay." After a second, he added, "As to dinner, if you can't make it tonight, how about tomorrow night?"

"Tomorrow night would be fine," Hilary agreed quickly.

Jay nodded and headed for the door. Hilary followed, wondering if he would turn back at the last instant and make history repeat itself by kissing her again.

He didn't. And fighting off her disappointment, she shut the door behind him.

The day inched by. Early that evening George Delacorte called and asked Hilary if she'd like him to bring over a couple of pizzas. Her answer was an unqualified affirmative. She yearned for something tasty and hot, but more than that, she wanted company.

She and George sat in front of a blazing fire, sipped red wine, munched pizza and talked. George had been a good friend for a long time, and he could be a great companion. Tonight, he didn't allow any personal feelings toward her to intrude—for which Hilary was thankful. To add to that, he was perceptive. Their kiss the other night had sent them both a message, and Hilary was certain George wouldn't again try to put their friendship on a more romantic footing.

George had lived in Devon most of his life. The only time he'd spent elsewhere was during his college years in western Massachusetts and, afterward, when he'd lived in Boston for a year, having taken a job with the IRS. His friends still loved to heckle him about that era in his life.

After his stint with the IRS, he returned to Devon and joined forces with another accountant. Eventually, he set up his own firm, a very successful move. Thinking this, it occurred to Hilary that George must know a fair bit about his fellow townspeople.

She sketched out her thoughts for a shop featuring strictly Cape Cod arts and crafts and lightly touched upon the concept—Jay's concept—of a tearoom. George was discreet and could keep a confidence. Hilary was sure he wouldn't tell anyone about her plans until she wanted him to. But much though she trusted him, it still took her awhile to get down to the nitty-gritty of questioning him about Jay Mahoney.

Even then, she proceeded very cautiously. She hoped she didn't sound *too* casual as she asked, "You do know Horace Mayo's successor at the bank, don't you?"

George was deciding between a piece of pepperoni pizza or a piece of mushroom pizza. He opted for the pepperoni, then said, "J. A. Mahoney? Yes. Most of my clients do their banking at Commonwealth. Also, J. A. belongs to the Cape Codders Club. Matter of fact, he's slated to become president at the next election."

"Hmmm." Hilary considered this, then asked, "Is he into a lot of other things?"

"J. A.?" George repeated, as if he'd already mentally changed the subject. He sat back, mulling over her question. "Well, I guess he's active enough, if that's what you mean. Into civic things, that is . . . but then that's the main purpose of the Cape Codders Club. I don't know about his private life. Come to think of it, I guess you'd say he keeps kind of a low profile."

"Oh?"

"Well, you know how it is in a town like Devon. Among the year-rounders, anyway," George amended, and grinned. "Little pockets of society," he said. "Sometimes lots of pockets in the same coat. Sometimes pockets that don't get mixed up with any others, if you follow me. I'm one of the lucky few who get invited across the board. . . ."

Hilary smiled. "Are you saying you wear a lot of different coats, George?" she teased.

"Not at all," he answered seriously. "I'm saying I know a lot of people who keep their hands in their own social pockets. Whereas I get chances to dip into all of the different . . ." He paused. "This is getting complicated."

"Well, I think I know what you mean," Hilary told him. "The same people travel in the same circles, but someone like yourself gets the chance to cross a number of the intersections. I should think the same thing would apply to Mr. Mahoney."

George glanced up suspiciously, then admitted, "I'm not much for the cocktail-party scene, but I make appearances for the sake of business. I seldom see J. A. at any of those shindigs. He doesn't belong to the Yacht Club, either, come to think of it."

"The Yacht Club where nobody owns a yacht?" Hilary joked.

George grinned. "Come on, Hilary, we have sailboat races out on Pleasant Bay, you know that. And I hear windsurfing lessons are in the offing this summer."

"Big deal," she applauded, kidding him. "To get back to J. A. Mahoney..."

"Why the interest in him?" George asked bluntly.

"I'm planning to do business with Commonwealth, if they want me as a client," Hilary allowed. "I'd like to get my shop started by this summer, including the tearoom. To do that, I'll have to raise some cash. Uncle Chad had his fingers in a lot of pies, but it's going to take time to convert this to that, if you know what I mean."

George nodded sagely. "I know exactly what you mean."

"When I came down to Devon this time," Hilary confessed, "I seriously thought of putting this place up for sale. I can hang on to the cottage out in Wellfleet, mainly as an investment. Now, George...well, the idea of starting my own business here—not to mention getting into the necessary renovations—challenges me."

"I can understand that."

"So, I think my best bet will be to go for a bank loan. That's where Commonwealth and J. A. Mahoney come in."

"Shouldn't be any problem," George told her, after giving the subject a moment's thought.

"I hope not."

"Might have been easier for you if Horace Mayo were still at the helm," he opined.

"Why is that?"

"Well, he knew your uncle. They'd done business for years. Not that you're apt to have any problems with Commonwealth, considering your family's record hereabouts. J. A. is kind of new around here, that's all."

"He's from the Cape, isn't he?"

"I believe so," George nodded. "I gather he's from Provincetown, grew up out there. He's half Portuguese..."

And would have been named Serafina, Hilary remembered, had nature decreed otherwise. She repressed a chuckle, but a special twinkle came to light her eyes.

"The more I think of it," George mused, "the more it hits me that J. A. really is pretty much of a loner. He lives in that new condo complex over by the harbor—Sand Terraces, I think it's called. He's always pleasant enough and active in civic affairs, as I've said. But he doesn't hang out with any particular crowd."

George's brow wrinkled. "Seems to me I heard a couple of things about him...."

Hilary leaned forward, silently willing George to reveal whatever those things were.

George either didn't remember, or he chose to keep the gossip to himself. And Hilary couldn't unduly prod him without arousing his suspicions, so she let it go. Not long afterward, George finished up the last of the pizza, decided they'd better call it a night and went home.

Hilary, perhaps subconsciously, had been clinging to the idea that snow melted quickly on Cape Cod because of that legendary salt air. She woke up the next morning to find she'd been putting her faith in a myth. The snow hadn't disappeared; it had increased. While she slept, a new layer of white fluff had drifted down from the heavens, creating Christmas-card scenes wherever she looked.

She was putting on the coffeepot when the doorbell rang. Again, no warning vibes sent out impulses that might have prepared her for the sight of Jay Mahoney.

He was wearing a bright red ski suit, the pants thrust into the same knee-high boots he'd been wearing yesterday. A matching knit cap was pulled down over his dark hair. He radiated health, vitality and a sex appeal that was entirely too overt for Hilary to handle, especially at this hour of the morning when she'd only just got out of bed.

She suddenly became conscious of her appearance and instinctively retreated. Jay took this as an invitation to enter and, knocking a final clump of snow off his boots, strode into the hall.

He cast an approving eye at Hilary's pink wool robe, then swept her face with those arresting dark eyes and observed, "You look sleepy."

Hilary had splashed her face with cold water and had given her hair a quick brushing, but her face was devoid of makeup. Her eyelids probably looked as heavy as they felt, she thought dreamily, as she yawned, then awkwardly cupped a hand over her mouth.

Jay laughed. "Did you just get up?" he asked.

"Just about."

"Well," he drawled, "I decided to verify our dinner date for tonight in person!"

He was closing the door behind him as he said this, and Hilary got another revealing glimpse of the world outside. She shuddered, then managed weakly, "I can't go out with you tonight, Jay."

The door thudded, and Jay turned to her, his face darkening. "Hey, what is this?" he demanded.

"I ... I just can't go out with you tonight, that's all."

"Why not?"

"I don't like to go out in the snow."

He stared at her. "Good grief, why?"

Hilary shrugged unhappily, and Jay pressed, "Didn't you tell me you've lived in Boston most of your life?"

"I don't know if I told you that or not. Maybe you plucked it out of your dossier on me at the bank," she retorted defensively.

"It could hardly be called a dossier, Hilary," Jay countered stiffly.

"No?"

"I read the file on your family before I met you," he said, summoning patience. "I knew we'd be meeting because of your uncle's estate—"

"And you wanted to be prepared?"

"Hell, yes, I wanted to be prepared. It saves a lot of time all the way around if you've done your homework before you meet a person."

"And with that weird memory of yours I suppose you only have to read through things once?"

Jay did grit his teeth at that. Then he said tightly, "Just what is that supposed to mean?"

"Nothing, really." Facing him, Hilary knew an argument wasn't what she wanted. "I'm sorry, Jay."

He expelled a deep breath, then stated, "We'll get back to that another time. Right now, I want you to put some warm clothes on..."

"And come play in the snow with you?"

"Exactly." He added, ominously, "If you can't get dressed by yourself, I'll help you."

Would he dare? Hilary looked at him, and knew he would definitely dare. "All right!" she blurted.

Her legs were shaking as she headed upstairs to do Jay Mahoney's bidding. Once she stepped outside and faced that winter world, she was sure she'd go to pieces. She'd make a fool of herself in front of someone she wanted so much to impress. Jay would think her an idiot. Or worse, a sniveling coward. Two sorry options.

She took a long time putting on a few layers of clothing. At one point, she heard Jay call, "Hey, there, don't take all day! I have to be at the bank in an hour."

Next he'd be threatening to come up and get her!

Hilary tried to hurry, but her fingers fumbled and she twice fell over her own feet. She was miserable, and desperately wished that she could summon up an imaginary yet convincing sore throat, as she'd done so often when she was younger and couldn't face going to school in the snow.

Chapter Five

Hilary's snow costume would have given any self-respecting couturier a nightmare. She'd spied a pair of boots and other winter paraphernalia in an upstairs closet while looking for extra towels the other day. Now she appropriated these items of dubious vintage and layered herself for her unwonted outdoor rendezvous with Jay.

Her bulky down parka reeked of mothballs, and the boots were too big, so she stuffed socks in the toes and donned an extra pair of socks herself. Finally, she clumped down the stairs.

Jay was not in the hall. Hilary called his name, but he didn't answer. Perplexed, she opened the front door and peered out cautiously. She saw footprints—actually, foot *impressions*, she amended. The snow was too deep for mere footprints. These elongated "holes" started at the door and continued down the front path. She couldn't tell whether Jay had made them coming or going. In fact, there was no

solid evidence to verify that they'd not been made by some
neighborhood abominable snowman!

Hilary advanced apprehensively, edging forward and
making her own mark with first one foot and then the other.
The snow, even on the front steps, was so deep it nearly went
over the top of her boots. She reached the bottom of the
steps and paused to steady herself. At that instant, a mass
of cold white fluff spattered her square on the shoulder.

It took a moment to register that someone was throwing
snowballs at her. Someone? Jay!

The effect of his action was more of a curative than anything else could have been. Hilary, possessed of a basic
Yankee fighting spirit, was at once motivated to retaliate,
regardless of this snowy environment.

When Jay emerged, laughing, from around the side of the
house, she was ready for him. She let him have it with two
hard-packed fistfuls of snow that exploded against his chest
and sent him staggering backward.

He swiftly regained his balance and advanced toward her,
an impish grin on his face, a threat in his eyes. Hilary tried
to retreat, but with the steps at her back, there was no place
she could go. Jay lunged and grabbed her, and they went
tumbling into the snow together.

His merriment was contagious. And as they rolled over
and over, Hilary found herself laughing uncontrollably.
Then they came to a stop, halted by a clump of snow-
covered bushes.

Jay, at that point, was on top of Hilary, his arms still
around her, his face dangerously close to hers. Hilary gazed
into his mesmerizing eyes, and every detail of his handsome face seemed etched especially for her.

She thought, weakly, that if she could find a white flag to
clutch she'd flutter it at him because she could think only of
surrender. Surrender in the snow. It was crazy. She detested
snow. But this felt fantastic . . . because of Jay, because he

was so near her. Because the slow, insidious warmth of her desire for him was chasing away the coldness of nature.

Their mouths touched. His lips were cold, but as they meshed with hers they began melting into a warm and velvety softness like eating a spoonful of rich vanilla ice cream. Hilary became dazed by what this man was doing to her, even with both of them wearing enough clothes to dress half an army!

She entwined her arms around Jay's neck, bringing him even closer, and sought his lips with newfound hunger, sensuously twisting to keep pace with the ardor of her embrace. When she drew back for a breath of air, she heard his wicked chuckle.

"Boy..." he murmured huskily. "If the neighbors are peeking, they won't need to turn their thermostats up to heat their homes."

That did it. Hilary pushed him away from her and tried to get up with a show of dignity. Instead, she struggled, teetered and promptly fell into a deep drift. Forgetting about dignity, she simply tried to gain control over her clumsily-shod feet.

Towering over her, Jay commented, "You look like a teddy bear in hand-me-down duds!"

"Thanks a lot," she began, but her indignant mutter was cut short when he lifted her upright.

"Take it easy," he cautioned. "This stuff won't bite you."

"Maybe not, but you might," she retorted.

Again, she heard that wicked chuckle. "I'd love to."

Hilary stood, supported by his arms, and—regardless of any neighbors who might possibly be taking this in—let him hold her for a minute as she dared to look around. Her familiar yard had been completely transformed into a dazzling winter wonderland of unique beauty. Icicles spun from the eaves of the big old house, long frozen needles glittering in the sun. The frosted tree branches etched surrealistic patterns against a sky that was incredibly blue and totally cloudless. The air was fresh and clean, piercingly cold to Hilary's lungs but wonderfully exhilarating.

Suddenly she felt like a blind person who, upon being given a pair of special glasses, could miraculously see. It was because of Jay. He'd lured her out into the dreaded snow; he'd dispelled memory's shadows. And he'd made her open her eyes to the exquisite glory of a world she'd considered totally repugnant for so many lost years.

Gratitude for him stabbed at her heart, but there was something else, too. An emotion she was almost afraid to identify.

Love?

How could she be falling in love with him? She scarcely knew him!

As Jay helped her back up the steps, brushed the snow off her clothes and then followed her into the hall, Hilary felt her head clicking out indecipherable messages, and her heart was reeling. She was out of touch with reality, so the thud was hard when Jay abruptly brought her back to earth.

"Hell," he muttered reluctantly, "I've got to get to the bank."

Hilary's chaotic thoughts eddied around, then settled into a ragged semblance of order. "Would you...um, like some coffee or something before you go?" she suggested.

Jay shook his head. "I'm late as it is, and I've got back-to-back appointments scheduled." He paused in the doorway. "Shall I pick you up at seven?"

She'd forgotten all about his dinner invitation, but she dimly remembered refusing him. Still, that was because she hadn't wanted to go out in the snow. Now, she'd *been* out in the snow and, with Jay along for moral support, there seemed no valid reason for not venturing forth again.

"All right," she managed.

He kissed her briefly. Too briefly. "Until tonight, *cara*," he murmured, in that soft tone that would melt an iceberg. And before she could rally, he was gone.

By the time Jay Mahoney got to the bank that morning, he was glad he had a busy schedule ahead of him. If it weren't for a number of appointments he had with people who he knew were relying on him, he would have tossed business to the winter wind and returned to the Forsythe homestead.

He wanted to sit in front of the fireplace with Hilary and talk about all kinds of things. He wanted to know her a thousand times better than he knew her now. He yearned to make love to her, but not yet. He instinctively sensed that she was somehow important in his future. Very important. Too important to rush things.

Without conceit, Jay knew there was a good chance he could sweep Hilary off her feet. But one reason for a swift acquiescence on her part might have to do with the fact that she was still recovering from her unhappy experience with Roy in Boston. Also, she was still bruised by the trauma of her uncle's long illness and death. Subconsciously, she might be seeking love and affection to fill the void left by that loss.

Jay wanted *Hilary*. He didn't want her on the rebound.

The morning passed slowly. People came to consult him about everything from getting a car loan to setting up a trust fund, and several clients were impressed by the way his trick memory worked. But, except for the delight that registered in their faces every time Jay pulled a personal fact from thin air, these sessions were boring him.

He dispatched Eleanor Roberts to pick up the calzone and black coffee he'd ordered from a nearby deli. Then, brown bag in hand, he closeted himself in an upstairs room the bank normally used for conferences. As he ate, he reflected on his extraordinary ability to recollect seemingly useless bits of information.

He ruefully conceded that it was a mixed blessing. Sometimes it was a curse. Other times, almost a miracle. Automatically remembering facts like people's birthdays and wedding anniversaries, or the names and ages of their children, had a decidedly plus advantage.

Everyone, Jay realized, liked to feel that someone else cared. Even the friendly neighborhood banker!

In the middle of the afternoon, George Delacorte came to see him. George had long ago inherited a piece of property in nearby Orleans, and he was wondering whether to sell it undeveloped or build a house.

Jay, leaning back in his chair, surveyed the popular accountant after hearing this and privately wondered what was making him so itchy. Ordinarily, George Delacorte was the prototypical Yankee, presenting a calm facade and a taciturn nature. But today he was restless and on edge, tapping his fingers against the arm of his chair and favoring Jay with some rather speculative glances.

Jay said thoughtfully, "Well . . . I'd say it all depends on what you want to do."

George had been studying his fingernails so intently that Jay thought he might begin biting them any second. But now his head shot up, and he demanded, "What's that supposed to mean?"

"Just what I said," Jay answered patiently, restraining the impulse to ask George just what the hell was eating him. They weren't close friends, but they'd worked together on several committees in the Cape Codders Club. And he liked George.

"Look," George said, uncharacteristically abrupt, "if I knew what I wanted to do, I wouldn't be here."

Jay tried a different tack. "What I mean to say is, if you want to build, go for it. If not, you might do well to sell the

nd as is. There's a big market currently for property in the
rleans area, and your tract is in an excellent residential
ection."

George picked up on part of Jay's explanation. "Why
ould I want to build another house?" he asked. "I've al-
eady got one."

That was true. George shared an old Cape Cod house
ith his widowed mother. She spent her winters in Florida
nd frequently traveled during the rest of the year, visiting
er other children. Most of the time, George lived alone.

"Well," Jay tried again, "you can make big money on a
ouse, assuming it sells. Or you could keep it as an invest-
ent, with several options. Since this property is near the
each you'd have a maximum summer rental poten-
al...."

"I'm not interested in being a landlord," George stated.
Oh, what the hell," he added. "I guess I'll just hang on to
e land a while longer. The taxes on it aren't that bad."

Jay looked at him curiously. He'd wedged George in for
is meeting because on the phone this morning the ac-
ountant had sounded as if whatever was on his mind was
rgent. Now...

Resignedly, he sat back and let George bide his time, even
hough he knew that this would make him late with his other
ppointments. There was nothing pressing on his personal
genda, though, until seven o'clock when he'd be picking
ilary up. He reminded himself that he must call and make
eservations for two at the Pilgrim's Path, or else have
leanor do it.

He was tempted to press his intercom and request this of
leanor when George asked, unexpectedly, "What about
ilary Forsythe?"

Jay was staggered. It hadn't occurred to him that George
ould even know Hilary. He temporized by posing the ob-
ious question, "Are you her accountant?"

"Not so far. Her uncle used a Boston firm. If Hilary wants me to handle her affairs, I will, of course."

"What's your interest, then?" Jay queried, and immediately wished he hadn't.

"Well, I've known Hilary...a long time," George hedged. "Since she used to come here summers as a kid, in fact." He paused, then continued carefully. "I understand you're encouraging her to start a business here, and I gather it'll be with the bank's backing. I just wondered how you stand on the issue, that's all," he admitted, then finished, almost defiantly, "Hilary's a pretty great person. I just don't want to see her make a mistake."

Jay drew a long breath. Then he asked, "Are you saying you think she'd be making a mistake to open up a business in Devon?"

"Hell, I don't know. I don't have to tell you how many damned gift shops and souvenir shops and artsy-craftsy shops there already are around the Cape. I mean, they're practically falling over each other. It amazes me so many of them make it, but there are plenty that don't, as we both know. As for Hilary—I know she had a shop in Boston which sounds good, but...she didn't need to make a lot of profit. She always had her uncle to watch out for her."

"Are you saying she operated at a loss?" Despite his personal feelings for Hilary, Jay's caution flags went up.

"I don't know," George conceded. "The thing is, it seems to me it would make more sense for Hilary to sell the old Forsythe place and get some money out of it while there's money to be got."

"The house needs a fair bit of work, you know. As it is now, Hilary wouldn't get anywhere near the price she could if it was fixed up."

George shrugged. "She'd make enough. And, personally, I think it would rid her of a tremendous burden. She's got a summer cottage out in Wellfleet she can use if she wants to come to the Cape...."

Jay's mounting tension began to abate. If George wasn't interested in having Hilary become a permanent resident of Devon, then maybe he didn't have that much of a personal ax to grind.

"To tell you the truth," George confided suddenly, "I guess what I'm most interested in is seeing Hilary happy. She's pretty much alone in the world now, and there a lot of people out there who wouldn't hesitate to take advantage of her. I'd hate to see her go out on a limb with a big bank loan and maybe wind up losing everything."

"I couldn't agree more," Jay replied levelly.

A moment later, they switched to a problem involving the Cape Codders Club; then George left. As he bade him goodbye, Jay was convinced that George's entire purpose in making his emergency appointment that day had been to voice his fears for Hilary. He cared for her a lot, Jay realized. Possibly, too much. He only hoped that Hilary didn't return any of the romantic feelings he intuitively sensed George was harboring for her.

He flicked his memory switch. No, Hilary had not, so far, mentioned George Delacorte to him. But then he didn't know that much—he didn't know *anything*—about the people in Hilary's life, aside from her late uncle and the callous, self-centered Roy.

Maybe tonight, Jay thought, as he finished up his day's work, he'd have a chance to fill in some of the gaps.

The day passed as slowly for Hilary as it did for Jay. In the late afternoon she luxuriated in a long, hot bubble bath—fortunately, the hot-water heater in the house, though an old one, still worked well. Then she took her time deciding what to wear.

Finally, she slipped into a stunning gray wool dress cinched at the waist with a wide silver belt. But it wasn't until she was fastening on complementary silver earrings that Hilary realized that the floppy old boots she'd worn in the morning were the only footwear she had, suitable for the outside weather.

She discovered that the boots were big enough to pull right over her slim silver slippers. That problem solved, she further topped her fashion picture by opting for the bulky old down parka she'd worn earlier, instead of the chic black cashmere coat she'd brought down from Boston.

When Jay appeared at seven, Hilary was ready for him. She thought about offering him a predinner drink, then decided against it. She needed to keep a level head because she really did want to discuss business with him tonight. Thus far, too much proximity to Jay had only served to make her feel as if her IQ suddenly had been cut in half!

Jay was again wearing his furry boots, his red ski jacket and the matching knit cap. Hilary had never lived in a small community in winter, but it was easy to see that "country" people dressed practically while the remnants of a minor blizzard still covered the ground.

She would've fallen into snowdrifts any number of times on her way to Jay's car but for his steadying arm. Incredible, how *warm* his hand was. His body heat surged right through the thickness of her parka, making her feel like a self-contained cauldron slowly being stirred to a boil. This sensual, potent awareness of him could easily eclipse the far more mundane details she wanted to work through with him, Hilary warned herself.

She was so absorbed with trying to remain cool, calm and reasonably collected in Jay's car that they were almost at the door of the restaurant before she realized he'd chosen The Pilgrim's Path for their dinner.

The restaurant had valet parking. Jay turned his keys over) an attendant, then came around to offer Hilary his hand. .s she took it, she murmured, "Great, I really like this lace."

He stood stock-still. "You've been here before?" he asked uriously.

"One time," she nodded, tugging slightly so that he'd inish the job of getting her on her feet. Her boots were unooperative at best. She felt as if she had a rocking horse on ach foot.

"Oh...well, it's a fairly new place," he allowed blandly. I've only been here once before myself, at a dinner with ome bank people."

Hilary didn't answer him. She was too preoccupied with rying to make a reasonably graceful entrance into the resaurant, and she couldn't wait to get the boots off so she ould walk with considerably more poise.

Jay was quiet after that. As they were seated at a table for wo, Hilary suddenly realized that the vibes between them ad changed. There was a shuttered look to Jay's expresion, and waves of an emotion emanating from him washed ver her. Disappointment? Why should Jay be disapointed? Because she'd been here before?

He asked if she'd like a drink, and she said she would. Jay ave the order for two whiskey sours, then sat back and tudied the cranberry-colored tablecloth, his brow furowed.

"All right," Hilary said, deciding on a frontal attack. 'What's gone wrong?" When he looked up, startled, she miled wryly and added, "Do you think you're the only one vho can be perceptive?"

His ensuing smile matched hers. He said softly, "No, of ourse not. I...well, I wanted this to be a first for you. This lace, I mean. It's our first date, so I wanted to take you

somewhere that would become memorable. You know, late:
on we could look back and say, 'Our place'..."

"Can't we?" she asked innocently.

"Depends."

"Depends on what, Jay?"

"On who you were here with previously, I suppose," he
admitted. "It's a new place, Hilary. It wasn't even here las
summer."

"My, but your curiosity is showing," she teased. "Very
well, I was here the other night with George Delacorte.
imagine you know him?"

"Yes, I know him." The words thudded like stone:
dropped into a still pool.

"George is an old friend of mine," Hilary went on
"We've known each other for years."

"I know," Jay stated abruptly.

"You know?"

"Don't sound so surprised. George was in to see me thi:
afternoon. Allegedly, about some business of his own. Actually, about you."

"George went to the bank to see you about *me*?"

"Well, I doubt he'd admit it if you asked him," Jay told
her, "but that's why he was there." He sighed. "George
seems to think the world may be out to take advantage of
you."

"What?" she scoffed. "That doesn't sound like George."

"Doesn't it?"

Jay's jealousy was showing. He'd picked up his knife and
was bending the blade as if he'd like to see it break off. Hilary smiled. The thought that Jay could be jealous of her
shouldn't make her happy, but it did. Outrageously so.

She said calmly, "I suppose I do love George."

Jay's eloquent eyebrows arched uncomprehendingly.
"Love?" he queried.

"I was an only child," Hilary evaded, "but you already know that, of course." She hadn't meant this as a dig at his proverbial memory, but seeing Jay's mouth tighten, she added quickly, "I love George like the brother I never had. Seriously—" as pure disbelief now registered "—he's a very good friend. The kind of person I know I could always turn to if I ever needed help. I admit that maybe George has had a few other thoughts about me, especially since I've been back in Devon. And...I settled that early on. There's nothing between us but friendship, and there never will be."

Suddenly Jay smiled, that fantastic smile that started pinwheels whirling all the way from Hilary's heart to her head. "May I have a guarantee of that in writing?" he asked.

"Honestly, Jay!"

He shrugged. "So, I'm being obvious. I'm being childish. Maybe I'm even being a bad sport," he conceded. "But...you're doing things to me, Hilary. I don't entirely understand it myself, this effect you have on me."

That makes two of us, Hilary phrased silently.

"It's very seldom that I let a woman into my life," Jay informed her with a solemnity that surprised her. "I have my reasons, and maybe someday I'll tell them to you, but not tonight. I've put a blight on the evening as it is. So from here on in, could we just forget and enjoy?"

He reached an imploring hand across the table, and Hilary clasped her fingers through his. Her skin was very white against the stunning olive of his. The contrast reminded her that she really barely knew Joaquim Alvaro Mahoney, as outwardly charming, sometimes zany and thoroughly fascinating as he appeared.

That was an odd statement he'd made about letting women into his life. It indicated that there'd been someone. This wasn't the first time that thought had crossed Hilary's mind from something he'd said to her. Still, he was right. Tonight wasn't the time for serious exploration. Dredging up the past was the last thing she wanted at the moment, and she was sure Jay felt the same way.

She nodded her agreement, then gently disengaged her hand from his and raised her cocktail glass. "To enjoyment!" she toasted.

A candle flickered between them, and as they clicked glasses, Jay's face was brushed by its golden glow. Seeing him like this, Hilary had visions of that crazy episode in the carnival tent when he'd posed as Madame Zola. The memory elicited an amused smile, and Jay asked, "Can I share what you're thinking?"

"You made a great fortune-teller," she said wistfully, and laughed when she saw his startled expression.

Rallying quickly, he murmured, "But I have forgotten my crystal ball, though in your case I don't need one. Would you like me to look into your future, *cherie*?" he purred, adopting Madame Zola's phony accent.

"No way," Hilary told him. "I'm too happy with the present."

"So am I," Jay said softly. "So am I."

They drank, they ate, they talked about small, safe things, and they laughed—a lot. Dinner finished, Jay said, "I'm going to suggest we go somewhere else for a nightcap. Someplace, I hope, you haven't been to before."

"Well, now, let's see," Hilary began thoughtfully. "That does narrow the field, doesn't it? I'm such a night owl when I'm in Devon."

"Okay, have you been to our local version of the South Sea Islands, called Polynesian Paradise?"

"There's a place called Polynesian Paradise in Devon?"

"There sure is. It opened up in time for New Year's Eve, and you wouldn't believe the bash they threw."

"So, you were out celebrating!"

"Was I ever! Once again, I violated my annual promise to myself not to start the New Year off with a hangover," Jay admitted. "Anyway, it might be fun to stop by for a drink."

Once inside the Polynesian lounge, Hilary found it difficult to believe she was still on Cape Cod. The place had a number of tropical props including a mock volcano that belched smoke at regular intervals, and hostesses who wore grass hula skirts and flung artificial leis around customers' necks.

Jay ordered a rum and fruit juice concoction called an Exotic Ambrosia for Hilary and something entitled Fog Cutter for himself. As they were sipping, again in candlelight, a combo started to play. Hilary, watching other couples glide through the amethyst haze provided by the dim lights edging the dance floor, looked across at Jay and asked, "Shall we?"

She added, impishly. "Though I'm not blessed with your kind of a memory, I do recall your saying that dancing is not your forte. Even so..."

"You'll be sorry," he told her dolefully.

"You, with all that Latin blood?" she challenged. "I've always heard that Latins are natural dancers."

"Then I must have been given a transfusion at birth, and the donor had two left feet," Jay informed her.

"Jay, you can't be that bad!"

He rose reluctantly. "All right, you asked for it."

That there were many people dancing now, didn't help the situation. But after they'd done a couple of turns around the floor, Hilary had to admit Jay definitely was not the world's best dancer. Twice he actually stepped on her feet, and she had to repress a potentially fervent, "Ouch."

Each time, he apologized abjectly and asked her if she wanted to go back to their table. On the third occasion, she said, "No, I'm going to make you suffer through this."

"Me, suffer? It's you who'll wake up in the morning with badly bruised toes."

"Jay, I can't believe this. Usually you seem so..."

"So what?" he prodded.

"Well, so sure of yourself, so absolutely self-confident and in command. And so well coordinated. But when you dance..."

"Yes?"

"You're tight as a drum," she accused. "If you'd just relax and let yourself go..."

"Those are dangerous words, *cara*," he warned her. Nevertheless, he tried. And a short while later, when the combo launched into a bouncy disco melody, he was definitely doing better.

Jay sidestepped a third dance by telling Hilary he was keeping her up past her bedtime. She knew that he had to be at work in the morning, too, so she didn't protest. Anyway, she'd had a fantastic evening, despite its rather unsteady beginning. And Jay... Jay, she thought, as he drove her home along the snowy streets of Devon, was unlike anyone she'd ever known before.

As he helped her up the steps of the Forsythe homestead and waited while she unlocked the big front door, Hilary's head was swimming with treacherously sensuous thoughts. If she had felt less intense about him, she would have suggested he come in for a nightcap. As it was, she knew what would happen if they found themselves alone in her darkened house.

Jay was too special to chance letting her surging emotions toward him take over. Hilary didn't want to be swept away by a sex-inspired tidal wave. She amended that. She wanted very much to be swept away by Jay's lovemaking. But she and Jay first needed to establish a foundation so that they wouldn't suddenly find themselves far out at sea.

Jay's arms encircled Hilary, cutting short her rationalizations. He kissed her temple, and she wouldn't have believed that particular little zone was capable of such an erotic response. Then his mouth moved across her cheek and brushed back toward her ear, leaving a trail of small fires along the way. Delicately, he encircled the inner edge of her ear with the tip of his tongue.

Hilary moaned involuntarily and instinctively clutched him, plunging her fingers into the dark thickness of his hair while her body edged closer and closer toward places of ultimate contact with his.

Abruptly, his mouth claimed hers. And as her lips opened, as she and Jay mutually took the first step on a sensual voyage that could easily reach a point of no return, Hilary's desire became a force unknown to her. She'd thought she was experienced. But now she knew she'd only touched the edges of what passion could truly be.

She was willing. She wanted Jay to take her in his arms and carry her upstairs. She wanted him in her bed. She wanted *him*. She was shocked by the fire of her wanting, but the warning signals exploding in her brain were becoming more inaudible with every passing second. Her body and her heart were taking over. Executing an emotional coup that would be impossible to resist.

Then Jay stopped. He shuddered briefly and then relaxed. Holding Hilary gently, he whispered, "I'm going to leave you now."

Her heart was where her voice should be, preventing her from speaking.

Sensing this, Jay said, "I want tomorrow for us, Hilary. Many tomorrows. Let's not spoil them by taking too much too soon, okay?"

She nodded slowly, still unable to speak. She knew Jay was right, but as he headed back down the path they'd carved through the snow, Hilary wished, for an agonizing moment, that his heart had prevailed over his logic.

Chapter Six

I know Mr. Mahoney has a busy schedule. But I wonder if there might be a chance he could fit me in for a few minutes some time today,'' Hilary said sedately.

There was a pause. Then Eleanor Roberts suggested, ''Let me ask him, Miss Forsythe. Frankly, I don't see any available slots on his calendar either today or tomorrow. But I'll double-check with him and call you back. If you'll give me your number...''

Hilary was tempted to say that Mr. Mahoney already had her telephone number, but she suppressed the urge. She rattled off the digits politely, answered with equal politeness when Ms. Roberts asked her if she'd be at the number for a while and then rang off.

Only a minute later, the phone began pealing.

''What is this?'' Jay Mahoney demanded, sounding frazzled.

''What's what?'' Hilary countered innocently.

"What's this about your wanting an appointment with me here at the bank?"

"I want an appointment with you at the bank. It's as simple as that."

"Why at the *bank*? Why can't I come to your house? Why can't you come over to my place, for that matter? I keep a reasonable supply of food and drink on hand."

"I don't want to eat or drink, Jay. I want to talk business with you."

He groaned. Lowering his voice, he said, "Anything even remotely approaching business tends to flee my mind when I'm with you, *cara*."

"That's what I'm afraid of," she admitted.

"Am I that transparent?"

"Sometimes you are, but that doesn't matter. What matters is that we...well, we seem to have a certain effect on each other."

"Tell me about it!"

"I can't think when I'm alone with you," Hilary confessed. "I know that's a terrible admission to make, but..."

She heard the devilish chuckle she'd come to love. Then Jay murmured sweetly, "It's the best admission I've heard all day."

"Seriously, Jay..."

"Seriously, Hilary..."

"If you haven't time for me today or tomorrow, I'll wait," she decided, ignoring his teasing. "Just put me down for the first free slot you have."

"Is that an invitation?"

"Jay, I'm not playing games." Hilary tried to sound severe, but it was almost impossible to keep any kind of grip on logic while she was listening to Jay's sexy voice. It would be even more impossible to get down to a business discussion with him if they were together anywhere except within the relatively austere confines of his office. Even there it would be hard.

Jay said, "I was planning to call you as soon as I had a minute. I'd like to persuade you to drive out to Provincetown with me tonight."

"Drive out to P-town, in the middle of the winter?" Hilary echoed, aghast at the thought. "Jay, there's still snow all over the place."

"I think I saw a robin today," Jay countered, "so spring can't be far away."

"Someone told me that many robins spend the whole winter on the Cape," Hilary remembered.

"Maybe. I guess they're hardy birds. Anyway, I have some relatives down in Provincetown. They're getting on in years, so I like to look in on them now and then. But Provincetown can wait a while longer if you'd rather do something else. How about me fixing dinner for us at my place?"

"You can cook?" Hilary blurted, and nearly added, "too."

"Yes, I can cook. A lot of men my age can cook. In case you didn't know it, many of us have had to learn how to be self-sufficient."

"That's a subject I refuse to pursue," Hilary warned him.

"Listen, I have to cut this short, much though I hate to. Eleanor will be breathing fire down my neck any second now. There are at least three people waiting to see me. Suppose I pick you up around six. Is that too early?"

"Jay?"

"Yes?"

"I'd really like to get through my business appointment with you before we make another date."

The silence that instantly stretched between them weighed a ton. Then Jay, his normally expressive voice void of emotion, said, "Can you come in at one o'clock?"

He would be cutting his lunch hour short, Hilary realized, or skipping it entirely. But she wasn't about to protest. "Yes," she answered quickly. "Yes, I'll be there at one."

It wasn't until after she'd hung up that it struck Hilary she would be forced to drive in the snow. Not in the snow, precisely. But certainly in a winter setting. Still, it was too far to walk, considering the weather, and her only other option—calling George Delacorte for a ride—was out of the question.

Summoning courage, Hilary struggled into her oversize boots and tramped out to the garage. Her car had been idle for more than a week, but finally it started. Gingerly pressing the gas pedal, she cautiously backed out of her driveway, trying hard to ignore the crunching sounds of the clumps of snow and ice beneath her tires.

Her hands were clammy as she drove down Sea Street toward Main Street. Nevertheless, she'd just achieved a victory. Not very long ago, she would have freaked out completely before she'd even cleared the garage. Her tussle in the snow with Jay the other day had done wonders. She smiled at the memory and began to relax.

The main roads were clear, as was the bank's parking lot. Shutting off the motor, Hilary expelled a breath of relief. And as she approached Eleanor Roberts's desk, she was riding a tidal wave of triumph.

She addressed the secretary cheerily. "Mr. Mahoney said he could see me at one," she reported, slanting a glance at the large wall clock above Ms. Roberts's head. It was precisely two minutes to one.

"I believe Mr. Mahoney's at lunch," the woman informed her coolly. "But, I'll check. Miss Forsythe, isn't it?"

"Yes."

As Jay's secretary buzzed the intercom, some of Hilary's ebullience began to dissolve. Was it possible that Jay had forgotten he'd told her to come in? Had he gone out to lunch . . . with someone else?

The answer was no, to Ms. Roberts's chagrin. Jay answered the intercom promptly, dispelling Hilary's anxiety attack, and a moment later he appeared in his office doorway.

He looked incredibly handsome. Wearing a brown tweed jacket and dark brown slacks, he could have stepped out of a top fashion ad. She had to remind herself that he wasn't entirely perfect. When it came to dancing, he really did have two left feet.

"Please come in," he invited curtly.

Hilary tried to detect a little warmth in his usually mellow voice, but there wasn't any.

Jay waved her to a familiar chair, then assumed his own place, facing her across the polished expanse of wood that separated them. Abruptly, Hilary became aware of the distinct advantage the person behind the desk always has. Almost like a king or queen on a throne. Jay certainly looked, at least, as if he were in command.

To make matters worse, he evidently was waiting for her to speak first. She cleared her throat and tried to think out a succinct statement, something that would have an impact.

All she managed was, "Jay, I'm sorry if I've messed up your lunch hour."

He picked up a slim gold pen and twirled it between his fingers. Watching him, Hilary decided this was a learned executive gesture. She'd noted this type of behavior every time she'd been in a similar situation. Now she wondered if the inevitable use of a small prop by desk-bound professionals was a cloak for nervousness or perhaps for impatience?

Jay said tersely, "You haven't messed up my lunch, Hilary. But I can only give you half an hour. I really do have a

full schedule this afternoon, and I'm already running late."
So saying, he put the pen down, folded his arms and waited.

Hilary searched frantically for the right words. But right
words were never more elusive.

Finally, she blurted, "Jay, I'm going to need to borrow
some money from your bank. Quite a lot of money, actually."

He shot a startled glance at her, and Hilary instinctively
drew back. For about two seconds, Jay's mask dropped,
and he looked frustrated and unhappy. Then he became as
urbane as ever.

"I presume you feel you're going to need some financing
for your shop, is that it?" he asked.

"I'll need more than 'some' financing," Hilary told him
honestly. "I'll need a large amount of cash to get things
going properly."

Jay frowned and picked up the gold pen again. "As I understand it, Hilary," he said, "you are your uncle's only
heir. Perhaps I'm mistaken, but I thought he left you quite
a bit of money."

"Not exactly," she replied. "That is . . . yes, I did inherit
the total of uncle Chad's estate and, yes, the estate has
considerable assets. But most of the available cash went to
pay his medical expenses, which were very heavy, and my
lawyer has warned me I must keep a large reserve for inher-
itance taxes. All in all, I guess you could say that my cash
resources have become...strained. Almost everything at this
point is tied up in investments. And I really don't want to
sell off any of those unless I absolutely have to."

She waited, but Jay didn't reply. He was staring at a spot
somewhere in the middle of his shiny desk top. Studying his
inscrutable mien, Hilary felt a surge of resentment toward
him. He certainly wasn't making this any easier for her!

She said, "I don't know exactly how much I'm going to
need. As you've seen for yourself, there's a lot of work that

needs to be done on the house. I can concentrate initially on the downstairs and on getting the veranda glassed in for the tearoom. But I'll need entirely new kitchen equipment to handle even a small amount of cooking, plus...oh, any number of other things."

"What will it cost to have those necessary things done?" Jay asked bluntly.

"I can't be precise," Hilary admitted. "I won't be able to give you exact figures until I've consulted with carpenters, plumbers, electricians and restaurant supply houses, for beginners. But, based on my experience with the Boston shop, I'd say I'll need in the neighborhood of fifty thousand dollars."

She met Jay's eyes as she said this and wondered how she'd ever thought they were warm enough to melt an iceberg. Right now, his steady gaze made her shiver.

"You must know," he said, "that although your ideas for a...gallery, let's call it, and a tearoom are interesting, you'd actually be embarking on a risk venture."

"You were the one who conjured up the idea of a tearoom," Hilary retorted, stung.

"We were just...talking," Jay answered, rather lamely. "I still think the porch could become quite a drawing card, and I like your idea of featuring strictly Cape Cod arts and crafts."

"So what's the problem?"

Jay collected his thoughts, and said, "Don't misunderstand me, Hilary. But when we discussed those things, I was under the impression that you were a wealthy young woman who could afford to put up a fair amount of cash on her own without going into hock."

Hilary froze. "Are you saying you consider taking a bank loan for business purposes going into hock?"

"In this case, yes. You're not dealing with a sure thing, and the location..."

"What's wrong with the location?"

"Maybe nothing, but that's only a guess. Sea Street is still primarily residential, even though businesses have crept in, as you previously pointed out to me. People do go right past your place on their way to Maushope Beach; I admit that. Nevertheless, while you're not off the beaten track, you're not entirely on it, either."

"What are you saying? That I would have a treasure of a place apt to remain undiscovered?"

"Not exactly. Whether or not you were discovered would depend on many things—publicity, a good advertising campaign, a really exceptional line of merchandise and a tearoom that featured consistently excellent food." Jay calmly ticked these points off on his fingers.

"You seem to think I'm incapable of achieving those things," Hilary commented coldly. "Well, Jay...you've really surprised me."

"I'm sorry, Hilary, but I can't be other than honest when it comes to business."

When it comes to business? The statement penetrated, stuck and nettled her with little stabs of doubt.

"Look," he said reasonably, "suppose I went along with you and said I'll put in a request to the bank for a fifty thousand loan? You'd have to put up something in the way of collateral. You do realize *that*, don't you?"

"I haven't thought the details through," Hilary muttered.

"Then you should, beginning now. Does your house have a mortgage?"

Hilary shook her head.

"Then you might put the house up as collateral to secure the loan, right? Well, suppose your shop doesn't work out? Suppose you go into the red, the first season at least, and can't keep up your loan payments? A year from now the bank could be owning the old Forsythe property."

Hilary's laugh was short and bitter. "Obviously," she commented tautly, "you expect me to fail."

"Oh, for God's sake!" Jay exploded. "Of course I don't *expect* you to fail. It's just common sense to look at both sides of the coin. If you came in here thinking I'd say, 'Sure, Hilary, the bank will be happy to hand you fifty thousand dollars,' then I have to tell you you're sadly mistaken. I wouldn't hold this job much longer if I was that irresponsible."

"Then you're turning me down?"

He glared at her. "No!"

Sitting across from Jay, Hilary felt that her arms and legs had turned to stone. So had her head, and...her heart. She flexed a hand experimentally and was surprised to find that the joints all worked. Never in her life, she thought painfully, had she felt so humiliated.

A small, sad smile played around Jay's lips. "It would seem that the ice maiden hath returned," he said softly.

"Not funny," she retorted.

"I wasn't trying to be funny. You should see the way you're looking at me. Those winter eyes of yours are chilling me right to the bone. Dammit, Hilary, I didn't want things to be like this between us."

Neither did she. But the old Forsythe pride was surging through her, stiffening her spine. "I'm sorry, Jay," she said coldly.

"Yes, you really sound sorry," he mocked. He sighed heavily. "I'm the one who's sorry. I can't think of anyone I've ever wanted to help more than I want to help you. And I'm certainly not closing the door, Hilary, don't misunderstand me. The thing is, we need to get together and go over details. Maybe with all the facts at my command I can present your loan request to the bank with some validity."

"I wouldn't count on it, Jay," Hilary stated icily. She stood up. "Thank you for your time," she managed.

Jay leaned back in his chair and surveyed her with smol
dering eyes. "If you think I'm going to leave it like this
you're very wrong."

"I don't think there's anything more for us to say."

"About business? Or about us?"

"About both." It took all of Hilary's willpower to expe
those two words, but for the sake of her self-respect, she
did.

To her surprise, the anger faded from Jay's midnight eye
and he actually chuckled. "If you think that, you really ar
out of your head, *cara*," he told her, his voice infused with
that sensuous quality that never failed to turn her on
"Business is one thing, Hilary. What you and I have be
tween us is something else entirely. I'm not about to giv
that up easily."

"If you don't trust me . . ."

"What in hell does trust have to do with it? So I'm no
sure you can start a new shop in Devon and make a profi
fast enough to repay a loan. So I'm not sure you can com
up with a cook who can make blueberry muffins like m
grandmother did. All of that's beside the point when i
comes to us."

"I don't think so."

Jay's lips tightened. "Am I to take it that you're going t
insist on putting business before pleasure from now on?" h
demanded, his exasperation reaching the boiling point.

Again, it took all of Hilary's willpower to answer, "Yo
could say so."

"Then I suppose we'll have to get the business over with
as soon as possible," Jay decided. "When can I come ou
and go over things with you? Tonight?"

Hilary had to bite back a laugh. The last thing she coul
envision was going over things with Jay tonight. This ses
sion had unnerved her. What she needed was his arm
around her, not a lecture on the risks of running a business

What she needed was his tenderness, mixed with the hot passion of his kisses. What she needed was...

She shut off this untimely investigation into her personal needs, and said, "Why don't you come out for brunch on Sunday?"

"Sunday?" he repeated, staring at her. "Do we have to wait that long?"

"Four days is not that long," she informed him. She was thinking that a midday brunch would be the safest time to be with Jay at her house. Daylight hours. Sunlight streaming through the windows.

"Very well," he conceded stiffly, "what time?"

"How about eleven?"

"Eleven o'clock, Sunday," Jay concurred, plainly annoyed.

Hilary began to think that Sunday, literally, would never arrive. Every hour seemed to drag twice as much as the one just past.

On Saturday, she got the car out of the garage again and went uptown to do some grocery shopping. She'd opened several cookbooks the night before and had concluded that it would be folly for her to attempt any new recipes. Cooking wasn't her forte, nor experimenting in the kitchen at the eleventh hour.

She'd never needed to cook, nor was she encouraged to learn how. As a child, then later when she'd gone to live with her uncle after her parents' deaths, there was always a hired person to concoct the Forsythe meals. There'd also been a nanny and a maid.

Still, she wanted to prepare something for Jay that wasn't completely off the frozen-food shelves. On several prior occasions when she'd had the yen to play chef, she'd made a mock cheese soufflé that had turned out reasonably well. It was easy and tasty, so she decided to go for that. She could fill out the menu with bakery croissants, fancy jam and fresh-ground coffee.

Jay, she was remembering as she headed back home with her provisions, had blithely said he could cook. Judging by how well he did everything else—except dancing, Hilary amended, suddenly thankful for that imperfection—he was probably a very good cook. Maybe even a gourmet chef. In any event, she knew he liked to eat.

The cheese dish was best when made a day in advance, then stored in the fridge until baking time. Hilary worked her way through the recipe without too much difficulty, then was appalled at the mess she'd made in the kitchen.

That was another thing. Because there'd always been people around to pick up and clean up after her, Hilary had never felt the need to do those things for herself—until now. Her mind had been so occupied since her return to Devon, she hadn't especially noticed how the house had gone well past an acceptable slightly-dusty point.

She looked around with growing annoyance. The downstairs wasn't too bad, but the upstairs was a disaster zone. And Jay would certainly want to see the upstairs in order to properly assess the value of her property.

It took Hilary all Saturday afternoon to clean the upstairs. Then she moved back to the first floor and worked until almost ten with the radio blaring for company. By then, muscles she didn't even know she possessed were protesting vehemently, and she ached from head to foot.

She soaked for a long time in a hot bath, thinking about tomorrow, now only hours away. It had been agonizing not even to talk with Jay during the past four days, and the thought of seeing him again was like having fireworks held in abeyance for the Fourth of July, knowing that with just a quick touch of a match they'd burst into showers of magnificent color.

On the other hand, she dreaded meeting with him under these circumstances. It had become obvious in the bank the other day that they were skating on thin ice, possibly in more ways than one.

Hilary recalled the old cliché about not mixing business with pleasure. She'd never had to test this in Boston, but now she could see why such verbal chestnuts endured.

It would've been better if she'd gone elsewhere for a loan, she realized. Maybe one of the other banks with which her uncle had done business. But she could also imagine Jay's fury if she'd done something like that without telling him first. She was sure he'd have considered it a stab in the back.

It seemed like a classic no-win situation, Hilary concluded dismally as she climbed into bed that night.

In the morning, she awoke to discover a suspiciously gray and whirling world outside her window. It was snowing again, and as she watched the flakes dust the ground with new accumulation, some of the old fear returned to clutch her.

She wished that Jay were at her side to chase away her apprehensions and encourage her to be brave. Thinking of how far she'd come because of him, Hilary drew a deep breath and mentally pushed those tragic memories away. She knew they were hanging over her, but...they'd stopped haunting her. Now she was able to look at snow and still function.

Later in the morning, checking out her game plan in the kitchen, Hilary glanced out the window and spied something decidedly yellow blooming to one side of the garage. It was a protected area that also got the full daytime sun—when there was any sun! Nevertheless, it seemed incredible that something could be flowering in the midst of a snowstorm.

Peering closer, Hilary realized she was looking upon an early-blossoming forsythia bush. It was possible to cut forsythia in late winter, she recalled, and force the blooming process inside a warm house. Evidently this particular forsythia had managed to force itself.

The splash of color was arresting. Hilary decided that a bunch of forsythia would make a great centerpiece for the dining-room table and also add a much needed highlight to the generally drab decor.

She calculated the distance from the house to the garage. It wasn't *that* far. Tim, a man who did odd jobs for people in the neighborhood, had shoveled out a path for her after the earlier snow. Today's snowfall had, so far, added perhaps two inches. But Hilary was sure she could make the trek without bothering with her boots.

That was a mistake. Midway along the path, she slipped and sat down on her fanny with a resounding thump that hurt clear through her hipbones. After that, she edged gingerly forward, wary of every step. She hadn't had the vaguest idea of where to find something like garden clippers on the premises, so she'd procured a sharp kitchen knife to do the cutting.

She hacked off several pieces of forsythia and was going for one last branch when the knife neatly sliced the side of her left thumb.

Blood spurted, and Hilary stared in disbelief as large crimson drops etched a gory contrast to the white snow. She had nothing with her to wrap around the wound, so she made tracks for the house, clutching the forsythia and carefully holding the offending knife.

She dripped blood across the kitchen floor before she made it to the sink. Then she washed the cut and covered it with a hastily folded paper towel. It was a clean cut and not that deep, but it had started to throb fiercely.

When the bleeding finally stopped, she taped a succession of bandages around her thumb. Then she cleaned up the kitchen floor and, glancing at the clock, knew that she had to start cooking the soufflé. She slid the large casserole in the oven, set the timer, then went upstairs to try to do something about her disheveled appearance.

Favoring her left hand, Hilary clumsily got out of the old slacks and wool top she'd been wearing and put on a rose-colored jumpsuit she'd bought in Boston. The color alone was a morale booster. With one hand out of commission, it was impossible to do much with her hair, so she settled for simply brushing it out and letting it swirl around her shoulders in a golden mass. She concentrated on a little eye makeup and some lip gloss, but a final glance in the mirror told her she still looked rather harried. The real problem was her mounting nervousness at the thought of her upcoming encounter with Jay.

Eleven o'clock came and went. The soufflé was definitely making its presence known with a delightful aroma that filled the air... but would be converted into the smell of scorch, Hilary knew, if she left the blasted dish in the oven any longer.

She'd timed the soufflé so it would be ready at exactly eleven. Now she knew she should have held off and allowed some leeway, since Jay was late. Also, what if he wanted a prebrunch Bloody Mary, something she'd be making for herself in another second if he didn't show up soon.

Chiding herself for her ineptitude, Hilary ferreted out a couple of pot holders from a kitchen drawer and opened the oven door. The grill stuck, so she reached for the casserole itself, as the cheese mixture was already getting dark brown on top. When she tugged, her hand made contact with the red-hot oven coil, and it was all she could do to control her movements as a searing pain shot through her.

Luckily, she didn't drop the dish on the floor. She hastily set the soufflé on top of the stove, then let her tangled emotions relieve themselves in a downright howl.

At that moment, the doorbell rang.

Hilary was close to tears as she went to let Jay in. She didn't realize what an abject picture she made as she opened the door and stood before him, a large bandage covering her left thumb while her right hand was stuck in her mouth.

A wave of tenderness rocked Jay from head to toe. He asked gently, "*Cara*, what have you done to yourself?"

Hilary looked up at him, and tears filled her ice-blue eyes. "Nothing," she wailed. "Everything."

A second later, Jay was holding her close, and she was sobbing out her saga.

Chapter Seven

Jay took charge. And Hilary was glad to let him take over, even though, under most conditions, she considered herself a very independent person.

First, he insisted that she sit down and relax while he fixed two stimulating Bloody Marys. Then he examined Hilary's wounds and carefully applied antiseptics and fresh bandages, which he had the good fortune to find in an upstairs cabinet.

The combination of Jay's presence and the heady drink he'd concocted gave Hilary the necessary boost to assert herself. With Jay's help, she put the soufflé back in the oven, but it was a sadly fallen, semiburnt offering that she finally placed on the table.

That didn't seem to matter to Jay. He ate it anyway, and relished the croissants, liberally spread with butter and boysenberry jam. He also drank three cups of steaming black coffee and arranged the forsythia centerpiece, all the while keeping a watchful eye on Hilary.

As they lingered at the table, he suddenly asked, "What is it about you and snow, Hilary?"

She was completely unprepared for the question. She stared at him dismayed, and instinctively tried to hedge. Snow was a subject she'd been dodging for the past sixteen years.

Jay, she soon saw, wasn't about to let her off the hook. Reluctantly then, she started telling him the terrible story of how her parents had been buried in an avalanche in Switzerland. She'd never fully revealed the incident to anyone, and she was surprised at the way her words were flowing. Still, she stared down at her bandaged hands as she spoke, afraid to meet Jay's eyes. She knew if she saw too much sympathy in their dark depths, she'd break down.

When she finished, Jay was silent for a long moment. Then he commented, "I can't even begin to imagine what you must have felt like. What a rough scene for a young girl in a foreign country to have to handle alone."

He spoke matter-of-factly. When Hilary glanced up, she saw that Jay was looking at her gravely but wasn't swamping her with pity or solicitude. For that, she was grateful.

"My Uncle Chad got there as soon as he could."

"Even so..." A remoteness swept over Jay's handsome features. "I suppose when something like that happens, you are essentially alone, no matter how many other people are around," he mused. "I'm sure your uncle did everything he could for you."

"Yes, he did," Hilary agreed. "He was a bachelor. He had to reshuffle whole portions of his life to accommodate a twelve-year-old girl."

"I imagine you made his life complete, Hilary," Jay said gently. "The bachelor state isn't always everything it's purported to be."

A momentary bleakness held his face in check. It was the same expression Hilary had noted the first time she'd been in his office at the bank. She wondered anew what had happened to Jay Mahoney to make him look like that. He seldom did. Usually, he was the most upbeat person she'd ever met—outwardly, at least. She wondered if his surface charm and zest for living was covering up an inner melancholy. If so, what had caused that melancholy?

He pushed back his chair and stretched. "How about looking over the house again, so we can come to some working conclusions?" he suggested, in a quick change of both subject and pace.

They toured the house, this time from top to bottom. Jay even navigated the shaky stairs to the attic and peered around in all the cobwebbed corners. Then he insisted on inspecting the cellar and taking a look at the furnace, which had been lumbering along for more years than Hilary herself but still was doing a good job.

"They made things better then," he concluded, his inspection finished. "Even so, it stands to reason that your heating system will have to be replaced, maybe sooner than later."

Like the attic, the cellar had been used for storage by many generations of Forsythes. Dusty furniture, moldy cartons filled with antiques, and literally hundreds of other items vied for space. These included everything from a rusted bird cage to an antique dressmaker's form.

Surveying this latter curio, Jay said, "One of your ancestors had quite a figure, Hilary. Ample, to say the least. I can only guess at that bust measurement, and will you look at that wasp waist!"

"Is there a joke I'm missing?" Hilary asked suspiciously.

"Maybe," Jay teased. He raked her with an appraising glance. "You wouldn't measure up to her in inches," he decided, "but I'd say the more important genetic attributes have been passed along reasonably intact."

Hilary felt herself flushing. Noting this even under the low-wattage cellar lights, Jay laughed. "Don't knock it, Hilary," he advised. "Be glad you inherited the right genes... or whatever it took to make you like you are." He added softly, "I wouldn't change a single cell."

He was standing very close to her, and in the next instant they turned to each other by mutual accord, and Hilary dissolved into his arms.

Jay's kisses were as hot as the snow outside was cold. Hilary became possessed by a raging fever that soon was well on its way to becoming an out-of-control fire. She felt Jay's hands clutch her shoulders as he tried to steady himself. She heard the rasp of his breathing and knew he was as intensely attracted to her as she was to him. In another second it would be overwhelmingly difficult for both of them to turn their emotional clocks backward. And everything in Hilary urged her to go forward, to take the next step.

Jay moaned huskily, "Oh, God, I've been trying not to give in to temptation, but now..."

"Jay..."

"Hilary, I've been trying to hold back, but I can't much longer. I want you so much. I find myself thinking about you at the damnedest times... with a potentially embarrassing lack of control coming along to dominate those thoughts. I don't want to rush you, I don't want to rush *us*." He laughed shakily. "Maybe it would be better if I simply give up and go crazy."

Hilary's voice was so low Jay had to press even closer to hear her. "Then I'd go crazy too," she murmured.

"Hilary, do you know what I'm saying? Do you know what *you're* saying?"

"Yes," she told him joyously. She rallied long enough to look around her, and her laughter rang out.

Jay pulled back and stared down at her. "What's so funny?" he demanded.

"Us," Hilary gasped. "Everything." She tugged at his sleeve, choking back her peals of laughter, her eyes brimming with merriment.

"I want you, Jay darling... but not in the cellar!"

Hilary's bedroom was neat that Sunday, almost to the point of being pristine. She'd cleaned it thoroughly, not because she had any idea she'd be leading Jay Mahoney to her bed, but because she didn't want him to see what a slouch of a housekeeper she was.

Her bed was an old four-poster, sans the canopy. Still, there was a virginal touch to the white eyelet bedspread and matching flounce that trimmed her girlish, kidney-shaped dressing table. Her uncle had given her carte blanche in redecorating this room when she was fourteen.

That had been during her frills, lace and furbelows period, and Hilary hadn't really changed anything since. It had been fun to return here every summer to this echo of her adolescence. Somewhere in her closet, she knew, there was a big album into which she'd long ago pasted pictures of all her favorite movie stars.

She'd never brought a man into this room. Even her uncle had seldom invaded these premises. As she crossed the threshold now, a funny feeling took over. Guilt? She was a grown-up woman, twenty-eight years old, for God's sake! Why should she feel guilty about inviting a man into her bedroom? Especially a man to whom she felt so strongly drawn. Especially Jay Mahoney.

He was holding her hands gently, taking care not to touch the bandages. Some nuance of expression must have given her away, because Jay asked, "What is it, Hilary?"

She didn't exactly know. She only knew that something had happened to that magic moment they'd shared in the cellar. Suddenly she felt curiously awkward and unsure of herself.

Jay asked softly, "Second thoughts?"

She turned to him. "Not really."

His mouth twisted ruefully. "I've simmered down, too," he confessed. "Funny, what a couple of flights of stairs can do, isn't it?"

"Jay..."

"*Cara*, you don't have to apologize. You never have to apologize to me. Remember that, will you?"

He flashed a devilish grin at her. "I should have made love to you right there on one of those heirloom couches of yours," he decided. "Dust, broken springs and all."

A smile lit up Hilary's eyes. "Yes, maybe you should have," she conceded.

They sat down side by side on the edge of her bed. Jay said, "I feel like I've broken into a dormitory at a select girls' school."

"Yes, it looks like that, doesn't it," Hilary agreed, appraising her room. "I should do something about it."

"On the contrary, maybe you should leave it exactly as is," Jay contradicted, his eyes absorbing the details of their surroundings. "It's a study in pale pink and white and girlishness." He glanced down at the bed. "You must have had many romantic dreams in this, Hilary. How many handsome young princes came here to court your favors?"

"I lost count years ago," she teased.

"Were you deeply in love with Roy?"

Hilary stopped short in what she'd been about to say. Jay had this uncanny habit of changing subjects so abruptly that she was invariably rocked off base.

"Were you?" he persisted when she remained silent.

Hilary shook her head. "You ask the damnedest things," she told him.

"You're not answering my question, Hilary... and it's something I need to know."

"*Need* to know?"

"Yes."

"Well, I thought I was in love with Roy. Otherwise I never would have moved into his apartment."

"Why did the two of you break up?"

"He locked me out," Hilary confessed.

"*What?*"

She'd thought this was something else she could never bring herself to talk about with anyone, but she recalled that even when he was acting the part of Madame Zola, spilling out forbidden topics to Jay was dangerously easy.

"Roy resented my spending more and more time with Uncle Chad," she stated, her tone edged with bitterness. "Uncle Chad was dying, dammit! I wanted to be with him every minute I could. Just then he needed me a thousand times more than Roy did. But Roy couldn't see it that way. After the funeral, when I went back over to Beacon Hill— where Roy has his apartment—the key he'd given me didn't work. He'd gotten back at me, if you can put it that way, by changing the lock."

"Selfish bastard," Jay muttered.

"Yes, you're right," Hilary agreed, with surprising objectivity. "That's precisely what Roy is. He has a tremendous ego, and like most tremendous egos it requires frequent feeding. I wasn't able to do that, so... let's say Roy got too hungry to wait for me any longer."

"What did you do when you found the door locked in your face?"

"I was tempted to break it down and then smash up everything in the apartment," Hilary recalled. "Instead I went back to Uncle Chad's town house in Back Bay, cried, paced the floor and raged about men..."

Jay nodded understandingly.

"Then I went out to a Chinese restaurant and got something to eat."

"Come on!"

"I'm not a total idiot, Jay," Hilary said levelly. "It didn't take me long to realize that Roy and I had had something pretty intense going, but it had nothing to do with love."

She ignored Jay's growl and continued, "Physical intimacy isn't necessarily love. Roy certainly proved that. There wasn't any caring or affection. There wasn't any *relationship*. When all that came home to me, it wasn't very difficult to wash Roy out of my hair."

"Have you?"

"I've given him a final rinse," Hilary concluded defiantly. "Believe me, there are no lingering suds."

"You're sure about that?"

"Positive."

Jay stared down at his hands and said solemnly, "I don't want there to be any doubts in your mind, Hilary. I need very much for you to be sure your heart is free." He raised his eyes to hers. They were very dark and deeply intent. "I'm running a little scared about this," he admitted.

"Scared?" That was the last word she would have expected Jay Mahoney to choose.

"Let's just say I don't fall in love every day."

Slightly dismayed by his seriousness, Hilary told him, "Neither do I."

Jay did another of his quick switches. Speaking in Madame Zola's voice, he intoned, "I see a tall man who came into your life as a stranger only recently, but soon he will be closer to you than anyone you have ever known. You must place your trust, your heart in this man's hands, *cherie*. He will guide you to the stars. . . ."

"Will he?" Hilary asked softly.

Jay reached for her, and she clasped her arms around his neck, not minding the slight sting of her wounds. He slowly ran his fingers sensuously across the back of her neck and shoulders. Then he trailed them downward to her waist, and began lightly kissing her velvet-smooth cheeks.

When he kissed her ear, Hilary felt a tremor infiltrate her entire body, and her desire for him mounted. She moaned and then whispered seductively, "I want you, Jay."

Jay answered by slipping a warm hand under her sweater. Then, after unclasping Hilary's bra with a deliberateness that only heightened her anticipation, he gently nudged her back on the bed until she was lying against the pillows, looking up at him with wide, expectant eyes.

He was very tender, very gentle. He touched here and kissed there, his hands and mouth playing on her body as if she were an instrument upon which he was about to perform a magnificent concerto. With each gesture the tempo gradually quickened, the melody became more wonderfully complex.

Hilary let Jay undress her, loved having him undress her, loved the look in his eyes as he caressed her body with an ardor that left her breathless. Those magical hands followed the path pioneered by his eyes, and finally he struck chords upon the most intimate of her secret places, orchestrating an emotional symphony within her that matched his tactile expertise.

She wanted to undress him, but her small injuries kept getting in her way. At last Jay laughed and said, "This time I'll do it." The gleam in his eyes was nothing less than erotic as he moved swiftly to rid himself of his clothes. Then it was Hilary's turn to let desire overwhelm her as she visually explored every inch of Jay's perfect masculine anatomy and reached out to touch him with tentative fingers.

It was snowing again, and the house seemed cushioned from outside sounds, wrapping Hilary and Jay in an inviolable cocoon of silence that only they could break. It was punctuated by the sounds of their breathing, their moans of

pleasure and, ultimately, their cries of ecstasy as passion
triumphed and they reached the peak of fulfillment.

In the aftermath of their lovemaking, they covered
themselves with the luxuriously soft comforter Hilary's
grandmother had stitched long ago and nestled within the
confines of each other's arms, silent and satiated.

These private minutes could have been the time for confidences, and Hilary began to wish that Jay would start
telling her more about himself. She wanted to know everything about him, beginning with the day he was born and
continuing right up to that crazy night she'd met him playing fortune-teller.

She was seeking for the right conversational key to open
the door to his past when she heard that the tenor of his
breathing had changed. Jay had fallen asleep—at entirely
the wrong moment!

Jay left the Forsythe homestead late in the afternoon that
Sunday, telling Hilary in rather vague phrases that he had a
previous engagement. He offered no further explanations.
He simply left with a brief wave over his shoulder. Feeling
both hurt and dismayed, Hilary resisted the urge to call out
any questions.

He hadn't said a thing about her request for the bank
loan. But as Hilary heated a can of soup for her supper and
munched a piece of cold soufflé, she had to admit that the
way the day had turned out, there'd hardly been an appro-
priate moment to discuss business.

Monday dawned bright and sunny, and three or four
inches of new snow had been added to the previous accumulation.

She was surprised when the entire day passed without a
call from Jay, and even more surprised when he didn't call
her Tuesday. By the time he finally phoned toward noon on

Wednesday, there was an edge of coolness to her voice that Hilary had no desire to suppress.

If Jay was aware of this, he didn't let on. Instead, he asked, "How about coming over to my place tonight, and I'll fix dinner?"

Did he expect they were going to repeat Sunday's performance? Hilary certainly didn't regret what had happened between them the other afternoon. She'd already filed her lovemaking episode with Jay under the "Unforgettable" category in her memory book. But it miffed her to think that he would deliberately let the better part of three days pass without even phoning to say hello.

"I think I'll stay in tonight," she responded stiffly. "I have a lot of correspondence to catch up on."

"That excuse probably has more holes in it than the instant-headache lie," Jay informed her dryly.

"I really do have a lot of letters to write."

"I don't doubt it. But that doesn't mean you have to write them tonight, Hilary. Why don't you want to come to my house for dinner?"

He could be so suave and diplomatic when he wanted to be but also incredibly blunt!

Right now that annoyed Hilary. She was thinking of a suitable retort when Jay sighed and said, "I know you're angry because I haven't called you. The reason I haven't called you is that I would have had to wake you up. I've been tied up in bank meetings from early morning until late at night. In fact, I just now skipped out of a meeting—" his brusque tone mellowed, and he concluded softly "—because I had to hear the sound of your voice."

Damn, but the man had an uncanny power to melt down her defenses just as she was getting them cemented into place! Hilary latched on to only part of what he'd just said and asked, rather coldly, "Is it customary to have so many bank meetings?"

"It certainly is not!" Jay snapped. "The president's down again from Boston, and the reason for the meetings is that there's a strong possibility we'll be merging with another bank. Actually, we'll be taking over the other bank, if things work out, which will push us into a very high echelon in New England's financial circles."

"Well, bully for you."

"Do I detect a note of sarcasm?" Jay queried, then continued before Hilary could answer, "Look, *cara*, this isn't just an ordinary merger...not that any merger is ever really *ordinary*. But in this case a lot of big changes will result. I could be involved in them. The specifics are highly confidential, but I might be transferred from our Devon branch to another branch who knows where. I could even be promoted to a job at Commonwealth's headquarters in Boston."

A big, black hole poked its way into Hilary's universe. She held the phone receiver away from her head as if it were responsible for making the hole and stared at it unhappily. Then she heard the faraway sound of Jay's voice finishing another sentence. "What?" she quickly asked into the mouthpiece.

"Did you vanish into thin air for a moment there?" Jay demanded.

"No, I didn't vanish."

"Look, Hilary, this isn't something that's going to happen overnight. The mills of banks grind slowly and not always exceedingly fine," he misquoted. "In the meantime..."

"In the meantime, what?"

"Will you have dinner with me tonight, at my place?"

"Why don't we just go out?" she temporized.

"Don't tell me you're afraid to be alone with me?" Jay taunted.

There were lots of possible answers to that, but Hilary didn't want to waste an hour deciding which one was the best. She simply said, "Yes."

For once, Jay was tongue-tied for an adequate reply.

For the rest of the afternoon, Hilary's efficiency quota was at a low ebb. Jay's disquieting news was the reason for her mental doldrums, she admitted unhappily. She'd just begun to carve a little niche for herself here in Devon. She'd taken it for granted that, for a while anyway, Jay would be part of her new life. Despite "Madame Zola's" predictions, Hilary hadn't allowed herself to peer too far into the future. She still wasn't that sure of achieving a long-term relationship with anyone.

Now, though, it looked as if she wouldn't have to worry about weaving a special fabric of togetherness with Jay, a fabric whose design should extend toward tomorrow. She felt sure that Jay wouldn't have brought up the matter of a transfer at all unless there was a very good chance it would happen.

When Jay came by at six-thirty that evening, she was ready for him. She'd ventured uptown during the afternoon and bought herself a pair of chic boots—boots that fit! She'd also chosen a full-length electric blue coat with a fake-fur collar and a matching fake-fur hat.

As Jay guided her down the steps, he grinned and said, "You look like a punk Eskimo! But that crazy hat is somehow absurdly becoming."

Hilary, afraid she was going to slip despite his firm grip on her arm, muttered, "That's a backhanded compliment if I ever heard one."

"Not really," Jay corrected blithely. "You're so beautiful in that stuff that I can't resist kissing you—immediately." So saying, he halted in the middle of the walk and quickly suited action to words before she could push him away.

After a breathless moment, Hilary privately conceded that she hadn't wanted to stop him anyway. The sensations aroused when Jay's lips caressed hers were one of life's finer pleasures.

Jay took her to a country inn that featured a Mexican Night in its cozy, casual lounge. They feasted on guacamole, enchiladas and refried beans, then topped everything off with a coffee concoction that blended brandy and tequila.

Staring wistfully at the blazing hearth that dominated one wall, Jay said carefully, "I think I'd better edge in a little business here, Hilary. Without mentioning any names—your name, that is—I discussed the subject of your loan request with a friend of mine who's an officer at the bank. He shared my opinion that you'd probably be putting yourself out on a limb."

Hilary opened her mouth to protest, but Jay raised his palm to shut her off. "Please," he urged, "hear me out first, okay?"

She shrugged, feigning calm, but inside she was dying to speak.

Jay continued, "He pointed out an alternative...one that I've also considered. That is, the bank would give you a liberal line of credit, meaning you can draw on money as you need it and pay back the principal as you go along. Meantime, there's a monthly interest payment, but it's surprisingly low."

"What's your opinion?" Hilary queried, trying not to sound overly enthusiastic.

"Personally, I feel it's still a risk for you. It would be much safer to liquidate just enough of your inherited assets to get the initial cash flow you require. Once your uncle's estate has been completely settled, you'll have additional income from the investments he made. I've checked on that. His portfolio is very sound. The majority of interests were placed through us, with additional financial planning accomplished through a major investment firm in Boston. But it all ties together, and as you already know, he appointed Commonwealth Bank as his executor.''

''Which gives you a lot of control over what are now my affairs,'' Hilary remarked resentfully.

Jay exhaled deeply and summoned his professional cool. ''I have no personal say or control over any of your affairs, Hilary, but the bank does. That sort of thing is handled by our trust department. So you can rest assured that there's no way I can stop you—on my own, that is—from doing whatever you want to do.''

Hilary felt curiously sad. ''I'm sorry, Jay. Frankly, I've been somewhat out of sorts the past couple of days.''

''How are your hands?'' he asked abruptly.

''My hands?'' Sunday's injuries were healing well, to the point that Hilary was barely aware of them. She modeled her palms for Jay in the flickering candlelight. ''See for yourself.''

''I'd noticed you'd taken off the bandages.'' He nodded approvingly, then looked up to meet her eyes. ''After I left you Sunday, I began to think maybe you should have seen a doctor for the cut. Probably it could have used a couple of stitches.''

''The cut's fine,'' Hilary assured him.

''Are *you* fine?'' he persisted, his voice low and husky.

Jay's meaning was clear, and Hilary's mouth tightened. She was tempted to make a flip answer, but then she decided to be honest. ''I suppose my problem is that I've missed you.''

''Don't you think I've missed you, *cara*? Do you think I wanted to be tied up in all those stupid meetings?''

A lump filled Hilary's throat as she whispered, ''No.''

Jay held her hand gently and stroked her fingers. "Every minute I'm away from you seems like an hour, Hilary," he told her quietly. "I know I've got some very serious thinking to do. We both do. We haven't known each other very long, but what we have can't be equated with mere time. You've edged completely under my skin," he murmured, slowly shaking his head from side to side.

Hilary's heart was pounding so loudly she thought Jay might hear it. Instead, he effected a rapid change of mood and favored her with one of his high-voltage smiles. "It's worse than having the seven-year itch," he complained.

Shortly after that Jay took her home, and Hilary was more than ready to ask him to come in. She wanted to relive Sunday all over again. But when they reached her front door, he bent to kiss her lightly on the lips and whispered, "This is where I take off."

"Jay..."

"*Cara*, don't tempt me," he urged. "If you keep looking at me like that, all my hard-fought-for resolutions will evaporate."

Hilary felt numb and sounded numb when she said, "Well, then... good night."

He hesitated, his eyes imploring her to understand. Then he said, "Look, on Saturday night the Board of Trade is putting on its annual Spring Fling at the Devon Yacht Club. Doesn't look much like spring around here yet, I admit. But they're a very optimistic group. Anyway, come with me, will you? It'll be a chance for you to meet some of the local business people, and that couldn't hurt you."

Saturday night? Hilary wanted to remind Jay this was only Wednesday. But she held her tongue, smiled as best she could and let him kiss her once more.

"I'd love to," she managed.

"Great," Jay told her pleasantly, not needing to add that he wouldn't see her again until it was time to pick her up.

Chapter Eight

The next morning, after a restless night's sleep, Hilary called George Delacorte and asked if he could come by her house during his lunch hour and talk. When George appeared at her front door that noon, she promptly suggested they drive out of town for lunch.

George's brow furrowed when he heard this, and Hilary added hastily, "Unless you have to get back to your office soon?"

"I took the afternoon off," George informed her. He didn't need to say that it was a rare occasion for Hilary to ask him for a date. She knew he intended to take full advantage—of her time, not of her.

"Great," she said, feeling a flow of affection for him. Why couldn't every relationship be like her friendship with George? Easygoing. Undemanding. Not causing a constant state of mental and emotional chaos.

"Any place in particular you'd like to go?" George asked.

"How about the Cape Cod Mall in Hyannis?" Hilary told him. "I wouldn't mind doing a little shopping...."

"Fine. We can go to that German restaurant there. And I'd like to pick up a couple of new cassettes for my stereo."

That settled, they started out.

It was a bright, sunny day. A lot of the snow had melted. Hilary could almost begin to believe that—as Jay had suggested several times—spring really was on the way. She welcomed the thought of getting winter over with. This past winter had been especially rough for her. She wanted to close the door on it. She missed her Uncle Chad deeply, and her sense of loss was certain to linger for a long time. Also, her memory of Roy's shutting her out still stung on occasion, despite her conviction that he himself was a closed page of her past.

It was Thursday. Two days until she'd be going to the Board of Trade's Spring Fling with Jay. She wondered if George would be going, too—certainly he must be a member of that group. But she decided not to ask him for fear that he might invite her to go with him.

There were many other things she wanted to ask George, however. She saved most of her questions until they'd done a little shopping in the mall and were sitting opposite each other in a booth in the German restaurant, sipping imported beer.

By way of a beginning, Hilary said, "I'm going to have to get my act in order."

George was surveying the lengthy menu, trying to come up with a decision about the kind of sandwich he felt like eating. Somewhat absently, he asked, "What's wrong with your act?"

"It's my business act I'm talking about," Hilary explained. "I was hoping maybe you could help me out."

"Oh? How so?"

"Well, you've lived in Devon all your life. I thought you might be able to recommend a good carpenter and a good electrician and a good plumber and..."

George suddenly looked very wary, and Hilary broke off. "What's the matter?" she queried. "Have I asked the impossible?"

"Impossible, no. Improbable, yes," he allowed. "The thing is, Hilary, I know a few carpenters, electricians and plumbers on the Cape. I went to school with a couple of guys who have their own businesses now. As to recommending them..." George shrugged uncertainly.

"Wow!" Hilary observed. "That's a strange attitude for you to take, isn't it?"

"Nope, not really. The fact is, I think the guys I know are *competent*, but I haven't found them dependable enough. In other words, the ones I know haven't shown up when they said they were coming. Once they walked off in the middle of one job to do another job that looked a little greener, if you know what I mean."

"More money?"

"Sure. Then they went back to the first job and turned a deaf ear when the people who hired them were ready to wring their necks. It's sort of a Cape Cod trademark to be...laconic, I guess you'd say. And, independent. Kind of an old New England tradition not to seem too eager to grab work."

"That's a broad generality to make from a couple of incidences," Hilary put in. "I mean, there's too much competition in today's world to goof off. Maybe you've seen some bad apples, but I can't believe the whole barrel is rotten."

"I'm not saying they're all bad, but in any business you have to do a bit of weeding out before you latch on to the right person for a job."

"Well, that's true, I guess," Hilary conceded. "Now that you've warned me, do you suppose you could give me a few names I can try out?"

Over the next fifteen minutes, George obliged with a series of names Hilary jotted down in her pocket-size notepad. He also pointed out that she could hire a general contractor who, for a few well-spent additional dollars, would handle the hiring and coordination of the individual tradesmen. Then he proceeded to put all the names in an order of preference. Finally he said, "Tell those guys I recommended them. That should put the fear of God in them and make them treat you right."

"Am I to infer that you're slow to wrath, but if they don't treat me right you'll take them apart?" Hilary queried sweetly.

"Exactly." George grinned.

Hilary poured more beer in her glass and watched the foam subside. Then she said, "I'm still trying to figure out the best way to finance this whole thing. I can take a line of credit at the bank, or I could sell off a few securities and use that money to get going."

"Don't forget there's a tax on capital gains," George warned, the accountant in him surfacing.

"I won't," Hilary assured him. She paused, then asked as lightly as possible, "George, how long has Jay Mahoney been at Commonwealth Bank and Trust?"

"In Devon, you mean?"

"Yes."

"Oh, about five months," George said, ticking off the months on the fingers of one hand. "He took over right after Horace Mayo had his heart attack."

"Do you know where he was before he came here?" Hilary pressed.

"He was at a branch of Commonwealth in Fall River—said they put him there because he can speak Portuguese.

Then they transferred him over here and promoted him to manager." George took a sip of beer, then added matter-of-factly, "He's what you call up-and-coming. I hear the bank bigwigs in Boston think pretty highly of him."

Hilary was tempted to tell George about the possibility of a bank merger, and the chance of Jay's being transferred again, but she decided not to. Jay's words were confidential. And, if the merger went through, George would surely know before much longer.

She wondered if George knew that it was Jay who'd played the role of Madame Zola at the Cape Codders Club carnival. But she decided against bringing that up, too. What she really wanted to learn were personal things about Jay. She badly needed to fill in certain gaps in her knowledge of Jay Mahoney.

"You mentioned Jay is active in the Cape Codders Club...in the civic things the club does. But I think you said he doesn't socialize much."

George nodded. "He does tend to be a loner."

"Is he sports-minded?"

"Huh?"

"I just wondered if he was...well, especially athletic. Like you. You jog all the time."

"I haven't been running for over a week," George reported. "I slipped on the ice one morning and damn near sprained my knee, so I've had to lay off for a while." He frowned. "I don't think J.A. runs, or I probably would have seen him by now. Seems to me, though, he was kind of an athletic star when he was in college."

"An athletic star?"

"Yeah," George said, wrinkling his brow as he worked on his memory. "Swimming, that's what it was. He was on a college team, and he made it to the Olympics...I think it was the summer after his junior year."

"Jay Mahoney was an Olympic swimmer?" Hilary blurted unabashedly.

George's usually placid blue eyes narrowed slightly. "If you don't believe me, Hilary, why don't you ask him yourself?"

Hilary was brought up short. "Er," she stammered. Then began, "Well..."

"Hilary," George said patiently, "it might be a good idea if you fix it in your mind that Devon's a very small town. The other night Ed Bentley stopped in at the Polynesian Paradise to pick up a takeout order. He saw you in the lounge, dancing with J.A."

Hilary stared at George. "I'll be damned!" she muttered.

George grinned. "Once," he confessed, "I kissed a girl in the high-school parking lot. It was midnight, but there was moonlight. She was wearing a white dress. The next day when I got home from school my mother told me all about it."

"I get the message."

"I just don't want you to be embarrassed," George said, still grinning. Then, pretending not to notice Hilary's suspicious glance, he tactfully changed the subject to something close to his heart—video cameras and VCRs.

"What I'd really like is to make a short film one of these days," he confided. "Just something I could play at home for friends. Or, if it turned out good enough, use as a fundraising project for the Cape Codders Club. J.A. would make a great hero type, don't you think?" he asked pointedly.

"Yes," Hilary countered without hesitation. And it was the last time during their "date" that Jay's name was spoken by either of them.

Hilary spent the latter part of the afternoon on the phone, calling some of the names George had given her. She had no luck at all with the four general contractors she tried. Two had left rather disinterested-sounding speeches on answering machines, and the other two were completely tied up through the summer! Finally, she set up appointments for the following morning with a plumber and a carpenter. Another carpenter and an electrician said they would stop by on Saturday.

As George had warned, some showed up, some didn't. But by the time she started to dress for the Spring Fling Saturday night, Hilary had compiled a new list of men who'd promised to stop by the first of the week and give her estimates.

Rather triumphantly, as they were driving to the Devon Yacht Club, she brought Jay up to date on her progress.

He'd been slanting appreciative sidewise glances at her, glances that only served to make her even more aware of him than she already was. He was wearing his thick wool parka so she couldn't rate his choice of clothes for this evening. But he was so *damned* attractive she didn't need a complete fashion picture to set her pulse rate accelerating. Being this near to him made her wonder if maybe she'd developed a case of early hypertension.

When she announced her success in lining up some workmen, the gleam in Jay's eyes faded. He said, in a tone that bordered on asperity, "I thought you were going to let me help you with that, Hilary."

"I thought you'd be too busy, Jay."

"Is that supposed to be funny?"

"No, of course not," she protested, his attitude puzzling her. "You *have* been especially busy, haven't you?"

"Yes," he agreed, his words clipped, "I have. But I never could be too busy to find time to help you."

"Jay..." Hilary pursed her lips, not wanting to start the evening off by arguing with him. Still, she couldn't simply let his comment go by. "If I remember correctly, when you left me Wednesday night you made it pretty clear you wouldn't be free again until now."

"Did I?" He took his eyes off the road to favor her with an arched eyebrow, an intensely skeptical expression. "I seem to remember that you felt things between us were...overheating. And—if I may be allowed to read between the lines—that a slight cooling-off period might be in order."

Was that the way he'd taken it? Looking back, Hilary supposed he was right in a sense. Yet she'd never wanted anything as much as she'd wanted to ask him inside on Wednesday night. *He'd* nipped that in the bud!

"Look," he said hastily, "it's true that I've been tied up this week. Thursday and last night there were business dinners and conferences that lasted later than they should have. But even so..."

Jay paused. Then his face became so inscrutable it looked as if he'd put on a mask. "How did you latch on to people you know are capable of doing the jobs for you?"

"George Delacorte gave me some names."

"Ah," Jay murmured, as if that explained everything.

"Stop sounding as if a doctor's just asked you to stick your tongue out!" Hilary snapped waspishly.

"I didn't realize you were still seeing George."

"George is a good *friend*," she stated defiantly. "I've never made any secret of that."

"No, I suppose you haven't. I didn't think you'd still be dating him, that's all."

Hilary darted a suspicious glance at Jay. "What makes you use the word 'dating'?"

"The two of you were seen having lunch in the Wursthaus in Hyannis on Thursday," Jay informed her.

She sank back, aghast. "My God!" she exploded. "Can't anyone do anything around here without being seen and reported on?"

"Very little," Jay assured her. "One of the tellers who's seen you at the bank has Thursdays off. She happened to be in the mall, and first thing she told me yesterday morning was that she'd seen you having a great old time with George Delacorte."

"We were not having a great old time, for God's sake!"

"I guess it looked that way."

Jay sounded morose. He looked morose. Hilary stared at him in disbelief, then said, "You almost sound as if you're jealous of George."

He nodded, his midnight eyes ablaze. "I'm jealous as hell of George, or of any other man who does much more than look over the top of your head," he admitted.

A beautiful warm glow invaded Hilary. She felt as if a candle had been lighted deep within her and was spreading lovely apricot light through her veins. "That's wonderful," she said simply.

Jay glared at her. "Wonderful—to be turned inside out to the point I could hardly keep my mind on bank business yesterday?"

"It's absolutely marvelous," Hilary nodded tranquilly. She looked at Jay, her ice-blue eyes melting. "I love having you jealous of me," she told him.

Jay muttered something in a language she didn't understand. Then he pulled over to the side of the road and slammed on the brakes.

"Lucky you didn't pick an icy spot," Hilary reproved, "or we might have skidded from here to eternity."

He didn't answer. Instead, he reached for her...and his kiss transformed the single candle inside her into a sparkling candelabra. Every inch of her became consumed by glorious flames.

She'd wanted to look different for Jay tonight. Especially beguiling. So she'd arranged her hair in an intricate chignon that had taken quite some doing. She was sure he was mussing it now and couldn't care less. They twisted in each other's arms until Jay exclaimed, "Damn these modern car seats! At least I don't have bucket seats, but even so..."

His statement brought them back to a semblance of reality. Hilary, still breathing hard, gently pulled away from him. After a moment, she managed to fumble with her hairdo until she was convinced she again looked presentable. She glanced in a pocket mirror and smoothed her lipstick. Then she assessed Jay and, taking a handkerchief out of her handbag, wiped off the lipstick she'd left on his cheeks and his mouth.

She said unsteadily, "I really don't think you'd better try that again when we're on our way to a public engagement."

"Don't you?" He chuckled. "Want to dare me?"

"I have no intention of daring you, Mr. Mahoney."

"You're a wise woman, Miss Forsythe," he approved.

By the time they reached the Yacht Club, the Spring Fling was well under way. Hilary soon discovered that Jay, in the short time he'd lived and worked in Devon, had managed to meet just about everyone in town. At least everyone in the Yacht Club seemed to know him. Many people shouted hellos or came over to greet him warmly.

For a loner—as George had accused him of being—Jay related surprisingly well to people. Yet as the evening passed, Hilary realized that, for all of his cordiality, Jay was holding a lot of himself back as he led her from group to group and chatted with the people he introduced her to.

There was no doubt about the women's reaction to him. Hilary couldn't blame them for looking at Jay as they did. A few times she even felt twinges of jealousy, and could better understand his feelings about George... and about Roy.

What surprised her was that the men, even those whose wives were staring at Jay adoringly, seemed genuinely to like him. It was easy to see why he was such an asset to the bank.

Toward the end of the evening, with the Spring Fling still in full swing, Jay whispered in Hilary's ear, "Would you mind very much if we cut out of here?"

"No," she answered promptly.

She didn't mind. But she was a little surprised at the urgency in his voice.

They left the Yacht Club and walked into a silver night. Moonlight brushed the last patches of snow and stroked the calm waters of Cape Cod Bay to a smooth sheen.

Gazing at the far-off horizon, Hilary murmured, "What a gorgeous place this would be for a home."

Jay nodded. "It's better this way, though," he decided. "A lot of people can enjoy the view, thanks to club ownership of this property."

"How democratic of you," she teased.

"I have good cause to be democratic," Jay answered seriously. "My grandparents—both sets of them—came to this country with absolutely nothing. My mother's parents took the boat from Portugal. My father's parents came steerage from Ireland. They arrived at Ellis Island at differing times, but under similar circumstances, to find that maybe this wasn't the promised land they'd imagined. Still, America offered far more hope than they would've found anywhere else. They worked like hell, so both my mom and dad grew up in relatively easy circumstances. Nevertheless, according to most American standards, they had pretty rough lives."

"What did your father do?"

"He was a longshoreman in Boston when he was still in his teens," Jay said. "He never finished high school. He was an incredibly strong man. Maybe that's why, when his heart wore out, it stopped so quickly. He dropped dead when he was forty-six."

"How did your parents meet?" Hilary asked.

Jay smiled. "One summer Sunday when my dad was in his early twenties, he took the day boat from Boston to Provincetown. My mother was working as a waitress in a little cafe on Commercial Street. He took one look at her and fell in love. He gave up his job in Boston and moved to the Cape. My mother's brothers had their own fishing trawler, and they took him on. Then, just two months after he died, the *Amalia* went down off Peaked Hill Bars. They later found some of the boat, but my uncles' bodies were never recovered."

Hilary stared up at Jay in shock, unable to speak.

"That," he went on, "literally killed my grandfather. When both his sons died, he gave up the will to live, and he didn't last very long. I guess you could say my grandmother was made of tougher stuff. She died only a couple of years ago. She outlived my mother, who was her only daughter, as well as her two sons."

"But you still have relatives in Provincetown," Hilary remembered. "Brothers and sisters?"

Jay shook his head. "I have a brother and two sisters, but none of them live on the Cape. My sisters are married. One's in New York, and the other in Oregon. My brother took off and went all the way to Alaska. He lives in Anchorage."

"Have you been out there?"

"Not yet, but someday, perhaps. About my relatives...I have cousins in Provincetown and an aunt by marriage, the widow of one of my uncles. She remarried after a few years—another fisherman, would you believe it? He's retired, now. They're both in their seventies. Their health isn't the greatest, and though they both have kids by their previous marriages, the kids have their own lives to lead. Some of them live around Provincetown, but to my mind they don't see as much of Maria and Phil as they should. Neither do I, for that matter. It's better since I've been here on the Cape. I get out when I can."

He turned toward Hilary. "So you see," he finished, "not all of us are born WASPs like you, *cara*."

"Ouch!" Hilary retorted. "That stings worse than a wasp could."

"I don't mean it that way. But from the dossier, as you call it, that the bank has on the Forsythes, it was easy to see that you qualify for membership in groups like the Society of Mayflower Descendants and the DAR—organizations that wouldn't let me in the front door."

"I'm not much of a joiner, Jay," she said levelly.

"Even so."

"People don't choose their ancestors," she reminded him. "Also, you seem to forget that those who made the kind of societies you mention worked pretty damned hard, too. My forefathers had to carve a country out of wilderness, without Ellis Island as a starting point. No immigration authorities either to help or mistreat them. Not much of anything."

"Touché," Jay said, and grinned. "Enough of our roots for one night, okay?"

"Agreed."

"*Cara?*"

"Yes."

"When we get to your house, I want very much to come in. I want very much to be with you tonight. In fact, I think I'll go crazy right on your doorstep if you shut me out."

For answer, Hilary opened her handbag and found her house key. She held it out to Jay in place of words.

Later, upstairs in her old four-poster bed, she and Jay entered a new dimension in their lovemaking. Although the feelings between them were stronger than ever, they were both more relaxed. Physically, they were no longer strangers to each other. So it became natural and beautiful for them to become lost in each other's arms, and start out on voyages of exploration that could only lead to the edge of the rainbow, then topple over into shimmering cauldrons of golden glory.

It was very late when they finally fell asleep in an interlocked embrace. It was late, too, when they awakened. Jay stared at Hilary sleepily, as if he couldn't credit her being in the same bed with him. Then he glanced at the clock on her dresser and let out a shout.

"My God!" he groaned. "Look at the time!"

Hilary gazed up at him rather groggily and groped for a fact that was hanging over her but seemed to be escaping her power of reason. She found it and clutched. "This is Sunday," she said.

"I know, I know. But the bank president stayed over for the weekend with his wife. He said he's been away so much he was afraid if he didn't give her a taste of the Cape, she'd divorce him. I was supposed to meet them at nine o'clock for breakfast. They wanted to get an early start back to Boston."

Hilary glared at him. "Damn your bank," she muttered resentfully.

He was pulling on the black slacks he'd worn last night, but paused to look down at her in surprise. "Why damn the bank?" he asked mildly.

"It takes up your entire life."

With a swift gesture, Jay slipped off his slacks and sat down on the edge of the bed. "Does it, now?" he asked lazily.

Hilary saw the gleam in his eyes and backtracked. "Look, Jay," she said hastily, "don't be rash. I know all this is very important to you."

He cast an appraising glance at the bed, then at her. "Yes," he agreed deliberately, "*this* is very important to me."

"I'm not talking about me, dammit! I'm talking about your job."

"Yes, my job is very important to me," he said, with that same deliberateness. "But a person can always get another job, Hilary."

She'd been about to sit up, but the way he was looking at her made her sink silently back into the pillows.

"There will never again be anyone like you," he stated simply.

Hilary's love for him overflowed, and she didn't try to fight the flood. She let love wash over her, penetrating every pore in her body.

She loved him completely. There would never in her life be anyone approaching Joaquim Alvaro Mahoney. Several times during her twenty-eight years—culminating with the disastrous experience with Roy—she'd thought she was in love, had even seriously believed she was in love. Now she knew that everything she'd previously felt for a man had only been a rehearsal for the real thing.

This was the real thing. Looking up at Jay, Hilary was more vulnerable than she'd ever been in her entire life.

She forced herself to query, "Jay, what are you going to do?"

He smiled devilishly, and gave her the full impact of his wicked chuckle. "Do you really need to ask that question?"

"Seriously, Jay...you can't just not show up when you told your boss you'd have breakfast with him."

"Well," Jay said judiciously, "what I'll do is wait about forty-five minutes. Then I'll call the restaurant where we planned to meet and have him paged."

"What are you going to tell him?"

"I'm going to tell him I overslept."

"What?"

He looked at Hilary, a picture of mock innocence. "I did, after all."

"But..."

"He will be on his second cup of coffee," Jay mused. "He and his wife will have decided to go ahead and have breakfast without me. Probably, he'll be replete with blueberry muffins and all sorts of other good fare, so he should be in an excellent mood. He will thank me for my thoughtfulness and tell me he'll be in touch as soon as he knows when we should arrange another meeting."

Jay slipped under the bed covers, stretching alongside Hilary so that she could feel his warmth and the smoothness of his skin.

"I'd say," he told her, "that forty-five minutes should be just about the right amount of time. Wouldn't you?"

Chapter Nine

Jay phoned Hilary late Monday morning. She'd just hired a plumber and an electrician, and was feeling reasonably proud of herself. She'd been dubious about the carpenter who'd first appeared an hour late and then had been hazy in his estimates. He'd been placed on hold until she talked to the other carpenters she expected to see in the next few days.

Jay's voice warmed her, as it always did. So did the memory of the long and wonderful Sunday they'd spent together. Only yesterday? Already, she missed him as much as if they hadn't seen each other for years.

He'd gone back to his condo last night at the reasonable hour of ten-thirty. Remembering this, Hilary smiled. Jay had confessed that he'd never get up and make it to work on time if he stayed over again.

Now he asked, "Do you suppose you'd have a minute this afternoon to talk to someone about the tearoom?"

"What about it, Jay?"

"About this person taking it over for you."

"Taking it over for me? I don't understand you."

Jay sighed deeply, alerting Hilary to the fact that he had many things on his mind at the moment, including the bank merger. She didn't want to add to his problems by being dense, but she honestly didn't know what he was driving at.

He explained patiently, "It so happens that a woman who has some capital to invest came into the bank this morning. She wants to establish her own business, and with a loan from us to match her cash, she'd be in a good position to do exactly that."

"Lucky her," Hilary commented bitterly, and immediately wished she hadn't.

Jay got the message, and his voice took on a sharp edge. Hearing his crisp tone, Hilary realized anew how difficult it was to combine business and personal relationships. Perhaps it was as well Jay had turned her down on the loan, she mused. She amended that. He hadn't exactly turned her down, but he'd certainly discouraged her.

"Are you saying this woman wants to start a tearoom?" she asked, his gist suddenly registering.

"Yes," Jay answered, noticeably relieved. "She and her husband ran a successful restaurant up on the north shore above Boston for a number of years. Her husband died a while back and left her fairly well-fixed. She doesn't have to work, but she's bored and restless and too young for retirement."

"How young?" Hilary asked suspiciously.

Jay couldn't repress a chuckle. "Old enough to be your mother," he allowed. "I'd say she's pushing fifty."

"Hmmm." Hilary was beginning to feel a bit bewildered. "I can hardly stop her from opening a tearoom in Devon, Jay," she pointed out. "I suppose she's going to offer all the old New England favorites, as you suggested I do."

"Does that imply I was giving out trade secrets when I met with her?" Jay asked quickly. "Never mind, skip that. Look, Hilary, what I'm suggesting is that she opens *your* tearoom. In short, that she takes over and runs it as a concession. The risk will primarily be hers. If she makes a profit—as I honestly suspect she will—you'll get a hefty cut. It seems to me this could be a good arrangement all the way around."

"Maybe," Hilary muttered, her doubt showing.

"Your enthusiasm is overwhelming!" Jay chided.

"Thank you."

There was a heavy pause before Jay said, "Please realize, Hilary, I'm not trying to push you into anything. I just think you should talk to Mrs. Daniels and hear what she has to say."

"Mrs. Daniels?"

"Yes. Elizabeth Daniels. I think you'll find her a very pleasant person. If nothing else, she'd be a good source of advice."

"Is she there with you now?"

"God, but you can be a suspicious little wench," Jay retorted kiddingly. "No, she is not here with me now. She's going to call me at noon. I told her I'd try to reach you by then. If you'd like me to, I'll say you're not interested. Okay?"

"No, it's not okay."

He was making her feel like a naughty child, and Hilary was torn between resentment and the nagging knowledge that Jay honestly believed he was suggesting something for her benefit.

"Tell Mrs. Daniels I'll see her around four," she capitulated. "We can have a cup of tea together."

"How gracious of you," Jay commented dryly. It wasn't quite a sneer, but it came close to one.

Hilary knew he was miffed, and she couldn't blame him. To try to make amends, she asked, "Would you like to come over and take potluck tonight?"

She had visions of a charred cheese soufflé as she spoke, and nearly retracted the offer. Jay, she suspected, had also thought of that sad culinary effort because he said, "I asked you first, remember? That's to say, I think I've suggested more than once that you let me cook supper for us one night. So... shall I pick you up around seven?"

"I can drive to your place myself, if you'll give me directions."

"Whatever you wish," he agreed, then told her the best route.

Hilary was ready for Mrs. Daniels when the doorbell rang at four that afternoon. The teakettle was simmering, and she'd put out a teapot, cups and saucers. Also, she'd arranged some store-bought cookies in a pretty pattern on an antique Limoges serving dish.

She hadn't formed any preconceived idea of what Mrs. Daniels was going to be like or look like. Nevertheless, she was surprised. Elizabeth Daniels was definitely not old enough to be her mother. She resolved she'd have a word with Jay about that!

Tall and statuesque, with beautiful dark red hair, green eyes and a flawless complexion, Mrs. Daniels looked more like a professional model than a restaurateur. Her clothes were also model chic. She was wearing a forest-green wool suit with a matching cape, and black leather boots that graphically outlined the contours of her long, shapely legs.

Hilary suddenly decided she should have planned to offer her guest a martini instead of a cup of tea! She did suggest sherry, but Mrs. Daniels opted for the tea. Then the two women settled in front of the fire Hilary had started and played conversational table tennis for a while before getting down to the subject of the tearoom.

Within minutes, Hilary discovered that she was dealing with an expert in the restaurant business. And that she, herself, had been in danger of invading an area in which she had no experience whatsoever.

They finished second cups of tea, then Hilary took her guest on a tour of the premises, concentrating on the kitchen and the veranda. The veranda was still partially covered with clumps of snow that now looked like little icebergs.

The kitchen would have to be totally renovated. Elizabeth Daniels made that abundantly clear despite Hilary's assurances that she completely agreed with her. She'd already realized that her kitchen equipment not only was outdated, but didn't have nearly the capacity needed to sustain the food production of a restaurant.

"The veranda's perfect, though," Hilary was told, after Mrs. Daniels insisted on opening the door and walking around the slippery deck, bracing herself against the blasts of arctic air blowing in from the north. "And I can visualize a charming outdoor dining area for good weather, just as Mr. Mahoney mentioned."

She turned to Hilary. "There's excellent access to the veranda," she stated. "A door from the kitchen, which would be essential of course, but also that nice wide doorway from your center hall."

"The French doors in the dining room also open onto it," Hilary pointed out.

"That's what I was thinking about. Any chance you'd be willing to give up your dining room, Miss Forsythe?"

Hilary hadn't thought about *that*. She'd been concentrating more on plans for her shop than on plans for the tearoom. She was going to use the front and back parlors for the shop, and maybe the library. The only thought she'd had about the dining room was that she'd convert it into living space for herself.

When she said as much, Elizabeth Daniels answered thoughtfully, "I can understand your leaning in that direction. Personally, though, I've found that when one converts part of a home into a business establishment, it's wise to move the private living space as far away as possible from the business area.

"In this case," she went on, "we're dealing with the creation of not one but two businesses. Two separate entities that must fuse. In fact, they must blend beautifully. Each will be an adjunct to the other, each will complement the other." She paused, then asked, "You have quite a large upstairs, don't you?"

"Five bedrooms and three baths," Hilary nodded. "There's a full attic, too."

Mrs. Daniels thought for a moment, and then queried, "Would it be possible to tear down a wall and combine two of the bedrooms into a large living-dining area? Then you could convert another bedroom—hopefully an adjacent one, of course—into a kitchen. That would still leave a bedroom for yourself, plus a guest room," she concluded practically.

"I don't know," Hilary said slowly. "I hadn't thought of anything like that."

"Well, there's surely no hurry," Mrs. Daniels put in smoothly. "I was thinking ahead, that's all. If the tearoom does as well as I'd like to think it will, it would be nice to expand into your dining room. It's a large, very pleasant room, and even has a lovely fireplace. It might be possible to stay open right through the Christmas holiday season. From what I hear, Cape Cod doesn't close down on Labor Day as it used to."

"That's what I hear, too," Hilary admitted.

"Anyway," Mrs. Daniels continued, "the veranda could be heated. You might say that in using the dining room we'd be exchanging the outdoor summer space with an indoor year-round space. Do you follow me?"

"I think so, yes."

Elizabeth Daniels smiled disarmingly. "I'm not trying to rush you, Miss Forsythe," she said simply. "But for my own purposes, I want to get into something definite that can be started by summer, and summer isn't that far away."

"I know," Hilary agreed sullenly. In talking to the workmen she'd interviewed, she'd come to the conclusion that summer was just around the corner, and had begun to wonder how she could possibly put together a shop in time for the prime tourist season.

As if reading her mind, Mrs. Daniels said, "It *can* be done. I have contacts in the restaurant-equipment business, and Mr. Mahoney tells me he can help out in getting women who can make their local specialties for us. He mentioned that your idea was to emphasize traditional New England dishes on the menu. I thoroughly agree with that."

While Hilary's feeling of helplessness increased, her go-getter guest looked at her and asked brightly, "Well, what do you think?"

Hilary was in an odd mood as she drove across town to Jay's apartment that evening. She knew that he would question her about her meeting with Elizabeth Daniels. And that he would probably also question her about not having given Mrs. Daniels a definite answer.

She'd hedged but wasn't sure why she reacted that way. She stood to benefit by having an experienced restaurant operator handle the tearoom. She knew that. Still, Hilary felt a peculiar obstinacy about letting a stranger in on a project she'd considered entirely her own.

Condominiums were fairly new to Devon, and Sand Terraces was one of the newest. The attractive buildings had been well designed, combining gray-green clapboards and beige shingles that blended nicely with the Cape's natural palette. Jay's unit was at the end of a docklike area that overlooked the water. Surveying the exterior, Hilary was sure she'd find an interior—in his apartment, at least—as contemporary as today, even tending toward the futuristic.

She was wrong. As Jay led her into his spacious living room, her immediate appraisal of his surroundings only served to make her more aware of how little she really knew about Joaquim Alvaro Mahoney.

His apartment was modern only to the extent of having stark ivory walls and glass sliding doors that opened onto a balcony facing the water to the west. Twilight was merging into deep dusk as Hilary entered the room, so the view was dim. Still, she could imagine the splendor of the sunsets from this vantage point.

In his choice of furnishings, Jay had borrowed from his roots—at least, those on his mother's side of the family. When Hilary marveled at a fascinating, carved sideboard, a refectory table and the exquisite prints lining one wall, Jay told her that he'd bought most of the things in Portugal.

"Actually, I've been to Portugal three times over the years," he allowed. "Rather a lopsided score, as I've yet to visit Ireland."

Hilary looked around the room and asked innocently, "You mean you don't even have a replica of the Blarney stone?"

"No," he answered, then countered, "Are you saying there's a bit of the blarney about me?"

"Well..."

"Sure and faith," Jay told her, "you'd better watch that tongue of yours, *mavourneen*, or I shall prove to you the veracity of my feelings before we even have dinner!"

"Sure and faith," Hilary mocked, affecting her own phony brogue, "when you speak to me like that I may be moved to make further accusations."

Jay swung toward her, a smile on his lips, a gleam in his dark eyes. In another instant, Hilary was in his arms, returning his passionate kiss with a searing fire of her own. Then he released her abruptly and, favoring her with a wicked leer said, "Much though I desire you, my lovely colleen, I'm damned if I'm going to let my dinner be burned to a crisp."

"Is that a dig at the dinner I served you?" Hilary retorted promptly.

"Absolutely not," Jay insisted. "You, after all, were a wounded chef, remember?" He glanced at her hands. "All better?" he queried.

"A couple of minor scars," she conceded. "But I imagine they'll fade with time."

"Would that all scars could fade with time," Jay said, frowning slightly. "At least, most of them do." He smiled sadly, then instructed, "Sit down, *cara*, and I will get us some wine."

A minute later, Jay returned bearing a carafe of golden wine and two stemmed glasses. *"Vinho verde,"* he stated, as he poured. "Which translates as green wine."

"But it isn't green," Hilary observed.

"No, it is merely delicious."

Hilary sipped the chilled wine and began to relax, while Jay strolled across to the glass sliding doors and drew the pale amber drapes. The room seemed to take on an added glow. Being with Jay in his own realm, in the midst of objects that eminently suited his personality, Hilary felt warm, comfortable and . . . beloved.

Jay had prepared a succulent casserole of clams spiced with chunks of a Portuguese sausage called *linguiça*. The dish was definitely gourmet in quality. With it, he served

warm, crusty Portuguese bread, and a tossed salad with a
tangy dressing that he modestly said was something he'd just
"conjured up."

Hilary privately conceded that when it came to culinary
capabilities, she was definitely not in his class.

He was a casual host. Putting a great meal together and
then serving it perfectly obviously occasioned no anxiety in
Jay whatsoever. Once again, Hilary was glad he had a faulty
sense of rhythm.

As she waited for him to bring on their dessert, she also
remembered Jay's saying he couldn't carry a tune. This was
more than adequately confirmed when—as he whipped up
some cream to top the fresh fruit he'd soaked in Madeira—
he began whistling a song Hilary might have recognized if
his rendition hadn't been so off-key.

Hilary was smiling as he returned carrying the dessert
dishes. In the candlelight, her smile softened her features
and brought a special light into her unusual blue eyes.

Jay caught his breath at the sight of her and felt a chill run
through his entire body. He'd loved a woman very deeply
only once before in his life. He'd never expected to know
that kind of love again. Now, unexpectedly, he was overwhelmed by the surge of emotion he felt for Hilary. It
rocked him totally. So much so that he sat down quickly for
fear of losing the strength in his legs.

God knows, she did not remind him of Donna. She was
as different from Donna as any woman could possibly be.
But then Donna had only been nineteen when she died.

At the memory of this, a spasm of pain crossed Jay's face.
Donna had still been a girl when he married her, and had
never had the chance to blossom into a mature woman like
Hilary.

He tried to visualize Donna as she might have appeared
today had she lived. How old would she be? Thirty-three,
going on thirty-four, Jay told himself. She'd been six

months younger than he was. They'd gone through school together in Provincetown and had graduated from the same high-school class.

Donna had been entrancingly beautiful. So was Hilary. But Donna had been of Portuguese descent on both sides of her family. Like himself, her hair was jet and her eyes a near match. Hers had been glorious eyes, deep velvet fringed by incredibly long lashes that swept her cheeks, which were always tinged to a soft, rosy hue.

She'd been shorter than Hilary, and more...voluptuous. Probably by now, Jay thought wryly, she would have been struggling to maintain the figure that had excited him so much when they'd been teenagers. Teenagers consumed by a passion neither of them had been able to resist.

But...their passion had been the passion of youth, desire raging out of control. It was fortunate, Jay realized retrospectively, that Donna had been possessed of such an innately ardent nature. He'd been anything but experienced as a lover. It had been up to her to keep pace with him, because he didn't know any better way. Most of the time, she'd succeeded....

They'd wanted to get married the same day they graduated from high school, but their parents had been adamant about their waiting two years...until Jay was twenty. Patrick Mahoney, glowering, had said he considered even that too young. A man, he'd added, needed some knowledge to make his way in today's world. He'd wanted Jay to go on to further education.

But Jay'd had other ideas. He'd gone to work on the *Amalia*, the fishing boat that would later sink, taking her crew to the bottom with her. Two years later, he'd amassed enough money to make the down payment on a small house in Provincetown which he and Donna lovingly furnished in the weeks before their wedding.

They'd opted to go directly to their new home after their wedding, rather than set forth on a honeymoon they couldn't afford.

Jay had taken the next three days off, but on the fourth day he'd gone back to work. As it happened, there was a hurricane edging up the coast. That morning the wind had begun to blow steadily and the rain fell in a thin, tropical drizzle. The *Amalia*'s crew had holed up at a tavern near the docks, drinking beer and swapping stories to pass the hours away.

At home, Donna had decided to clean and polish her house so it would be shining for her young husband when he came back that night. There were bright yellow chrysanthemums blooming along the picket fence, and Donna must have suddenly decided to pick a bouquet to brighten up the living room. She'd been nearly through with her vacuuming at that point, as far as anyone could ascertain.

She must have unplugged the vacuum when she'd paused to get the flowers. Then she'd evidently come back into the house from her small expedition, soaking wet—her clothes had still been wet when they found her. She put the chrysanthemums in the sink and returned to finish her cleaning.

When she plugged the vacuum in again, something happened. A flow of current. Maybe the machine had been faulty, or the wiring. It didn't much matter. She'd been electrocuted.

All of these memories whirled through Jay's head with a relentless force he couldn't push back. When he visualized the tragic end to his bride's life, he shuddered convulsively, unaware that this motion was as physical as it was emotional. He'd thought that he'd long ago gained enough self-control so that those terrible shudders were confined inside his psyche, invisible to the rest of the world.

Struck by Jay's sudden silence, Hilary had been watching him closely. Transfixed by the emotions that played over his face in a few seconds, she was instantly assailed by a deep inner pain. Hilary knew the reason she was hurting was because Jay was so obviously and so visibly suffering.

She reached out an imploring hand and gently touched his wrist. "What is it, darling?" she urged.

Jay started. Then he looked up at her blankly, as if he'd been overcome by amnesia and didn't even know her.

"Nothing," he evaded, his voice husky.

"Jay, please," Hilary implored softly. When he didn't at once respond, she plunged. "You've learned a lot about me," she said, not chiding him, "while I've learned very little about you. But this isn't the first time I've suspected that you harbor a terrible secret. Can't you share it with me?"

She was telling him, without putting her thoughts into precise words, that she cared very deeply for him. She wanted to share the bad as well as the good. She wanted to share everything.

Some of the darkness drifted away from Jay's face, and he managed a small smile. Still, it was a smile that made Hilary want to cry. He covered her hand with his, and his mouth twisted slightly. He was trying to restrain emotions that threatened to overflow.

"I don't harbor a terrible secret, *cara*," he whispered tenderly.

"Please, darling..."

"I love to hear you call me darling."

"Jay, please don't go away from this. What were you thinking of just now?"

Jay sat back, propped his elbows on the table edge, and rubbed his temples. Then he regarded Hilary levelly. He said, his voice curiously toneless, "I was thinking of my wife."

Hilary froze. She would have sworn the blood was draining out of her veins. In the wake of this sensation, she became the ice maiden Jay had several times accused her of being.

Seeing her reaction, he quickly said, "My God, don't look like that! Donna has been dead a long, long time." The questions in Hilary's eyes prompted him to add, more slowly, "She's been...gone for fourteen years. I've lived the major part of my life since then."

Hilary was staring at him, speechless. She started to open her mouth, but words wouldn't come, so she looked away.

Jay flinched, and went on, "I was only twenty years old, Hilary. Donna was still nineteen. We'd only been married a couple of days."

Hearing that, Hilary involuntarily reached for her wineglass and drained the last of the *vinho verde*. But her throat was still dusty-dry as she asked, "Do you want to tell me what happened?"

"It was a freak accident." Jay sounded a lot calmer than she felt. "Donna was electrocuted."

"Dear God!" The words were wrenched out of her, and Hilary felt a sudden surge of nausea. Pushing her chair back, she walked toward the window, wishing she could tear away the drapes, break the glass and then gulp long drafts of the cold night air.

She felt Jay's hands on her shoulders. He tried to turn her toward him, but she stiffened. She knew she was handling this terribly, but she felt overwhelmed by what he'd just said. She didn't think she could bear to look at him.

He murmured softly, "I know it's a very bad time to say this, Hilary, but...I love you."

That did it. She swung around, and Jay was so close she had to tilt her head to study his face. He was tight-lipped, deadly serious, intense. He said, "I mean that."

"But..."

He shook his head. "No 'buts,'" he said. "As I was bringing in our dessert, I somehow became swamped by memories."

"Somehow?" Hilary echoed.

"Well, all at once I realized...how much you mean to me."

Hilary stared into the midnight eyes that confronted her and could feel the sincerity emanating from them.

"Only once before in my life have I ever really loved a woman," Jay confessed. "That's what I began to think about, and then one thought followed the other. I'm very sorry you had to learn about my...my past, in such an awkward fashion."

Hilary found words. "When I told you about the accident that took my parents' lives," she said, "why couldn't you have told me that you'd had a great tragedy in your life? Why couldn't you have shared that with me?"

"Because I was thinking primarily of you, I suppose," Jay told her. "I certainly wasn't trying deliberately to deceive you. Anyway," he added reasonably, "how many adults do you know who've never experienced some form of tragedy in their lives? I can't think of a single person."

Hilary concentrated on an antique Portuguese map of the world on the wall behind Jay's head. "The kind of tragedy you've just touched upon is different," she managed.

"Perhaps," he agreed, "but you really can't measure such things. You know that. Believe me, when Donna was killed I thought my world had come to an end. But gradually I began to notice the sunlight again. I began to smell the flowers. I began to see the stars. I didn't expect to ever *love* again, though. I suppose that's what came over me tonight. My timing," Jay concluded wryly, "couldn't have been worse. Now I've spoiled this evening for you because I wasn't able to control myself."

"That's not true, Jay."

Again, his smile twisted her heart. "Yes, it is," he corrected. "And that's as far as I'm going to go with it right now. It isn't that I want to hold anything back from you. You have to believe that! In due course I'll tell you everything you want to know about me, my life, about everything that's touched my life—and every person. But we'll start on a more even emotional keel, okay?"

Hilary didn't know how to answer him. The urge to know, the need to know, was fiercely gripping her. Yet at the same time she knew he was right.

"Now shall we have our dessert?" Jay suggested, abruptly changing his tack. "And perhaps some coffee?"

"I couldn't," Hilary murmured.

"All right then. Suppose we put a movie on the VCR and sit back and relax?"

That was a fair compromise. So for the next hour and a half they watched a comedy Jay had rented from the local video mart. Afterward, though, Hilary couldn't remember who'd starred in the film or what the plot had been about.

The evening hadn't been spoiled, but it had been traumatized. There was a considerable difference between the two adjectives, Hilary discovered, as she drove back across town to Sea Street. It was easier to deal with something that had merely been spoiled.

Also, she realized belatedly, they hadn't gotten into the subject of Elizabeth Daniels and her possible involvement in the tearoom. But those things, right now, seemed incredibly trivial.

Chapter Ten

Jay and Hilary drove out to Provincetown late on an April afternoon. Spring's promise was finally beginning to come true after several false starts. There was a fresh, tilled-earth smell to the air, the willows were dressed in green-gold fronds that rippled in the breeze, and crocuses—purple, white and deep yellow—turned expectant faces toward the vernal sun.

Hilary had been consistently busy. At last she was starting to feel that things were coming together. She'd accepted both her partnership with Elizabeth Daniels and the idea of giving up her dining room to the tearoom. Somehow these decisions were much easier to make after that traumatic evening at Jay's apartment.

She'd also decided to concentrate solely on her craft gallery. Getting the parlors ready and stocking them with merchandise was more than enough to accomplish over the next few weeks. Later she could convert the upstairs rooms into the comfortable living space Mrs. Daniels—Betty, she amended—had suggested. For now, the shop demanded top priority.

She'd yet to come up with a catchy name, as Nostalgia II simply wasn't right. George Delacorte had offered several suggestions, which Hilary had politely rejected, and for all of her resourcefulness, Betty Daniels was also stumped.

Jay had been constantly busy himself. He and Hilary had only seen each other in snatches since that night in his apartment. The bank merger appeared to be definite, but Jay's future role remained an uncertainty.

As they drove toward Provincetown, Hilary knew they had a lot to catch up on, but she had no desire to talk about business. Jay was interested in the renovations taking place at the Forsythe homestead and curious about her progress in locating suitable crafts to feature on her shelves. At the same time, she was more than anxious to be updated on the bank merger. Just now, though, she wanted to enjoy the peace of getting away from her Devon responsibilities, even if this was only a short reprieve. Most of all, she wanted to relish the time alone with Jay.

He'd greeted her with a smile and a kiss when he'd stopped by Sea Street to pick her up, and for this Hilary felt grateful. The wonderful rapport they'd achieved had been lacking in their sporadic, too-brief encounters of late. An uneasy constraint had inserted itself between them, a tenseness Hilary attributed to Jay's revelations about his youthful marriage. She still couldn't think about the tragic fate of Jay's bride without shuddering physically and emotionally. Worse...when she was with Jay, she felt an odd embarrassment, as though she should tiptoe softly around the issue of his grief.

He'd said it had been a long time. Fourteen years, during which time he'd grown up, attended college—Hilary still didn't know which college—and got into banking. Nevertheless, despite her efforts to fight away the images of the past, the ghost of Donna Mahoney had definitely come between Jay and herself, in Hilary's mind, at least.

He seemed so *normal* today that she almost felt that special camaraderie they'd achieved. She almost felt at ease. She stole a glance at him and discovered he looked anything but grief stricken. The day was warm, so he wasn't wearing the heavy wool jacket she'd come to think of as his trademark. Nor was he wearing one of the three-piece suits she privately termed "banker's clothes." His tweed sports coat combined muted shades of blue, his slacks were navy, his shirt bright royal. The color of the shirt picked up the gleaming blue-black highlights in his raven hair and the effect was sensational. Looking at him, Hilary felt a wonderfully familiar stirring.

As if he'd read her mind, Jay took his concentration off the road just long enough to flash her a dazzling smile. His expression evoked the image of Madame Zola, and Hilary wanted to ask what he'd done with the crystal ball he'd gazed into on that special night when they'd first met. A crystal ball would come in handy at this moment, she thought wistfully, then abruptly changed her mind. For entirely different reasons, she was no more eager to probe the future now than she'd been in Madame Zola's tent.

Maria—Jay's aunt by marriage—and her husband, Phil Gonsalves lived in a modest house perched atop a sandy hill on the eastern edge of Provincetown. The view of the harbor was spectacular, and the Gonsalveses had personalities that surpassed it. They were characters from a broken mold, and Hilary liked them immediately. Her constraint quickly faded as Maria poured her a plain glass full of Phil's homemade elderberry wine, then plucked some sugary Portuguese pastries from her quaint gas oven.

They settled around the kitchen table, and the Gonsalveses were at no loss for words in the presence of their

guests. Their warmth and humor and their innate hospital-
ity were just the cure Hilary needed for the bleakness tha
had been holding her so firmly.

Maria was short, plump and matronly. Though she'd jus
celebrated her seventy-first birthday, she was still very
pretty. Her face was surprisingly unlined, and her dark eye
were incredibly like Jay's. Her hair in earlier years woul
have been the same as his, too. Now it was streaked wit
strands of pure white, and the effect was stunning.

Phil was big and hearty. He'd been a fisherman all of hi
life and had quit only because he'd lost an arm. This ha
happened ten years ago, Hilary was told, in a midwinte
trawler accident out on the frigid North Atlantic. The story
made her shiver and admire Phil all the more for how we
he dealt with his handicap. So well, in fact, that she wa
barely conscious of it.

The conversation flowed easily, and the Gonsalvese
tactfully included Hilary whenever they spoke of someon
Jay had grown up with. Phil was particularly adept a
painting verbal character sketches of Provincetown's mor
memorable residents. Hilary found herself laughing una
bashedly, and wished she could tape his anecdotes, whicl
were made all the more unique by his gravelly voice.

They were talking about an old man who'd recently died
and Maria said, "I think Joe Perry must have been close t
a hundred."

"Ninety-six," Jay put in promptly.

"I suppose you remember what day his birthday fell on?'

"October sixteenth."

"That sounds right," Phil Gonsalves decided. "It was i
a bad October storm that Joe was nearly lost at sea. I re
member him saying he was spared because he still hadn'
celebrated his birthday. That was back when he was cap
tain of the *Three Sisters*."

"The *Two Brothers*," Jay corrected automatically. Then he scowled, and muttered, "Damn!"

His aunt laughed. "Don't fight it, Joaquim," she counseled affectionately. She turned to Hilary. "Never say anything to him you don't intend to stick with forever," she teased. "Jay never forgets a fact."

Jay's scowl deepened.

Phil quickly changed the subject. But as the minutes passed, Hilary couldn't help noticing that Jay said very little. Finally, Phil—a lifelong cigar smoker despite all the warnings about indulging in tobacco—announced that he had to go to the store for "some smokes," and invited Jay to tag along.

The two women were left alone, but the silence that fell between them was a companionable one. Into it, Maria said, "I'm sorry that came up. About Jay's memory, that is. He hates it when people make allusions to it."

"He really has that unusual a memory?" Hilary queried.

Maria nodded. "When he was a child, they called him a human encyclopedia," she said. "It wasn't a very nice nickname for a boy who desperately wanted to be just like all the other boys. Except for his memory, Joaquim was surely normal. The thing is . . ."

"Yes?" Hilary prodded.

"Well, I must admit that my sister-in-law Elena—Jay's mother—took advantage of Jay's gift. Because certainly it is a gift, when you consider it. I don't think Elena, or Jay's father, Patrick, ever *intended* to exploit Jay, mind you. It more or less just happened. Someone knew a Boston television producer and told him about this boy in Provincetown who stored facts in his mind the way squirrels store nuts. The producer's curiosity was aroused, and Jay was tested, with Elena and Patrick's consent, of course. As a result, he was featured on a New England TV show as the

Memory Midget. He was only eight or nine when all that began, and it went on for a couple of years.''

Maria sighed. ''The show was extremely popular,'' she went on. ''People began to act as if Jay were some sort of prophet because he had such an astounding memory. That wasn't the case at all, of course. By the time he was into his teens and in high school, there was talk of the show going national. At that point, Jay balked. His whole experience on TV had caused him far more pain than pleasure. The kids in school liked him, but they also looked on him as a kind of freak.''

Maria's smile was rueful. ''Jay fought some pretty heavy battles over that,'' she recalled. ''More than once he came home with a split lip or a black eye.''

''I take it the TV show never made it to a major network?'' Hilary asked.

''Yes and no,'' Maria answered. ''The network wanted to do it, but Jay quit.''

''His parents let him quit?''

''Yes, they did.'' Maria paused reflectively, then said, ''Even as a youngster, Jay was very perceptive. He was well aware that his family needed money. Patrick was working on the fishing boat owned by my first husband and his brother.'' Sadness etched a brief mark on Maria's smooth countenance. ''Times were sometimes hard; there wasn't enough money to go around. I'm sure Jay didn't get paid anything like he should have for his performances. Elena and Patrick didn't know very much about contracts, nor did it occur to them that Jay might need an agent. Even so, what he earned on those TV shows meant a great deal to the family income. Jay knew that, so it wasn't easy for him to tell them he was going to give it up. On the other hand, he'd come to a point where I think it might have ruined his life if he'd gone on much longer.''

Maria talked a bit about Jay's family and about life in Provincetown in those earlier years, especially when the winter weather turned stormy and the fishing boats didn't dare leave the harbor. Then, as Hilary was brimming with questions, Phil and Jay returned. She'd yearned to ask Maria about the girl Jay had married, but now the chance was lost.

Although the Gonsalveses tried to persuade them to stay for supper, Jay adroitly turned aside the invitation, promising to bring Hilary out to dinner one night soon.

As they started back along the shore road toward Devon, Hilary felt puzzled. She'd been enjoying herself with the Gonsalveses and would have accepted their invitation had it been left up to her.

Without warning, Jay said in a terse voice, "I hope I didn't put you through too much back there."

"I loved meeting Maria and Phil," Hilary told him. "I wouldn't have minded it if we'd stayed...."

"I thought you'd had enough of reminiscences."

Hilary looked across at Jay, but he was staring straight ahead. "Enough of reminiscences?" she repeated, feeling slightly hurt. "I loved hearing about Joe Perry and people like that."

"Loved, loved... why don't you say what you mean, Hilary?" Jay demanded.

Hurt changed to annoyance. "I don't know what you're driving at," she blurted. "I just said what I mean."

Jay darted a swift glance in her direction, and his stern expression began to fade. "I'm sorry," he murmured. "I guess I'd feel better if I'd kept my mouth shut when Maria and Phil were talking about Joe Perry. The name of the boat he captained and his precise age really didn't make much difference, did they?"

There was charm even in the way he apologized, and Hilary felt her heart swell. "But those were things you remembered," she pointed out.

"That's right ... *things* I remembered. Do you see now why this damned memory of mine can be a curse?" Jay muttered bitterly. "My subconscious is cluttered up with a lot of trivia!"

"Does it bother you?"

"What do you mean, does it bother me?"

"Exactly that. I suppose I'm thinking that all those facts, or whatever they are, must give you severe headaches sometimes."

Jay laughed shortly, and said, "No, facts don't give me headaches, severe or otherwise. Most of the time I'm not even aware of my memory. It's just there. But like an obnoxious jack-in-the-box, it can pop out at the damnedest times, like today. I suppose Maria told you about my childhood career."

"Yes, she did," Hilary admitted.

"What else did she tell you?"

"Not much."

"I thought she might fill in the gaps for you in the so-called story of my life," Jay said rather sarcastically.

"You and Phil weren't gone that long."

"Perhaps not, but sometimes women can cover a helluva lot of ground in very little time when they're motivated."

"And I suppose men can't?"

Jay grinned. "Let's not get into a battle of the sexes, okay? Look...I know I'm overreacting. I know I tend to be too sensitive about certain things. But what you think about me, Hilary...the way you feel about me, is very important."

He'd told her he loved her that night in his apartment. Hilary hadn't forgotten his declaration, even though the moment had been awkward. She'd still been reeling from the just-learned knowledge that Jay had been widowed at the age of twenty. He'd tried to convince her that he'd learned to cope with his sorrow, but she hadn't been able to accept that. She still wasn't able to accept it, she conceded dismally.

He was waiting for her to speak, but there was nothing Hilary could say without dissembling or sounding very trite. She settled for silence, and it stretched uneasily between them for the remainder of the ride.

Once they reached her house, there was the ready-made diversion of taking him around and showing him how things were coming both with the shop and the tearoom.

Neither enterprise had a name yet, Hilary confessed. Betty Daniels felt that the tearoom's name should complement the shop's name, and that the shop's name should come first.

"I've got to come up with something before much longer," she admitted. "We'll need to order everything from business cards to letterheads to menus...."

Jay paced around, looking for inspiration. He tossed out a series of potential names featuring "sea" or "sand" or "shell," but quick perusals of the phone book showed that the better choices had already been used.

They didn't get very far that evening with those ideas, or much of anything else. Once Jay had left, Hilary felt increasing waves of discouragement wash over her. She had to admit he'd tried. Except for his annoyance at Maria's reference to his memory, he'd acted as if nothing had ever happened to form a cloud between them.

As she got ready for bed, Hilary realized that she was the one who couldn't handle the echoes of Jay's past. She also realized she would have to do something about that. She cared too much for Jay to let anything damage their evolving relationship.

Jay called the next morning, surprising her. It was even more of a surprise when he asked her to play hooky.

"Now?" she blurted.

"That's right."

"But how can you possibly get away from the bank?"

"Well," he drawled, "I can walk out the front door. That's one way. Then there's always the back door, or the side door..."

"Jay, I'm serious!"

"So am I. I bought a boat."

He sounded like a boy caught stealing candy, and Hilary responded accordingly. "You bought a boat?" she asked suspiciously.

"A boat, not a yacht," he assured her. "A very small boat, with a very small outboard motor. But it's big enough for the two of us to putt across to the outer beach and get some sea clams. After that, we can go to my place and make a chowder for supper."

"How do you *get* sea clams?"

"You dig for them, Hilary," Jay explained patiently. "Though, with sea clams you do most of your work with your toes. They're big, and best found at low tide, when there's just a shallow cover of water on the flats. You feel for bumps with your toes, then you carefully explore with your fingers, otherwise they can get pinched. Nature has a way of protecting her treasures...."

"That's the name!" Hilary exclaimed excitedly.

"What name?"

"The name for my shop!" she bubbled. "Treasures & Tea."

"Not too bad," he conceded.

"Not too bad? I think it's excellent!"

"Then I'm happy for you." He chuckled. "Look, you can get away if you try, can't you? I happened to run into Betty Daniels a little while ago when she came into the bank to get a check cashed. She said she was heading for your place and would be there all afternoon.''

"Yes, but she's got her own work...."

"Must there be such a specific definition of interests?" Jay asked.

Hilary knew he was becoming nettled. "Well..." she began.

"What I'm saying," Jay cut in, "is...can't you cover for Betty sometimes, and let her do the same for you? Like today?"

"I suppose so," Hilary admitted grudgingly.

"Don't sound so delighted at the idea of sharing a small outing with me," Jay cautioned. "The thought of your pleasure might go to my head."

"You don't have to be nasty."

"And you don't have to balk at a simple suggestion," he countered. "The ocean water, shallow or not, is bound to freeze your toes. Maybe that's what you need, ice maiden, to start the red blood flowing again."

Before she could form an indignant answer, Jay warned, "I'll be by for you in approximately one hour and ten minutes."

Despite a natural impulse to make him wait, Hilary was ready for him when he showed up precisely on time. She was wearing old jeans baggy enough to roll up to her knees, stained sneakers and a faded sweatshirt.

Jay surveyed her costume, nodded approvingly and said, "You almost look like a native."

"I should look like one!" Hilary sputtered. "I've been coming here all my life, remember?"

"Well, being *born* here is what makes one a native," he told her with an exasperating smile.

Jay was right, Hilary admitted, feeling anew her love for him as they drove out to an area of Orleans called Nauset

Heights, parked at a town landing, then waded out into the inlet where Jay had moored his boat.

As he'd said, it was a very small boat. And though Hilary had spent time on everything from a canoe to a full-size yacht, she'd never felt as exhilarated as she did now, watching Jay pull the cord to start the outboard, then maneuver the motor's handlelike tiller as he headed toward the sand flats on the other side of the channel.

He beached the boat on a sandbar, stuck an anchor out for security, then offered his hand to Hilary as she climbed out into the ankle-deep salt water. As Jay had warned, the water was pure melted ice. Hilary winced as she stepped into the shallow ripples, thankful that the sun was out with a golden benediction of warmth.

As they walked along slowly, the water got a little deeper. Knowing Jay as she did, Hilary was reasonably sure he'd push her in all the way if she didn't advance voluntarily. So she followed his lead, and by the time she'd probed for and excavated her first sea clam, she was in such high spirits that she'd practically forgotten her feet were freezing.

In fact, she discovered, they were no longer really freezing. Cold, yes. But as Jay had suggested it might, her red blood had sallied forth to meet the challenge. It was flowing defiantly through her veins, warming her feet and ankles. The rest of her was heating up, too... as she literally rubbed elbows with Jay in their quest.

After a half hour, during which time they placed more than a dozen of the big sea clams in the metal basket Jay had brought along, he declared an intermission. He led Hilary to a sheltered spot at the base of some low dunes along the outer beach. Then, after making a brief pilgrimage back to the boat, he produced a picnic lunch that consisted of a can of root beer for each of them and two ham and cheese sandwiches on dark rye bread.

"Hope you like hot mustard," he said, as he passed Hilary's sandwich to her.

"I love hot mustard," she told him. "I thought you already knew that."

"No, I didn't."

She grinned. "Don't tell me your memory's beginning to fail you," she teased.

She was unprepared for his reaction. Sparks shot from his dark eyes, igniting the air between them. Stung, she protested, "Hey, look..."

Jay simmered down. "Sorry," he apologized, "but that's one subject I'm touchy about."

"To put it mildly," Hilary muttered, feeling as if she'd been showered by a Fourth of July sparkler.

"It is, however," Jay continued, very calmly now, "the only thing about which I'm touchy, Hilary."

"Oh?"

"You may talk to me about Donna," he explained. "Or about my parents, or friends...or anyone who's ever been a part of my life. Or about anything that's ever happened in my life. Do you get my message?"

Hilary looked at Jay across the small distance that separated them and said with a child-small voice, "Yes, I get your message."

"Then please believe me," he urged her huskily.

"Jay..."

He held up a hand and implored, "It's not fair to let Donna, of all people, come between us. Sooner or later you'll understand that. I only hope it'll be sooner. I've missed you like hell, Hilary. I think I've especially missed you the times we've been together lately."

She knew exactly what he meant. And as she looked at him, her mind and her heart suddenly became as clear as this cloudless day.

There was no reason in God's world why Jay Mahoney couldn't love her completely, from the depths of his soul. Just as there was no reason why she couldn't love him as fully as if there'd never been another woman in his life, Hilary realized. There was an edge of maturity to the love she felt for Jay far deeper than anything she'd known before. There was no reason, she told herself exultantly, why the same shouldn't be true for Jay.

He put his sandwich aside and stood up. Hilary was already on her feet, and met him more than halfway. They went into each other's arms, and their passionate kisses were like the ocean waves crashing on the other side of the dunes. The dunes were completely deserted, the sun was warm, the sand was soft. A perfect place for lovemaking. And, once they'd proved *that* to a satisfaction that left no room for doubt, Hilary wondered if there could ever again be a place half as good!

The climate of everything changed following that wonderful weekday escape. Jay put a new roof rack on his car for the lightweight fiberglass boat and stored the small outboard motor in the trunk. He stole time from the bank, Hilary stole time from her shop, and they both spent days together exploring meandering saltwater inlets and freshwater ponds as well as the depths of each other.

As the weeks of spring flew by, Hilary learned that Jay had been honest when he'd told her she could talk to him about anything. Their ability to communicate with each other reached new dimensions every day and was something Hilary treasured as much as their love.

He told her how he and Donna had been not only childhood sweethearts but high-school lovers. He had a box filled with old photographs in his apartment, and together he and Hilary pored through them. There were pictures of his parents, of his brother and sisters and of Donna.

Donna had been exotically beautiful in a dark and sultry Latin way, but Hilary felt no jealousy over this. Curiously, she almost wished she could have met the girl. Donna had been part of one phase of Jay's life, a past phase. Hilary had the wonderful knowledge that she was his present life and not a phase at all.

Chapter Eleven

By the middle of May, Hilary knew there was no way she could open her shop for the Memorial Day weekend. Betty had already decided the tearoom could not possibly be ready by then. They'd considered opening the craft gallery by itself and letting the tearoom follow later. But they'd dismissed that idea by mutual consent. It seemed obvious that the best choice would be a joint grand opening.

They aimed for the Fourth of July and were glad they'd allowed the extra weeks of preparation. There were any number of last-minute problems and a potential catastrophe with the delivery and installation of a large freezer—two doorways had to be widened to permit its entry into the premises.

By the first of the month, though, Hilary and Betty knew they were going to make it. They hugged each other in congratulations over late-afternoon wine coolers, Hilary heaping praise on Betty and receiving her share of compliments in turn. More importantly, she made a mental note never again to judge a person by a first appearance. The Mrs. Elizabeth Daniels who'd presented such a calculatingly suave mien was a professional front for the warm, generous, often impulsive woman Hilary had come to know by working next to her.

They featured a patriotic theme in their Fourth of July advertising, and Hilary wished they could dole out sparklers as gifts to their holiday customers. But fireworks of all types were prohibited by law in the Commonwealth of Massachusetts, so she settled for red, white and blue pinwheels.

The opening was a tremendous success, more than Hilary could have hoped for or predicted. The gallery and tearoom were thronged with people enjoying the hors d'oevres, sangria and cake that Betty had prepared especially for this occasion. Also, there was a steady flow of customers at the cash register, Hilary noted triumphantly, though the vast majority of purchases were small.

George Delacorte told her, encouragingly, that this was to be expected. "After all," he reminded her, "many of these people are longtime Devon residents who've been curious about the Forsythe homestead for years. This is their chance to venture inside."

When Hilary and Betty finally closed the doors of Treasures & Tea after the long holiday weekend, George drove them across town to Jay's condo. Jay had gone ahead and was waiting at his door to receive them. He'd casually suggested they celebrate with a couple of bottles of champagne, but in fact he'd planned a party!

As she crossed the threshold into his living room, Hilary saw that not only had he decorated everything to the hilt with red, white and blue streamers and balloons, he also had invited other guests. She recognized the contractors who'd come through for her on the job and three of the women who were making their culinary specialties for Betty.

Jay, outgoing though he was, was not normally a party person. Remembering this, Hilary doubly appreciated his efforts. Obviously, the party was especially for her, and she only wished she could find a way to be alone with him tonight after the others had left.

Her chance came easily. To her surprise, she noted definite sparks of interest between George Delacorte and Betty Daniels as the evening progressed, and suspected there'd be little resistance from George if she urged him to drive Betty home. There wasn't. George and Betty were the last to leave, happily and together.

Closing the door behind them, Jay turned to Hilary, his eyebrows arched significantly, and commented, "Well!"

"Well, indeed," Hilary agreed. "I seem to remember your saying that Betty Daniels was old enough to be my mother."

He grinned sheepishly. "A slight exaggeration," he conceded.

"A slight exaggeration?" Hilary challenged. "If you ever got that far off in your bank calculations, you'd have something to worry about."

Jay sat down in a comfortable armchair and thrust his long legs out in front of him. He'd poured himself a snifter of brandy and looked happy and relaxed. "If my recollection is correct," he said, slanting a mischievous smile in her direction, "you exhibited a touch of the green-eyed monster in your questions about Betty."

"Ah, your memory..."

"Don't you dare say a word about my memory," he threatened teasingly.

"I won't," Hilary promised, with mock meekness. "Seriously, Jay, how old do you think Betty is?" Without waiting for him to answer, she mused, "George is about your age. Maybe a couple of years older, say... thirty-six. I don't think Betty is much over forty, so—"

"Are you asking me or telling me?" Jay queried.

"Come on, Jay. I'm wondering, that's all. If George is thirty-six and Betty is perhaps forty-one, that isn't much of an age difference."

"Women," Jay groaned.

"What?"

"Even in supposedly *emancipated* women, the urge to matchmake appears to be irresistible," he stated.

Hilary sat down cross-legged on the carpet a few feet away from Jay and studied him dispassionately. "I suppose you've been subject to matchmaking attempts more than once," she allowed.

"Have I ever!" Jay scoffed. "You should see the candidates some of my best friends have chosen for me! I mean, I've never thought I deserved perfection, but..."

"They weren't pretty enough for you?"

"That's not the way I'd put it."

"Okay, they weren't gorgeous enough, then?"

"Physical beauty isn't everything," Jay intoned. "No, before you start giggling behind your teeth, I mean that. It so happens that you're beautiful. God knows, that's probably what attracted me to you initially, although..." He broke off, considering this. "Come to think of it," he went on, "that wasn't what first caught my eye."

"What was?" Hilary asked automatically.

"Well, you looked like a lost kitten back in Madame Zola's tent."

"Thanks a lot."

"It's true," he insisted. "I felt I should pick you up, soothe your bruises, smooth your fur..."

"I don't think I like that," Hilary decided. "I wasn't aware I was coming on to you in such a helpless fashion."

"Would that you'd come on to me in an even more help-less fashion now," Jay speculated, using Madame Zola's phony accent and favoring Hilary with a decided leer. "Though," he added, returning to his normal tone but keeping the leer, "it does seem to me we made out fairly well on that first encounter."

Remembering their embrace in the fake nomadic tent, Hilary knew she was on the verge of blushing. Her suppos-edly ice-maiden exterior hardly ever permitted such a visi-ble display of emotions... except with Jay.

"I'm glad George took Betty home," he said. "And, if you want my opinion, I don't think she's too old for him. From what I've seen of George, he's old for his age any-way. Betty might actually rev him up a bit!"

He took a lazy sip of his brandy. Then, as Hilary watched, he casually set the snifter aside and surveyed her. "Is there a chance you'd accept an invitation to spend the night with me?" he asked, with disarming simplicity.

Jay had stayed the night on Sea Street, but Hilary had yet to spend the night at Sand Terraces. She'd silently hoped he'd issue exactly this invitation and was at a loss to under-stand why she was hedging now that he had.

"What's the matter?" he queried softly.

"I don't know."

"Okay, something is. I get the impression you're not happy with my suggestion."

"No, it's not that."

"Well then, what is it?"

"I guess I'm leery of... oh, damn. Of staying overnight in a man's apartment, I guess," Hilary managed, mentally wrestling with her choice of words.

Jay regarded her calmly. "Am I right in assuming that you're thinking of our old Boston enemy, Roy?" The ques-tion was put urbanely. Still, there was a thread of tension running through it.

"If I was thinking of Roy, I wasn't aware of it," Hilary asserted.

"Subconscious memories and hidden doubts are the worst kind," Jay pronounced. "So, I'll take you home and spend the night with you at your place."

Hilary thought of the upstairs at the Forsythe homestead and flinched. Her bedroom was a disaster, her bathroom in utter chaos. The other upstairs rooms were presently being used as storage bins. Further, nothing had been cleaned or even superficially dusted for longer than she liked to think about. She tried to rationalize her haphazard housekeeping by reminding herself that she'd been too busy getting the shop ready to do anything else.

She said weakly, "Maybe I'd better stay here."

"Maybe," Jay decided darkly, "I'd better take you home."

Hilary didn't know just what she'd done. Dented his ego? Upset his confidence in her? Damaged his pride? Whatever it was, he was downright stern on the drive across town and left her at her door with a muttered, "Good night."

As she made her way up the stairs, it occurred to Hilary that underneath Jay Mahoney's usually controlled exterior there boiled a veritable cauldron of emotions. That mixture of Irish and Portuguese blood could be pretty lethal... while at the same time eternally fascinating. He had a hot temper, she'd learned, but had discovered his own way to control it. He also didn't stay angry very long, and there was no evidence that he bore any lingering grudges against anyone.

This was proved the next morning when he called her at the somewhat ungodly hour of six o'clock.

"Good morning," he said softly, then added, "I want to give you a windsurfing lesson."

Hilary's subconscious had been entirely consumed by the subject of Joaquim Alvaro Mahoney as she'd tried to sleep.

As a result, she'd tossed and turned, and was still groggy as she listened to his pronouncement.

"Huh?" she murmured sleepily, sounding like a girl.

"I'd like to take you out windsurfing today," Jay repeated gently yet insistently.

"But I'm not even a good swimmer," Hilary protested. Suddenly, a memory struck her. George, wasn't it, had told her of Jay's fame as a swimmer during his college days. Days, she now knew, that came after he'd recouped from Donna's death and had made up his mind to get on with his life and his education.

"Anyway," she said deliberately, "I have no intention of going swimming with you, of all people."

"What's that supposed to mean?"

"As I understand it, you're an ex-Olympic star. So I'd rather not have you watch me muddle around in the water."

"Where," Jay demanded, "did you get the idea I was an Olympic swimming star?"

"I think it was George who told me."

"Well, George had it wrong. Partially wrong, anyway. I was a swimmer in college, *cara*. I went to Dartmouth, by the way. And I did participate in the Olympic trials. However, I never even made it to the finals."

"You still must be very good to have gotten that far," Hilary pointed out.

"Reasonably good, yes. So that'll make you all the safer when you're in the water with me. If you start to drown, I assure you I'll do my utmost to save you."

"Are you sure about that?" Hilary teased.

"Yes," Jay said briskly. "Now, getting back to the point . . . can you snitch a couple of hours this afternoon? The tide will be perfect over on Pleasant Bay—a very safe body of water on which to learn how to windsurf. It's quite shallow, and the wind almost always blows onshore."

Hilary paused, then said, a bit more tautly than she intended, "Jay, it's kind of early to make decisions, don't you think? Anyway, I don't keep banker's hours...."

"Neither do most bankers keep the kind of hours they're reputed to," he shot back. "Anyway, I have some extra time just now because the top echelon is so involved with the merger. My branch is sort of on cruise control, at the moment."

"That's great, Jay. But you seem to have forgotten that I've just opened my own business," she reminded him. "I should be working every chance I get."

"Can't we compromise, *cara*? You have to arrange to take time off occasionally, you know."

"I will...once my act is together," Hilary told him.

She'd hired a couple of local high-school girls to help out in the shop. Both were excellent, having worked previous summers in other Devon establishments. Still, to arrange time for herself, Hilary knew she would have to have an older woman as her substitute. Betty Daniels had her hands completely full with the tearoom, so there wasn't any point in even asking her.

Hilary told Jay this, and he promptly said he had the perfect person in mind. By ten that morning, Olivia Harris was at the door. Olivia was middle-aged, an unnatural blonde, plump and delightfully outgoing. By ten-thirty, Olivia and Hilary had come to a mutually satisfactory agreement, with Olivia scheduled to start working afternoons at the gallery by the end of the week.

In the meantime, though, it was necessary for Hilary to stay at the helm. She put in long hours, and Jay formed the habit of showing up with take-out orders of fried clams, pizzas or far more delicious concoctions that he brought from his apartment. Plans for Hilary's upstairs renovations were in limbo at the moment, and the only place to cook anything was in the efficient, restaurant-type kitchen that properly belonged to the tearoom. That suited Hilary. There were always coffee and muffins available when she got up mornings, and she seldom had time to stop for lunch anyway. Fortunately, Jay was taking care of her evening meals.

Business slackened somewhat in the middle of July, but there were still plenty of people around and plenty of chores that required Hilary's attention, leaving her little spare time.

This was true the afternoon before Olivia was due to report for work. Hilary was in the shop by herself, her two young employees having gone off for a half-hour ice cream break. There were three or four customers browsing around . . . when Roy LeClair walked through the door.

A hazy moment passed before Hilary recognized him; then a curious kind of coldness set in. Fortunately, she was giving change to a patron and managed to stall as she counted out dollars and cents. She needed any time she could grab, to regroup before she faced up to Roy.

She didn't want to face him at all. It wasn't that she had any lingering feelings for him. She didn't. Rather, he was so completely a part of her past that she hated opening a lid she'd already closed.

He strolled around the long table she'd taken from the dining room to use for display and came to a stand beside the cash register. He waited quietly until Hilary had completed her transaction, and then moved into the vacant center space.

"Hello, Hilary," he said.

He smiled as he greeted her, but it seemed very strange to Hilary to hear the sound of her name on his lips. She had the crazy feeling it didn't belong there.

Like Jay, she noted objectively, Roy was tall, dark and handsome. There all comparisons ended. He wasn't nearly *as* handsome as Joaquim Alvaro Mahoney, perhaps because life had failed to stamp on his features the marks of character that were so much a part of Jay's beloved face.

Assessing him, Hilary decided there was something faintly garish about Roy. Maybe that was too strong a word, she conceded. But his clothes—from the bright plaid shorts to the tailored pink sports shirt he was wearing—shouted tourist. Nor did his Italian loafers, the logo on the sports shirt nor his carefully matched socks do anything to alleviate the image.

There was nothing wrong with being a tourist. It wasn't that. What mattered was the kind of tourist a tourist was, Hilary thought somewhat incoherently. She couldn't help but think that Roy would be the worst kind. Demanding, arrogant, yes... quite insufferable.

His smile was almost tender as he surveyed her, and that made her shudder. She'd realized quite a while before that when Roy smiled like that it meant he wanted something. His intense gray eyes swept her hair, her face, her figure... and, for no logical reason, Hilary felt like reaching out and slapping him once he'd finished his appraisal.

He said, "You look great, Hil."

She hated being called Hil. In fact, she couldn't think of anyone who'd every called her Hil, except Roy.

To her surprise, he glanced at his watch. Then, still keeping his smile in place, he said, "I wonder if we could talk—just for a few minutes. I can see you're busy."

"I really don't have time, Roy," Hilary rejoined promptly. "You're right, I'm very busy."

He wasn't fazed by her rejection, implied considerably more in her tone than by the words themselves. But that was Roy, she recalled, shaking her head. Roy had an alligator-thick skin. The emblem on his shirt suited him!

He said, with the show of charm he could switch on and off like lights on a chandelier, "This isn't personal, Hilary... though I think you know I'd dearly like to make it personal. What I want to talk to you about now is strictly business. I have something in mind I think would benefit us both.''

Hilary bristled. Roy, she thought bitterly, might have something in mind that would benefit *him*. She doubted very much that it could stretch also to benefit her.

"Look," he said, "I have some things I'm sure you're going to want for the gallery. I came in this morning and looked around. You were out at the time.''

Hilary's mind raced backward. True, she'd been out briefly during the course of the morning. And she'd taken a ten-minute break to go upstairs to the bathroom, brush her hair and touch up her lipstick.

"You have some very nice stuff," Roy conceded generously. "But nothing like what I have in mind. Anyway, I think you need the kind of thing I want to offer you.''

Hilary had no idea what he was driving at. She knew that some people considered Roy a good artist. Occasionally, he'd sold an oil painting to one of his "patrons" on Beacon Hill in Boston. But privately she'd never liked his work, even when she'd fancied herself in love with him.

That she'd made no secret of that fact had galled Roy considerably. She remembered this with satisfaction and stared at him, puzzled. Knowing the way she felt about his artwork, Roy wouldn't possibly suggest she take any of his paintings. Anyway, the subjects he delved into weren't even remotely related to Cape Cod.

"Look, Hil," he said, glancing again at his wide-banded platinum wristwatch. "I'll only take a minute.''

"Okay," she said resignedly, seeing her young helpers coming in the door. "But a minute is about all I can give you.''

She led Roy out to the veranda. It was a hot, sunny afternoon and people were still at the beach, so there were several vacant tables. One of Betty's waitresses came over quickly and greeted Hilary politely. Then she took Roy's order for iced coffee and blueberry pie. Reluctantly, Hilary decided on having an iced tea.

When the girl left, Roy leaned across the table and said, his voice low, "You pretty much did me in, Hil, when you left Boston as you did. You could have told me you were going."

Hilary took a deep breath. "You'd changed the locks on your apartment door so I couldn't get in, remember?" she observed coolly.

"Only because there'd been a rash of break-ins on the Hill," he objected, equally cool. "I had a duplicate set of keys made for you. If you'd just hung on . . ."

"I guess I didn't want to hang on any longer, Roy. Nor do I want to talk about *that*, now or ever. What is it you want to tell me?"

She saw him wince, but he quickly shrugged it off. "I've moved to Provincetown," he announced.

Hilary nearly choked on her iced tea. "When?" she asked.

"Oh, just a few days ago. I have a friend out there—another artist—who has a decent studio, but needed someone to help pay the rent. He's not even there most of the time. He has a concession of sorts. Paints tourist portraits, that kind of thing. So I have plenty of space in which to work on my own stuff."

"I'm glad, Roy," Hilary told him.

"I might add," he said carefully, "that my style has changed considerably. Of late, I've been going in for seascapes. That's one of the reasons I jumped at the chance to move to P-town, and I've already begun painting like crazy. I worked out on MacMillan Wharf yesterday. The atmosphere's terrific. All those trawlers and Portuguese fishermen, and the colors are fantastic. I've really got it down, Hil."

This news stopped Hilary cold. She was well aware that her shop was dismally lacking when it came to an art inventory. She'd acquired a few paintings from local artists on consignments, but none of them were seascapes. She badly needed water scenes, dockside scenes, harbor scenes . . . in short, anything evoking those aspects uniquely Cape Cod. Many customers had already made inquiries for exactly those themes.

But to take on Roy's work? The thought was untenable.

He was watching her closely. "Why don't you look before you refuse to leap, Hil?"

She thought about this. Because they'd had a miserable, messed-up personal relationship didn't mean they couldn't have a successful business one, she rationalized. Assuming that Roy really had something to offer, doubtful as that was.

Grudgingly, she said, "Well . . . all right."

In an earlier day, Roy would have commented caustically on her lack of enthusiasm. At this moment, he let it go. To her surprise, he produced a small leather portfolio she somehow hadn't even noticed and flipped it open. Then he extracted several instant-camera color snapshots.

He held them out to Hilary. She took them reluctantly. She was prepared to see something as little to her liking as Roy's previous work. That made the shock all the greater.

She studied each of the snapshots in turn, then stared across at Roy in disbelief. That was his signature in the corner of the paintings depicted, all right. Even reduced to this miniature replica, it was quite clear. But it was difficult, close to impossible, to believe that the Roy LeClair she'd known had done these paintings.

He'd handed her four snapshots, and all were great!

"These," Hilary managed, forcing herself to stay calm, "are quite interesting."

Roy grinned triumphantly. "I thought you'd see it that way," he said with satisfaction. "I didn't bring the paintings with me, but I'd be glad to let you see them as soon as you like.''

"Well, Roy," Hilary said warily, "I think deciding that depends on a few things."

"Such as?"

"Such as how much you're asking for them, and what kind of financial arrangement we could make." As she spoke, Hilary was struck by the fact that she wasn't actually operating on much more than a shoestring budget. She'd converted a conservative number of securities into cash, but she still owed money to the carpenter and the electrician. Most of her stock was on consignment. Nevertheless, the situation was already getting a little hairy. If she started making more money, the pinch would ease. Even so, she needed a cushion. She was coming to realize that more and more. What she needed, she thought grimly, was a bank loan. But that was not a subject she wanted to bring up again with Jay.

If Roy wanted to sell her his paintings outright, she knew there was no way she could afford them, even if his prices were reasonable. Knowing Roy as she did, she doubted his prices were apt to be reasonable.

Again, he was watching her closely. He said, "As I already mentioned, Hil, you have some very nice stuff in your shop. Top drawer, I'd say...when it comes to local crafts. I'd like to add my paintings to your list. I'm willing to go for a consignment deal with you. Provided you don't ask too great a percentage."

So, Hilary observed silently, this wasn't just fun and games with Roy after all!

"Well," he said, playing off her silence, "why don't I get back to you tomorrow? I'll bring the four paintings you've seen pictures of, and we can work out our terms. Over dinner, perhaps?"

"Thank you, no," Hilary said primly.

Roy arched an eyebrow and said easily, "Okay, then, whenever you say."

"How many paintings do you have on hand, Roy?" Hilary queried. "Seascapes, that is. Like the ones you just showed me," she added hastily.

"Several," he answered evasively. "This isn't the first time I've painted on the Cape, Hil. Anyway... would this time tomorrow suit you?"

She nodded, though she wanted to say there would never be a right time with him. Even if he proved to be the best, and most salable, marine artist in the world, she wasn't about to change her personal opinion of him.

Once he'd left, and she'd returned to her work, Hilary began to rue her agreement with him, tentative though it was. It did no good to reassure herself that she hadn't committed herself to anything. Just dealing with Roy at all was apt to be too much.

A deep resentment toward him still brimmed within her. She had to acknowledge that. Once she might have wanted to get even with him. Now it no longer mattered. Rather, she feared that having anything to do with Roy, no matter how much his paintings might enhance her shop, would prove to be disastrous.

Chapter Twelve

Roy's paintings were absolutely beautiful. The color snapshots he'd shown Hilary hadn't even begun to do them justice. She stared transfixed...and wondered how she could possibly handle this ironic dilemma she found herself in.

She was all too familiar with Roy's conceit, and unfortunately he was showing her exactly what she needed. She reminded herself that there were other excellent marine artists in the area. In fact, Cape Cod abounded with them. But few of this quality—none, she amended honestly—would be willing to place their work in a brand new shop on a consignment basis.

Hilary had never considered herself a good actress. Still, she drew on Jay's teasing about her ice-maiden exterior to present Roy with a show of indifference. Not indifference, exactly. Roy was too clever to be fooled by that. But she did manage to pretend that this was a matter she had to take under serious consideration.

"I have to allot my display space very carefully," she began, glad to be interrupted by a customer looking for a wedding gift, something truly reminiscent of Cape Cod.

"My friends met here," the woman babbled happily.

Hilary sold her a reproduction Sandwich glass vase that looked so authentic only an expert would have known the difference. She stalled as much as she could with the woman, then reluctantly went back to Roy.

To her surprise, he'd started stacking together the four paintings he'd brought with him. He said abruptly, "Hil, if you don't want these, say so. I'm sure I can place them elsewhere."

Could he ever! This rueful bit of knowledge stabbed Hilary's brain, already weary for a number of reasons. For one thing, Jay hadn't been able to come over last night. He'd called to say that the bank president was back in town and had "summoned" him to dinner.

"Speaking of dinner," he'd added, "just because I'm not going to be aboard, don't you dare skip yours! There must be something you can munch on in the tearoom."

Hilary had "munched," but it had been a lonely repast. She'd had too much time to think. Facing up to the fact that she couldn't possibly buy Roy's paintings outright made her realize anew that she needed ready money until the shop's cash flow put business in the plus. Otherwise, she'd miss out on important purchases such as this, as not all artists and craftspeople were willing to work on consignment.

Now, watching Roy get his art together, she suddenly realized she had to have his paintings. She *needed* them, dammit! He'd said he was willing to give her a sales percentage, and it was too good an opportunity to pass up.

Gritting her teeth, Hilary wondered why it had to be Roy, of all people, who'd created precisely what she needed. Then she forced herself to stuff her pride in her pocket.

She said levelly, "I think perhaps we can do business, Roy."

He didn't exactly smirk. But from the smug expression that crossed his face, Hilary knew she hadn't surprised him in the least. So, he was a better actor than she was! That, she told herself, was something she should have realized long ago!

They adjourned to the veranda again, where Hilary politely suggested that he might like to repeat yesterday's order of iced coffee and homemade blueberry pie. She opted for a dish of cranberry sherbet but merely toyed with it as they talked. She had too much on her mind to be hungry.

She'd noted, with amusement, the way her two teenage helpers—Thelma and Amy—had been ogling Roy. Viewing him objectively, she had to admit that he was, in his way, quite handsome. His dark, intensely physical good looks had attracted her to him in the first place. Funny, she mused, Jay was far better looking than Roy. And with Jay, there was so much personality and character that she sometimes forgot how really good-looking he was.

Hilary forced herself to concentrate on the man sitting opposite her. Roy was digging into his pie and paused between bites to say, "Delicious."

She nodded. Everything Betty served in the tearoom was delicious, as people were discovering.

She waited until Roy put down his fork. Then she said, "Suppose we work on a basis of sixty percent for you, forty percent for the gallery?"

He smiled. "I think that rather favors the house, don't you, Hil?" he drawled. "I'd say a twenty-percent commission is about what most places get."

That wasn't true. With consignment merchandise the percentage kept by the shop varied considerably. What she'd offered, Hilary felt, was essentially fair. If it had been anyone else, she would have stuck to her guns. With Roy, she wanted to get the details over with as quickly as possible. Then she hoped he'd go back to Provincetown and keep on painting. Whenever the shop sold a painting, she'd notify him. That was as much contact as she wanted to have with him.

She temporized. "I'll give you seventy percent," she said firmly, "but that's my max."

Roy smiled. "Since it's you, Hil," he said softly, "that's a deal."

She ignored his dulcet tone and asked briskly, "How many paintings can you leave with me?"

"Enough," Roy said succinctly.

"How many are enough, Roy?"

He frowned. "Okay," he capitulated. "I don't like giving away trade secrets any more than you do. Presently, I have ten paintings, Hil. You have four, and there are six more out in P-town. I can bring down two or three more in a day or so, and we can wait on the rest till you've made a sale. After that, I could fill in one at a time, unless you come upon someone who's so enamored of my work they want to buy the whole lot." He added, "And there will be more... once we clear up matters between us and I can get back to work."

Hilary was not about to explore what he meant by "clearing up matters." She hastily suggested that he help her work out an effective display for the four paintings she was starting with. They arranged wall space in the front parlor with a surprising lack of disagreement. Then, with a number of customers suddenly appearing, Roy took off.

About an hour later, Jay called. Looking back, Hilary decided that's when her world began to suffer a serious crack.

With very little preamble, Jay said, "*Cara*, I have to go to Boston. I should be back tomorrow afternoon. How about dinner with me tomorrow night? There's a Portuguese restaurant out in Provincetown I've been wanting to take you to. Maybe we can stop by and say hello to Maria and Phil, too.''

She needed him. That was the first thing Hilary thought when she heard Jay's voice. Right now, she needed him. She needed his arms around her; she needed to have him hold her while she babbled out a string of woes. Roy and his paintings were among those woes, though she realized how profitable Roy's paintings might be, even at a thirty-percent commission rate.

Dammit, she thought angrily, this was the worst time for Jay to take off to Boston!

"Look," he said, "if I can break away tonight, I'll call you. There's something wrong, isn't there?"

"Is the memory prodigy playing psychic again?" she asked nastily, and wished she'd bitten her tongue off. There was no excuse for taking out her frustrations on Jay.

After a moment, he said, "I don't think I'll bother answering that. You obviously have something eating you. Anyway, if I could get out of this, I would. So try to act like a grown-up about it, will you?"

That stung, even though Hilary knew she had it coming. Jay quickly tried to mollify her, but they needed a kind of communication that couldn't be achieved over telephone lines. After she'd hung up, Hilary couldn't shake off a feeling of mounting depression.

Evening arrived, and she snacked on leftovers in the tearoom. Then she settled down with the shop's books. Accounting was not her forte, and she was tempted to call George and ask him to come over and help her out. Then she remembered that George and Betty had a date tonight. Betty had confessed, her face aglow, that she and George were going to a very special new restaurant over toward Hyannis.

Hilary's consultation with facts and figures convinced her that she should take out a bank loan. But not through a bank in Devon, she decided. Nor did she have any desire to trek up to Boston where she'd have no problem, thanks to her late uncle's connections there. Thinking about Betty and George dining in Hyannis, she got the idea of seeking a bank loan there.

It was early, not quite eight o'clock. Having searched through the yellow pages for a couple of Hyannis banks to contact in the morning, Hilary headed upstairs to take a shower. As she undressed, she looked around her messy room and her spirits sank further. She'd intended to call Clara Chase—who'd housekept for the Forsythes during the summers for as long as Hilary could remember—but she just hadn't gotten around to it. Now, she would.

Clara Chase was delighted to hear from her. But the delight faded from the woman's voice when Hilary asked if she could start working for her within the next few days.

"Since I hadn't heard from you, it never occurred to me you might want me over the summer," Clara admitted. "So...I took a job with the Sand and Surf Inn out in Eastham. I'm really sorry."

"Don't be, Clara," Hilary said honestly. "It's all my fault. I'd intended to call you right after Memorial Day, but the house was undergoing renovations, and time just flew by in a big blur...."

"I know," Clara murmured sympathetically. "Getting a business started is never easy. My husband tried three times before he gave up and went to work for someone else. Anyway, I promised myself to these people, Hilary, and frankly I'd hate to let them down. The owner's a cousin of mine. He wouldn't take kindly to my telling him I was going back to my job with you, especially with the summer almost half over."

"I can certainly understand that," Hilary admitted.

So saying, she brought Clara up to date on her new business, and Clara promised to drop by. But it didn't help, once she'd hung up the phone, to be left alone in the upstairs rooms. Even casual inspection revealed they were at the point of needing a lot more than the basic cleaning she'd hoped Clara could provide. They needed fresh paint, new wallpaper, new shades and drapes, floor refinishing....

"Just name it," Hilary said aloud, dejectedly.

She took her shower, but it failed to mark the beginning of the relaxing interlude she needed. As she was toweling herself dry, the phone rang. She instantly thought it must be Jay and hurried to answer the phone's summons. In doing so, she knocked her toe into the wall. A searing bolt of pain shot through her, and it took fortitude not to groan audibly as she picked up the receiver.

"Hilary?"

That was not Jay's voice at the other end of the line.

"Yes," she said.

"Trevor Andrews, Hilary."

Trevor Andrews was the real-estate agent who had dealt with the various properties owned by Chad Forsythe over the years. Now, those properties were down to the Forsythe homestead itself and the summer cottage out in Wellfleet.

The realtor said cheerily. "I've been meaning to get over to your shop. I hear it's going great and the tearoom's guaranteed to put ten pounds on anybody in ten minutes."

Hilary managed a laugh. "Well, I hope that's not quite the case or we'll be losing business," she said.

"I'll drop in before long and find out for myself," Mr. Andrews promised. "Meantime, we've got a little problem out at your cottage."

Hilary had stayed with Trevor Andrew's agency when she'd decided to rent the cottage. Subsequently she'd given it little thought.

"We have three rentals this season," Mr. Andrews reminded her now. "The first people came in on June 14th. They're in until the end of this month. The next tenants have the month of August through the Labor Day weekend. Then we have a gap of a week before an older couple comes in for the rest of September."

"Yes, I got your note to that effect."

"Well," the realtor went on, "the present tenants had to move into a motel about an hour ago. I managed to get a unit for them, but it's not in the best of places, and they can only have it for two nights."

"They moved into a motel?" Hilary echoed.

"Water system's gone on the fritz," Mr. Andrews explained laconically. "Nothing's working. Looks as if the well has run dry. Means digging a new one because there's no town water to hook into, as you know."

She didn't know. But that sorry fact didn't make much difference.

"Water's been running brackish," the realtor went on. "Lots of rust in it. I told the MacIntyres I wish they'd let me know about it sooner. Thing is...this being what anybody'd call a dire emergency, I got in touch with a contractor I know who can start putting in a new well for you first thing in the morning. Problem is, it'll cost you a bit extra— he'll have to put off several jobs, you understand. So it's not going to come cheap, but frankly I can't see any other way around it. This time of year, if you wait, you'll wind up with a cottage without water for the rest of the season. Which'll mean refunding money to the present tenants, refunding the deposits the other people have made, and having a pretty empty investment, if you understand me."

"I understand you," Hilary managed.

"I hate to heap this on you, Hilary," Trevor Andrews said sincerely. "It's a rough one. And it's your decision."

"I understand that, too."

There was a pause, then Mr. Andrews said, "If you don't mind my saying so, your uncle would have given me the green light. The circumstances really don't leave you any alternative."

"I'm sure you're right," Hilary admitted dolefully, and added, "Okay, go ahead with it."

"Cash on completion of the job," the realtor warned. "Normally, you'd have to put a hunk down, but I know this man, and he'll wait."

"I'll have the money whenever you need it," Hilary promised, then hung up.

It was crazy, she thought, as she propped herself up in bed and stared into the darkness. She was supposed to be a very wealthy young woman, yet her bank account had dwindled to almost nothing. Once everything dealing with her uncle's estate was straightened out, she'd be as free of money worries as she'd always been.

She'd been insane to start a business in this interim period of financial transition, Hilary chided herself angrily. Particularly since she knew so damned little about money per se and even less about handling investments, she concluded grimly.

Despite her relative lack of experience, though, Hilary walked into a Hyannis bank at ten o'clock the next morning—having left Olivia Harris in charge of the shop—and an hour later had made arrangements for an extensive line of credit that she could draw on as the need arose. She could handle the new well at the cottage, pay the bills she'd accumulated in renovating the house, and still have enough surplus to maintain a petty-cash fund while the revenue of the shop sustained the business.

As she left the bank, she was aware as she'd never been before of how much luckier she was than so many other people. Her parents had left her well-fixed, but it was her

Uncle Chad who'd wisely managed the money she'd inherited.

Perhaps it was a good lesson to have got into a temporary hole with her business, and also to have been forced to deal with a problem like the well at the cottage. However brief the moment had been, Hilary now appreciated what it felt like to be in a financial bind.

She thought of Jay. According to what Maria had said, Jay had been a mainstay of his family's support while he was just a youngster, the child star of a TV show. True, Jay had eventually bowed out. But knowing him as she did, Hilary felt sure that by then his family were not suffering any real hardships.

Jay lived well, he dressed well, he'd traveled, but he was a self-made person. She, on the other hand, was a potentially wealthy woman who'd done nothing herself to earn any of that wealth.

The thought occurred that Jay might naturally resent her money. He knew very well what lay in store for her, through the "dossier" at his bank. But money, in itself, was the last thing Hilary could ever imagine coming between herself and Joaquim Alvaro Mahoney.

The first thing Hilary was told when she got back to the shop was that Jay had been phoning her. She promptly called him at the bank, weathered his secretary's unctuous tone and sat back with a smile on her lips when she heard him say, "Hilary?"

"Yes, darling," she murmured.

Jay's chuckle echoed sweetly through her receiver. "What a nice greeting," he commented.

"Well . . . it's good to hear your voice. I'm sorry I missed your call."

"Out early, weren't you?"

"Yes," she conceded. Suddenly, Hilary realized that she would have to tell Jay she'd taken a loan with another bank. Suddenly, it was beginning to seem like a rather rash action. She should have done him the courtesy of approaching Commonwealth Bank and Trust again first before going elsewhere.

But this, definitely, was not the time to go into that!

Fortunately, Jay didn't pursue the subject of her absence from the gallery on a workday morning. "Just wanted to verify our dinner date for tonight," he said, "and ask you for a favor."

"Oh?"

"I wonder if you'd mind meeting me at my apartment before we go out? I'm going to run late at the bank, and I'd like to go home and change into something comfortable. Anyway, we'll take my car from there. I thought if we pop in to see Maria and Phil before dinner we shouldn't be too late about it. So...suppose I make reservations at the Moors for eight-thirty?"

"That sounds perfect."

"Then suppose you meet me at Sand Terraces at five-thirty?"

"You'll be there?"

"I'll be there," Jay assured her, "though I should have given you a key, dammit," he added, reproving himself. "In the near future, let's get extra keys made to both our places, okay?"

"Agreed," Hilary told him, smiling as she hung up the phone.

The day ambled along with only a few bumps to mar it. One customer brought back a lovely quilt she'd bought, insisting she'd discovered a rip in it when she got home. It was an exquisite item, handmade and expensive. Though convinced that the woman had ripped the quilt herself, Hilary refunded her money. She'd already paid the quilt-maker and wasn't about to ask for any money herself, since the customer was to blame. Still, it was a loss she'd have to assume until the quilt could be repaired and, hopefully, resold.

Trevor Andrews called during the afternoon to say that the workmen were making good progress with the well. "In fact, the job should be completed by midday tomorrow," he added.

"Just tell me how much it is and, to whom to send the check," Hilary rejoined, feeling especially satisfied with herself.

Then, at four-thirty, Roy called.

"Hil, I'm passing through Devon in about an hour," he informed her. "I'm on my way to Boston. I'll probably be up there for a week, so I'd like to drop off the three paintings I promised you."

"Roy, I'm going out . . ." Hilary began.

"Will there be someone else at the gallery?"

"I'm afraid not. We close at five today and so does the tearoom."

"Hil," he pointed out, "I can't very well leave my paintings propped up against your door."

"I realize that."

"Well, unless I get them to you now, I don't know when I'll be able to let you have them."

Roy was on his way to being obnoxious about this, Hilary realized.

It made matters difficult. A wealthy couple who summered in Devon, and were friends of Chad Forsythe's had already expressed considerable interest in two of Roy's paintings. They weren't the only people who'd taken note of his work, although most of the others had frankly admitted they couldn't pay Roy's prices. This couple, though, had shown no qualms at all about the numbers Hilary quoted. They'd promised they'd be back tomorrow, and Hilary believed them. Also, her uncanny sense that they'd be making a big purchase made her all the more anxious to have the rest of Roy's work on hand.

"Couldn't you make it earlier than five-thirty, Roy?"

"For God's sake, Hilary...it's already twenty to five. It's at least an hour's drive to your place, and I'm not even ready to leave yet."

"Well, *I'm* supposed to be out of here before five-thirty," she shot back.

"That's up to you. We can wait until I get back from Boston, then. Matter of fact, I might take the paintings along with me and leave them with one of the galleries on Newbury Street."

It was a threat, and Hilary deeply resented it. This was a typical Roy ploy! She considered the play on words and wondered how she could've ever fancied herself in love with the man.

"Let's not play games," she said tersely. "If you'll be here by five-thirty, I'll wait for you."

"See you then, sweetheart," Roy assured her cheerfully, annoying her even more.

A moment later, Hilary dialed Jay at the bank. As she'd expected, she was connected with Eleanor Roberts. As she'd also expected, Ms. Roberts promptly informed her that Mr. Mahoney was tied up in a meeting.

"Please tell Mr. Mahoney that I'll be fifteen minutes late," Hilary responded sweetly, and was delighted to let Ms. Roberts stew in that one.

Ten minutes later, Jay called. "So what's the hang-up?" he asked.

"So how did you escape from your meeting so easily?" she countered.

"I had to go back to my office for a couple of papers. Eleanor said you'd phoned. Look, I have to get back to the meeting. What's come up?"

"Roy's stopping by here with a few more paintings," Hilary began, then realized that Jay knew nothing at all about Roy's being on the Cape or about her acquisition of the seascapes.

After a moment of heavy silence, Jay asked darkly, "Did you say Roy?"

She wasn't in the mood to deal with Jay's potential jealousy. "Yes, I said Roy," she told him. "Believe me, Jay, this is entirely a business matter."

"I'll bet."

Hilary ignored this. "Look," she suggested, "come over here as soon as you can. Roy said he'd be here at five-thirty, but he's always late. Anyway, you can be here and meet him and see his paintings...."

"I don't want to meet him, and I don't give a damn about seeing his paintings," Jay growled.

"Jay, please. I don't need this from you."

"Likewise," he assured her. "When Roy has departed," he added, "give me a call at home. I'll come pick you up, and we can take it from there."

Hilary could only begin to appreciate what that was apt to mean!

Chapter Thirteen

It was after six when Roy arrived at the shop, and Hilary was seething. Still, she didn't want to give him the satisfaction of seeing that he'd made her angry, so she played her ice-maiden role to the hilt. She was cool and polite, even slightly aloof . . . and managed to maintain that facade until Roy removed the protective wrappings from the new paintings he'd brought her.

Then she nearly gasped aloud.

These three were even more impressive than the first four. He'd done a winter scene of an old boat high and dry on a deserted beach. It was breathtaking and evoked a poignant mood of loneliness that astonished Hilary. She wouldn't have believed Roy had this in him and began to wonder if she'd misjudged him, artistically speaking.

The second painting showed the open sea on a stormy day and made such an eloquent statement about the power of nature that Hilary was again taken aback. The third was a more conventional dock scene. Fishermen dressed in yellow slickers were unloading the day's catch. Simple, yet the viewer could sense that these men wanted to finish their work, then stop at the local tavern for a beer or two before heading home to their families. Again, Roy had captured a special mood on canvas.

Hilary suppressed her rising elation and managed to say calmly, "They're excellent, Roy."

"Hmmm," he nodded, obviously agreeing with her. He peered into the parlor where they'd hung his other work, but Hilary had already turned off the lights so the room was dim. "Any sales yet?" he asked.

"A couple of nibbles," she reported noncommittally. "It's only been a day, you know."

"Just wait a while," Roy predicted succinctly. "You'll have people begging you to come up with a LeClair original."

Hilary made no comment. Roy's conceit was very hard to take and made her new respect for him fade.

He smiled at her ingratiatingly. "Time for a drink!" he decided brightly.

"Roy, I told you I had an engagement," Hilary retorted sharply. "I'm already late."

He nodded. "Business before pleasure," he agreed, infuriatingly. "All right, I'm off to Boston. As I said, I'll be away at least a week. I'll check in as soon as I get back, Hil. Maybe we can have dinner then."

"Maybe," she mumbled, simply to end the conversation.

The moment the door closed behind Roy, Hilary raced to the phone and dialed Jay's number.

He answered on the first ring and told her, "I moved our dinner reservations up to nine—that's as late as they'll take us. Will you be ready if I come by in twenty minutes?"

Jay's voice was cool, and Hilary knew she would have some heavy explaining to do. "Yes," she answered.

When the doorbell rang, she was ready. She quickly activated the security system she'd recently had installed in the shop, then followed Jay down the front steps.

He helped her into his car and closed the door after her. He was still tight-lipped as he took his place behind the wheel. But Jay being Jay, they hadn't gotten very far out of town before he burst forth with a heated, "Well! Exactly what is this all about?"

Hilary sighed. "Before I begin my explanation," she asked him, "are you going to listen to me?"

He shot a bristling glance at her. "Don't I usually?"

"I don't know. For a banker, you sometimes leap to conclusions."

"I wish to God you'd stop typecasting me," Jay stated bitterly. "Actually, for a banker, I should be more astute. Then maybe my competition wouldn't get the chance to steal business away from me."

Hilary froze, then stared at him, appalled. She'd been thinking that she'd only tell Jay about Roy and his paintings tonight. But now...

"Okay, Miss Forsythe," Jay said, his tone clipped. "Shall we work up an agenda? I've got pretty good at doing this lately, so let's decide how we'll arrange our priorities, shall we? Should we discuss Roy first? Or your bank loan? Which do *you* think should rate number one?"

Hilary sank back and wished she could melt into the upholstery. Jay was very angry. And he had every right to be.

She said meekly, "I'll accept your priorities."

"Fine. Then since it's the matter of lesser importance, suppose we deal with your bank loan first. Why, Hilary?"

"Because I needed some quick money," she confessed.

"And you couldn't come to me?"

"You'd already turned me down, Jay."

"I did not turn you down!" he corrected her angrily. "When you came in to see me you wanted to *discuss* taking out a loan. I did what I would have done with anyone. I listened to what you had to say; I went over your premises with you. At that time my feeling was that I didn't want you to stick your neck out. Maybe I was overly solicitous about your lovely neck, Hilary, because you certainly had no problem getting a whopping line of credit with a rival bank. They called me for a credit check, you know. Or perhaps you don't remember filling out that part of the application?"

"I remember."

"Well, you might consider how this makes me look in the eyes of my superiors, when Commonwealth has been doing business with the Forsythes for longer than either you or I has been around."

"I never thought about that," Hilary confessed, her spirits sinking still further.

"I think you never think about a lot of things," Jay accused. "But then you weren't born with a silver spoon in your mouth. Yours was platinum! I should have realized how impossible it would be for you to run up business debts that couldn't be handled by your uncle's estate. More the fool, I!" Jay concluded, expressing a cynicism Hilary had no idea he was capable of.

Somewhere along the line, she'd lost her voice. She groped around, found it, and quavered, "I wish you wouldn't put it that way. You should know I would never do anything to hurt you," she reminded him, her voice getting stronger. "Certainly not anything deliberate. An emergency came up at the cottage...but maybe you already know about that, too."

"As a matter of fact, I do," Jay informed her shortly. "Trevor Andrews called me about something else, but your name came up. If I hadn't been late for a meeting, I would have phoned you. Were you really that afraid of approaching me for a loan?"

"I—I'm sorry, Jay," Hilary murmured abjectly.

"So, you're sorry. You didn't have enough confidence in me to tell me of your needs."

She sat up straighter. "It had absolutely nothing to do with confidence," she denied.

"No?"

"No!"

"Then just what did it have to do with?"

Hilary wished his voice would mellow. She wished he'd call her *cara*. She loved it when he used that soft Portuguese term of endearment. She loved him, dammit, and he loved her. He'd told her so.

Had she ever spoken those exact words to him? She racked her brain, recalling times and places. Briefly, she wished she could borrow Jay's memory. To leave no doubt, she whispered huskily, "I love you."

The car swerved. Jay corrected quickly and pulled over to the side of the road. Glaring at her, he demanded, "Is my hearing going bad?"

"Don't look at me like that!" Hilary protested, stung.

"How the hell do you expect me to look at you?"

"Like you believe me. I mean, I just told you..."

"I heard what you just told me," he interrupted. "Your timing is terrific."

"I just thought...maybe you didn't know," she fumbled.

Jay looked totally dumbfounded. After a moment, he observed thoughtfully, "Well, maybe you're right. Maybe I didn't know."

She fought back tears. "Oh my God, Jay, I love you so much!" she moaned.

"Then why have you let Roy into your life again?"

It was as if he'd thrown cold water in her face. "I haven't let Roy into my life!" she insisted. "Roy walked into my shop a couple of days ago, unannounced. That's a lot different from letting him into my life."

"How did he find you?"

"It wasn't a question of his finding me. I asked him about that. He assumed I'd come back to Devon. I don't think he'd had any intention of contacting me, though, until a friend of his—a Provincetown artist—read in a local paper about my opening the gallery. He mentioned it to Roy because he knew Roy knew me. Roy took it from there."

"Okay," Jay said tightly. "Okay, so he stopped by to say hello. Why was he coming back today?"

"To bring more paintings. I told you that."

"Not precisely," Jay retorted. "Anyway, what do Roy's paintings have to do with you?"

"I've put a few out for sale...."

"You're selling Roy's art?" Storm clouds gathered again on Jay's face. "I can't believe this!" he commented to the air at large.

"Jay, wait till you see them," Hilary implored.

"I don't want to see them. I don't care if he's Picasso and Titian and Rembrandt rolled into one. I have absolutely no interest in his damned paintings!"

"Jay, don't be so limited!" Hilary wanted to beat her fists against his chest, but she knew it would be a losing battle. "Look, the thing is . . . they're seascapes. And they're very good. They're also exactly what I need to give the shop that extra touch of . . ."

"Of what?" he asked suspiciously.

"I hate the expression," Hilary admitted, "but the paintings do give the gallery that extra touch of class."

"You have all the class you'll ever need," Jay replied flatly. "Any place you're involved with is bound to have automatic class. So why do you need something extra?"

"Jay, you're not being reasonable."

"No, I'm not. Would you be, *cara*, if you were in my shoes?"

Hilary began to relax. Jay's voice was mellowing despite himself, and he'd just said the magic word. But her relaxation was short-lived when he asked, curiously, "Why did you feel impelled to tell me you love me? You're not trying to convince yourself by any chance, are you?"

"What?"

"Don't sound so surprised. I *know* you love me, Hilary. But the more I think of it, I'm not sure you know it. Perhaps seeing Roy again has opened up a window that you don't really want to close."

"I resent that, Jay. It's not true, and you know it."

He surveyed her for a long moment, and then he smiled. His smiles always affected her, and there was a special tug to this one. "It's lucky I know you so well," he told her. "Otherwise, watching you right now, I'd say you couldn't care less. But you do care, don't you? So pretend I'm drowning and toss me a rope, will you? Tell me you care!"

There was devilry in his eyes and Hilary, besotted with his charisma, couldn't help but laugh. Wickedly, she teased, "You know... I think I'll keep you guessing."

Hilary was unable to keep Jay guessing very long, not that she really wanted to. As the evening passed, she gave away her feelings with every word she spoke, every gesture she made, every nuance of expression that crossed her lovely face.

As they left the Gonsalveses' house, Jay chuckled and said, "I'm sure Maria is already hearing wedding bells."

Strange things happened to Hilary, hearing that. She imagined that an X ray taken of her right then would show everything within her turned upside down. She had a sudden vision of herself garbed in white, walking down a long aisle, at the end of which Jay waited for her. She smelled orange blossoms in the salty Cape Cod air. She felt giddy, girlish and on the verge of a spell of teenage giggles.

If Jay had asked her to marry him at that moment, she would have scattered affirmatives in his path like confetti. But he said nothing more.

They had a delightful dinner at the Moors, and the moon was high in the night sky when they finally started back to Devon. By unspoken consent, they'd avoided talking about business or about Roy. And, by the time Jay pulled up in front of her house, Hilary had become lulled into a lovely sense of tranquility.

Switching off the motor, he turned to her and asked, "Hilary, where do we go from here?"

The moon was hiding behind a cloud, so there was no silvery light by which she could scan his face. But the cool tone of his voice alerted her that they'd not finished with their problems. Not by any means!

When she failed to frame an immediate reply, Jay added, "Obviously, we can't leave things the way they are. I mean, this has been a great evening. At least it became one, once it got going. But midnight's about to toll, and I don't want Prince Charming to turn back into a pumpkin."

The analogy might have been amusing at another time, but it wasn't funny now. Hilary said slowly, "As far as I'm concerned, Jay, nothing has changed—between you and me, that is. As for my getting the bank loan...I can only say I'm very sorry. I can't undo it."

"Agreed," he stated tersely.

"As for Roy, it happened just as I told you. Why don't you come in and look at his paintings? Then maybe you'll understand why I was motivated to do business with him."

"I told you, I don't want to look at his paintings," Jay responded roughly. "Nor do I want you doing business with him. Maybe that sounds primitive of me, but I find it impossible to accept the idea of your ex-lover getting into any sort of partnership with you.''

"It isn't a partnership, Jay," Hilary pointed out. "All I've done is taken a few of his paintings on consignment. Believe me, he'd have had no problem placing them elsewhere if I'd turned him down. They're that good."

"Then let him place them elsewhere," Jay advised.

Hilary considered this, then shook her head and said, "I don't believe you. What are you suggesting I do? Call Roy and tell him to take his paintings out of the shop?"

"Exactly."

"It's not really an issue. Roy went up to Boston this evening and he won't be back for at least a week. And before you pose the question, no, I do not know where to get in touch with him!"

Hilary's exasperation was plain, and surveying her shadow thoughtfully, Jay very nearly backtracked. It was so dark he couldn't see her face, but the agitation in her voice told him he was making her miserable. Right now he couldn't help that. He'd been pretty damned miserable himself all day, and there were still things he needed to tell her he hadn't yet got around to talking about.

The bank was opening a large branch out in western Massachusetts, in Springfield. The bank building itself would center a major new mall-type complex. This was a multimillion-dollar outreach on Commonwealth's part, and the fact that he'd been asked to assume the post of vice-president of operations there was quite a plum.

He smiled wryly as he thought of how he would have jumped at such an opportunity just a bit over four months ago. But then Hilary had walked into his life, and her effect on him had changed everything.

He thought back to her troubled declaration, recalling her words with the accuracy that came to him so easily.

Oh my God, Jay, I love you so much!

Her anguish had been self-evident, and he'd been a stubborn fool. He should have bagged his pride immediately, taken her in his arms and given her the reassurance she'd so plainly needed. Instead of that, he'd behaved like a jealous idiot over the issue of Roy and a couple of paintings.

It had been a double dose, though, hearing that Hilary had gone to another bank, then learning that Roy had crept back into her life. Nevertheless, that was no excuse for his having handled his reactions so badly.

He said, unhappily, "I'm going to be in Boston for a few days myself, *cara*."

"Now?" she pleaded.

"Tomorrow, yes."

Suddenly it didn't matter whether he could see her expression or not. He could read her heart, and that's what counted.

"Dearest," he murmured huskily, reaching over to touch her arm. "Let's forget everything except ourselves for tonight, okay? Let me stay with you."

There was nothing Hilary wanted more. She'd never needed Jay so much. Then she thought of her room and flinched.

"What is it?" he asked swiftly.

"I'm such a messy housekeeper!" Hilary wailed.

Jay burst out laughing. It was genuine laughter, and it swept away all the small strands of discord that had been weaving a web between them. He said, loving Hilary as he'd never loved anyone else, "Sweetheart, I really don't give a damn!"

Hilary awakened early the next morning and remembered, of all things, that she'd left Roy's latest pictures propped up against a wall downstairs.

A glance at the clock on her bedside table showed it was only six. She'd become accustomed to waking up early because there was always so much to do before she opened the shop for the day. Also, Betty was usually on the scene quite early to supervise activities in the tearoom.

At Hilary's side, Jay stirred. She heard him mumble something, but his eyes were closed as she gazed at him lovingly. Dark lashes fanned his cheeks, and she leaned over to gently kiss him. Then she pulled back slightly and found herself staring into the midnight depths from which Jay saw his world.

"So," he observed softly, "that wasn't a dream."

"No," she smiled, "it wasn't."

"It isn't every day a man's awakened by an ice maiden whose kisses are filled with fire," Jay murmured. He sat up, stretched, then instinctively glanced at the clock. "For once," he observed contentedly, "we have a little spare time."

"And what do you want to do with that spare time, milord?" Hilary purred.

"Need you ask," Jay answered.

He pulled her into his embrace and snuggled back under the covers with her. Then, though the interval wasn't nearly long enough, they were again transported through an entirely wonderful realm of lovemaking. . . .

Later, trying to get her feet back on earth's ground again, Hilary plugged in an electric hot pot she'd bought and made two cups of instant coffee.

Jay wrinkled his nose over the brew. "With a whole damned restaurant downstairs?" he complained.

"Hang around for another couple of hours, and I'm sure Betty will see that you get a gourmet breakfast," Hilary teased.

"I'd better be long gone before Betty gets here, or there are apt to be some raised eyebrows," Jay muttered.

"I doubt that."

Jay ran a hand over his cheeks. "I do need to get going, Hilary," he told her reluctantly. "I'll have to stop at my place to shave, change and toss a few things into a suitcase."

"You really are going to Boston today?"

"Did you doubt it?"

"No. I just hoped it wasn't definite, that's all."

"I'm afraid it is. And I'm afraid some even more definite decisions may come out of it," Jay admitted.

"Such as?"

"Oh, hell," he said. "This is crazy. It should be an occasion for rejoicing, and it's anything but. It's pretty certain I'm going to be offered a promotion. We're opening a branch bank—a western headquarters, really—out in Springfield...."

"Springfield!" Hilary blurted. He might as well have said he was being exiled to the moon.

"It's not the end of the earth," Jay put in hastily. "Only a three- or four-hour ride from the Cape..."

"It must be quite a step up," she managed weakly, wishing she could smile but feeling that she wanted to cry.

"It is," Jay admitted. "Not that managing the branch here in Devon is insignificant," he added quickly. "Look, let's wait till the powers that be have muddled around a bit more before we get uptight, okay?"

That, for Hilary, was impossible. She slipped on a lounging robe and followed Jay downstairs, having the crazy feeling that every step was taking him farther away from her. They were passing the front parlor when she stopped abruptly and said, "Jay, I'd like to ask you a favor."

"Yes, *cara*?"

"I'd like you to look at the paintings. Forget Roy painted them and just give me your opinion. I've never liked any of Roy's work until now, and that keeps nagging me. I suppose I'm afraid I'm making a mistake, so I'd really like to know what you think."

"Well...since you put it that way," Jay conceded, and grudgingly followed her into the shop.

First, she showed him the four paintings already on display. Then she turned to the more recent acquisitions, saying as she unveiled them, "Excuse me just for a minute, will you? I really should throw something on..."

She stopped short, suddenly aware of Jay's peculiar silence, and saw him staring at the painting of the beached boat, a strange expression on his face.

"What is it?" she asked quickly.

"I don't know," he said. "At least...I don't think I know."

"What do you mean?"

"I'm not sure, but..." He glanced at his wristwatch, then said impatiently, "Hell, I wish I had more time. I need to think about this."

"Think about what, Jay?"

"Let me look at the first ones again," he said.

"Be my guest."

He nodded silently. Then, like a customer about to make a serious purchase, he moved from the paintings hanging on display to the three propped up inside the door, studying each one meticulously.

Hilary stood back, watched him and suddenly began to feel troubled. Very troubled.

"What's wrong, Jay?" she implored. She couldn't help but think that if he wanted to get back at her for doing business with Roy, he was succeeding.

But Jay silenced her with a curt, "Wait a minute."

He finished his perusal of the collection in general, then returned his attention to the painting of the boat on the beach. "It's been a long time," he said then, stepping back and shaking his head.

"What's been a long time?" Hilary demanded, feeling totally exasperated.

"It's been a long time since I saw these...or some of them, anyway."

She stared at him. "What are you saying?"

"Your friend Roy didn't paint these pictures, Hilary," Jay informed her. "Not the originals, anyway."

"How can you say that?" Agitated, Hilary rushed to the nearest painting and pointed to the signature. "Look, right here. It's signed Roy LeClair."

"Yes, it is," Jay agreed evenly. "But that doesn't prove a damned thing."

"Are you saying Roy stole these paintings?"

He shook his head. "No."

"Jay, if you're joking with me, it's not very funny."

"I'm not joking, Hilary," he said. "I love you too much for that. It's just...I've seen these paintings before, a long time ago."

"Why don't you tap into that weird memory of yours?" Hilary challenged.

"Weird, eh? Look, Hilary, I'm deadly serious. I've seen these before. I just can't remember where."

"And when you do remember, Jay? What then?" she demanded, feeling her sanity unravel.

"Then the mystery will be solved," he answered calmly.

Hilary picked up the dock scene and anxiously studied it. "This is...impossible," she choked. "Do you know what you're saying? You're accusing Roy of being a fraud. Some kind of an art pirate."

"Right now, I don't know what I'm accusing Roy of," Jay interposed. "All I can tell you is that I'd bet everything I have in the world that he didn't do the originals."

"In other words, you're saying these are copies?"

"Forgeries, copies, I'm not sure what the hell they are," Jay admitted. "If they are the originals, then somehow he's blotted out the name of the real artist and substituted his name. Maybe these canvases were never signed in the first place. If I could only..."

"Search your memory?"

"Since you put it that way, yes."

Hilary closed her eyes and shook her head. "I could be perpetrating a fraud," she murmured, half to herself.

"We don't know that yet," Jay said firmly.

"Still, what should I do? Hide these until you've tested your blasted memory? There's a very good chance a couple's coming in today to buy two of them."

Jay surveyed her coolly. To her dismay, he said, "That decision, Hilary, is completely up to you."

Chapter Fourteen

Jay walked into Treasures & Tea at eleven-thirty in the morning, two days after he'd planted doubts in Hilary's mind about the authenticity of Roy's paintings.

She was showing a customer a lifelike wood carving of a sandpiper done by a local craftsman. Jay virtually elbowed his way between them, murmured "Excuse me" to the customer, then said to Hilary, "Let's get out of here!"

He was tight-lipped and unsmiling, and his tension caused her already stretched nerves to shriek silently. A thousand questions raced through her mind, but she staved them off. "Sorry," she said icily, "but I'm busy."

"This is slightly more important, Miss Forsythe," Jay muttered between clenched teeth.

The customer—an affable, middle-aged tourist—looked amused. "It's all right," he assured Hilary. "I'm going to buy this anyway, so I'm sure the young lady over at the cash register can help me."

Thelma was at the sales counter, while Amy and Olivia worked the floor. At the moment, all three were occupied with other customers, this being one of the busiest mornings the shop had had thus far.

Thinking this, Hilary murmured resentfully, "Your timing's just perfect, Jay."

"Too bad," he said, making no effort to sound apologetic. He glanced around the room. "What have you done with those paintings?" he demanded. Before Hilary could answer, he spotted Roy's seascapes and snapped, "So, you didn't take them down."

"No, I didn't!" she snapped back. "I put Sold signs on them, instead. That way, anyone who's interested can make inquiries."

"Very clever of you," Jay commented dryly.

"Thank you."

His dark eyes swept her face and softened as they usually did when he looked at her for more than a second. "Look," he said. "I'm sorry about barging in here like this. I can see you're swamped, but please...let the others handle the shop for a while, will you? We need to talk."

"About the paintings?" Hilary asked fearfully.

"Yes, about the paintings."

"Can't we just go out on the veranda and have a cup of coffee?"

He shook his head. "We need to get away from here, Hilary. You're not going to like what I have to tell you."

She'd already guessed that. She'd discovered that she and Jay had their own kind of private telegraph system, and right now it was working at full voltage. Despite her resentment at the way he'd intruded so high-handedly upon her sale, she'd known from the instant she'd set eyes on him that something was very wrong.

As they got into his car, Jay said, "I wish there was a deserted beach we could walk on, but that's impossible around here, this time of year. All the bars and restaurants are crowded, too. So, I think we'd better hole up in my condo."

"Why do we have to go anywhere?" Hilary asked. "Why can't you tell me whatever it is you want to tell me while we're driving around?"

"Because I'd like to loosen my tie and have a drink first."

"Jay, it's not even noon."

"Well, I'm sorry if I can't pace my feelings to a clock dial," he stated testily. "And I can't see what people think they're proving when they do!"

"All right!" Hilary muttered. "You've made your point."

Jay held to his word. He refused to discuss anything until he had not only loosened his tie, but had also taken it off and flung it across his refectory table. It slid off the edge and onto the floor, but he didn't bother to pick it up, to underline the fact that he was deeply upset.

Next, with a leisurely calm that nearly drove Hilary crazy, he mixed two tall vodka and tonics. She accepted her drink without so much as a murmur and waited for him to speak.

The day had started out sunny. Now, though, huge dark clouds were taking over, filling the sky all the way to the horizon. Rather a symbolic coincidence, Hilary thought unhappily as she looked out through the glass doors at the bay. The water had taken on an ominous gray sheen.

Following her gaze, Jay observed, "We're going to have a storm."

As if Madame Zola herself had predicted this, jagged lightning suddenly streaked across the sky, followed by the menacing growl of thunder.

"Just as well we couldn't find a deserted beach," Jay decided.

Hilary nodded. When Jay remained silent, she asked, "How did you get down here today?"

He glanced up in mild surprise. "I drove."

"That's not what I meant, Jay. You told me you were going to be tied up in Boston for most of the week."

"That *was* the original plan," he agreed, "until Phil called me last night."

"Phil Gonsalves?"

"Yes."

Hilary was instantly alert. "Nothing's wrong with Phil or Maria, is there?" she asked anxiously.

Jay shook his head. "No, they're both fine. I'd asked Phil to check out something for me, that's all."

He set aside his drink and stared moodily at the old Portuguese map of the world on the wall behind Hilary's head. "After I heard what Phil had to say," he confessed, "I knew there was no way I could get through any bank meetings today. So, I told Mr. Doane—he's the president—that there was a family emergency I had to attend to here on the Cape, and that I'd have to take the day off."

"He agreed?"

Jay smiled a brief and utterly mirthless smile. "What was he supposed to say?" he asked rhetorically. "Anyway, I had to see you. I couldn't let you risk keeping those paintings in your shop under the circumstances."

"Just what are you saying, Jay?"

He sighed heavily, then admitted, his voice as heavy as the sigh, "I don't know how to handle this, Hilary. I wish there was some tactful way of putting it to you, but I can't think of one. And that puts me at a hell of a disadvantage."

"Tactful way of putting what?" she asked, totally baffled.

"Well...I'm sorry to be the person to expose your friend Roy for what he really is," Jay said unhappily. "A couple of days ago, if someone had given me this chance, I might have grabbed it. What I didn't realize is that it puts me in quite an unenviable position. I mean, he was your lover, dammit!"

"Oh, come on, Jay," Hilary sputtered indignantly. "Roy and I have been history for a long time, and you know it."

"I hope so," Jay said dully. "I'd hate to think you still harbor any feelings for the guy."

She bristled. "Will you make your point, please?"

"He's a fraud, Hilary, just as I thought he was."

"Are you saying Roy stole those paintings?"

Jay shook his head. "I said fraud, not thief...though the line between what he's done and thievery is a pretty thin one." He picked up his drink again, but without pausing to sip it, continued, "While I was driving up to Boston, I had some time to think. This goes back a long way, Hilary. Way back to when I was a kid in Provincetown."

"What does?"

Jay ignored her question, took a generous sip of his drink and said, "One day, my Uncle Manny took me to see a friend of his, a guy who lived alone in a shack out on the dunes near Race Point."

"Your Uncle Manny?"

"Manny Medeiros," Jay explained patiently. "Maria's first husband, my mother's brother, one of the men who went down with the *Amalia*..." He paused for a moment, then went on, "Manny had a heart somewhat bigger than the great outdoors. This friend of his, the man we went to see that day, his name was Ernie Arruda. He was sort of a godfather to me, a great guy. He'd never married, so I guess I was kind of like the kid he never had. I used to love to go visit him because he'd take the time to tell me all sorts of stories—sea stories, mostly—and he always had some little treasure to give me."

Jay reached in his pocket and produced a small silken pouch. "I got this out to give you an idea," he said, as he withdrew a delicate, gold-filigreed medallion that dangled from the end of a gossamer-thin gold chain.

Hilary took the medallion and studied it closely. In the center there was a golden circle on which was etched a ship that might have been a Spanish galleon. In this case, though, Hilary knew it must be Portuguese.

"Ernie got that on a trip back to the Azores," Jay reported. "He came from the island of Saint Michael but told me he traced the medallion's origin to Lisbon. As you can see, it's quite intricate and very old. He bought it for his fiancée, but he never gave it to her."

"Why not?" Hilary asked.

"Because he came back from a fishing trip out to George's Bank one day, and she'd run off with a truck driver, a guy who carted the fish down to the market in New York City. Evidently, this guy filled up his truck and persuaded Ernie's fiancée to go with him."

"Oh."

"Anyway, she never came back, and Ernie never had eyes for anyone else," Jay said. "You know, that would have wiped out a lot of us mortal men but not Ernie. He wasn't bitter about women; he wasn't bitter about anyone. He was just a great, generous, loving kind of guy... and he had a very rare talent."

Something about the way Jay said this made Hilary sit up straighter. "Painting?" she ventured softly.

"Painting," Jay said simply. "He'd never had any formal art training, but what happened to him was something like what happened to Phil. There was an accident aboard a trawler, and Ernie was severely injured. His leg was crushed, and he was badly crippled. He had to use a crutch to get around, but somehow he managed, living out on the dunes by himself. In much later years, he couldn't handle it any longer, and a niece of his, Rose Cordeiro, persuaded him to take an apartment in a house she and her husband Nick had off Bradford Street, not far from the center of Provincetown. It was more of a studio than an apartment, actually. But big enough for Ernie to set up his easel. He painted as if God were guiding his hand and gave it up only when his eyesight began to fail.

"The most beautiful seascapes I've ever seen," Jay finished solemnly.

Hilary was shocked. "Did Roy somehow steal Ernie Arruda's paintings?" she asked, after a tense moment.

"I think he copied them," Jay confessed. "Granted, that in itself requires considerable talent. I take it Roy does have a fair amount of talent of his own?"

"Yes, I suppose he does. Still, I can't understand any of this. How would Roy have come upon Ernie Arruda's paintings? How could he have got possession of them long enough to copy them? How—"

"Hold it," Jay cautioned. "I can't answer everything at once. I don't even know all the answers, yet. But I will," he promised grimly. He looked at his nearly full drink and set it aside again. "I told Phil we'd get out to his place by the middle of the afternoon," he said.

"I can't..." Hilary began, and then amended that to, "Why?"

"Why? Because Phil checked this out for me, Hilary. I thought you understood that," Jay pointed out, the threads of his patience unwinding. "I told you he phoned me in Boston last night."

"Yes, but I still don't know what he told you."

"The year-rounders in Provincetown, especially the people who've lived out there a long time, are pretty close-knit," Jay said. "They all know each other. Ernie Arruda died about ten years ago, but his niece and her husband still live in the same house. They have an attic full of Ernie's paintings, all stashed away. They never gave them much thought until recently, when there was an illness in the family and a lot of bills to pay. Rose got the idea she might raise a little money by selling off some of Ernie's paintings. She didn't expect they were worth much—you know how families often underplay the efforts of their own relatives—but she thought maybe they'd bring in a few dollars.

"Anyway, Nick Cordeiro is part owner of a little restaurant on Commercial Street. He knew a local artist who comes into his place frequently and told Rose he'd bring up the matter of the paintings next time he saw him. The artist in question is Garry Hinfield, who happens to be Roy's friend."

Jay paused. "Does this begin to make sense to you?"

"It's beginning to," Hilary admitted.

"Well, what happened was that Nick took Hinfield over to his house, took him up to the attic and showed him the paintings. Evidently, it was all Hinfield could do to keep a poker face. Nick told Phil, when they spoke about this yesterday, that Hinfield seemed kind of excited, but he didn't say much.

"A few days later, Hinfield appeared at Nick's house with Roy LeClair in tow. He said Roy was from New York...."

"New York?"

"That's what he said. He said Roy was from New York," Jay repeated, "and that he knew some people in art circles down there. He said if Roy could take a few photos of the paintings, he'd show them to his friends, and they'd know if they were worth anything."

"Oh, God!" Hilary moaned.

"The picture is beginning to emerge, isn't it?" Jay said, and added, "and that could be a lousy pun, couldn't it? So, they set up several of the paintings in Nick's living room, and Roy took more than a few photos of them. Then he and Hinfield left, telling Nick and Rose they'd get back to them as soon as they had any word. That was three months ago."

"And nothing's been said to Nick and his wife since?"

"Nothing. After a couple of weeks, though, Rose had the feeling that both Hinfield and Roy had been much more interested in Ernie's pictures than they'd let on. She still wanted to help with the medical bills her family owed, so she called a woman who's involved with the Provincetown Art Association and told her about Ernie's paintings.''

"And then what?"

"Well, this woman was nice enough to say she'd come over to the house and take a look at them as soon as she got a chance."

"Did she?"

"Just last week, yes. And she took one look at the paintings—and set some *real* wheels in motion. Now, dear Hilary, Ernesto Juan Arruda is about to come into his own. There will be a one-man show of his work at a leading Provincetown gallery in two weeks. Something tells me that the art critics from Boston and New York will be flocking down to see it. Something tells me that Ernie Arruda's paintings are going to be worth a mint . . ."

"And Roy's . . ."

"Roy's forgeries, or whatever you want to call them? I don't know what to say to that, Hilary. I think the first step is to fill in the gaps. That's what I'm hoping we can do out in Provincetown this afternoon."

Hilary's mind was spinning like a giant top. The mental gyrations were making her dizzy. She looked so distraught that Jay said compassionately, "I'm really sorry, *cara*."

He was. Naturally, jealousy *had* surged when he'd learned Roy had reappeared in Hilary's life. But he'd had the sense to thrust aside any doubts. He was as sure of Hilary's love as he was of the sun coming up tomorrow.

At first Jay had cursed his memory, as he had so many times before. Yet now, he knew he should be thankful for this gift. If he'd not remembered seeing those paintings long ago, Hilary would have sold them as originals. They were too good to remain unsold for very long, Jay realized, and shuddered to think of what that might have led to. Hilary, of course, would not have been to blame. But once the Arruda one-man show opened in Provincetown, someone would sooner or later make the connection between the originals and the replicas Hilary was selling. Even though she could be proved totally blameless, that kind of publicity heaped on her shop would do her harm. It could hardly be otherwise.

Jay asked gently, "*Cara*, where's Roy right now? Do you know?"

"Somewhere in Boston," she replied dully. "He said he'd be there a week, at least."

"I suppose that gives us a few days grace," Jay mused.

"What do you mean?"

"We're going to have to face him with this," Jay said, "and I'd like to have a few more facts under my belt before I lay this out to him."

Hilary shook her head sadly and said, "You're not going to be the one to lay it out to him, Jay."

"I think I should be."

"I disagree. I got you into this, so it's up to me to blow the whistle."

"Whatever," he said. He stood, his restlessness taking over, and added, "First let's drive down to Provincetown. We can stop somewhere along the way for a bite of lunch...."

"There's no way I could eat anything," Hilary stated flatly.

Jay proved her wrong. He pulled off the highway in Wellfleet and took her to a little place in the town center where the clam chowder was pure ambrosia. As Hilary stared at the steaming bowl placed in front of her, Jay said sternly, "You need some nourishment."

Not usually the obedient type, Hilary nevertheless complied, knowing Jay had her best interests at heart.

In Provincetown, Phil must have been at the window watching for them because he opened the front door before they had time to knock.

"Come in, come in," he invited heartily. He clasped Hilary with his one sound arm and kissed her firmly on the cheek. She smiled up at him, feeling a surge of genuine affection. This emotion was duplicated when, a moment later, Maria embraced her.

"I asked Nick and Rose to come over," Phil said, "but they thought maybe it would be better if we went over to their place so you can see the paintings for yourself, Hilary. They haven't been moved to the gallery for the show yet, so it's a good chance to have a close look."

Hilary stumbled on a question she hated to ask. "Do Nick and Rose know about Roy LeClair's paintings?" she queried.

Phil shook his head. "Jay said we'd get to that later. All I said was . . . you have a shop, and you're interested in acquiring some oil paintings."

"We're going to have to tell them the whole story," she said slowly.

"Let's take it a step at a time," Jay put in.

"I don't know." Hilary's eyes were troubled, and it was Phil to whom she spoke. "I don't want to deceive these people," she said firmly.

Phil smiled. "I never thought you did," he assured her. "Maria and I . . . we're both pretty good judges of character at this stage of our lives, Hilary. You know, you're the first girl Jay ever brought here. We like to think Jay considers our place his home—one of his homes, anyway. So when he came here with you, we took a very good look. Eh, Maria?"

"Indeed we did," Maria agreed, laughing.

Hilary stole a quick glance at Jay, and saw he was actually flushing! For once, Jay had been put on a definite spot, and she had to smile. In many ways he had it coming!

"So we liked what we saw," Phil told her, his grin widening. "Hey, Maria, how 'bout putting on some coffee?"

Maria nodded and headed for the kitchen, her smile as wide as her husband's.

Temporarily, Hilary forgot about all the problems involving Roy and the paintings and let herself bask in the warm glow that Phil and Maria's approval was giving her. She wanted to be close to these people. She wanted to hear all the things they could tell her about Jay as a little boy and as a young man.

One day, she wanted to have a baby who looked just like Jay....

As she thought this, Hilary looked up directly into Jay's midnight eyes. Now it was her turn to flush. Then he grinned, a slow, lazy grin that was completely captivating. And she knew he'd somehow read her mind.

With the coffee, Maria brought out a tray of Portuguese pastries called *trutas*, tarts filled with a spicy pumpkin-based mixture. Then, because Nick and Rose Cordeiro lived a fair distance away, they piled into Jay's car and drove down Provincetown's Commercial Street, which was choked with both cars and pedestrians.

It was a colorful, zany scene. In earlier years, Hilary had occasionally visited P-town with her Uncle Chad, but seeing the town with Jay at her side was an entirely different experience. She wished they had nothing more serious to deal with than playing tourist. She dreaded meeting the Cordeiros because she knew that sooner or later she was going to have to tell them about Roy's copies.

Rose and Nick Cordeiro, though, proved to be as easygoing and friendly as Phil and Maria. They welcomed Hilary into their home and insisted that everyone have a glass of Madeira before going up to look at the paintings.

By the time they mounted the stairs to the attic, some of Hilary's qualms had dissipated. Even if they hadn't, she unquestionably would have forgotten them once she saw the late Ernie Arruda's paintings.

She'd been amazed at what she'd thought was Roy's work. But his copies faded totally in the light of these originals. She wasn't negating that what Roy had given her was very good. But Ernie Arruda had been a man possessed of a rare talent, and he'd captured his native Provincetown and the surrounding sand and sea as few others had.

As she gazed at one painting after the next, Hilary wondered why Nick and Rose hadn't realized what a treasure they were hoarding in their attic. Perhaps it was what Jay had suggested about family downplaying family, or the fact that objects often become invisible after being right under a person's nose for very long.

How seldom we fully appreciate the things most dear and familiar to us, Hilary thought.

She heard Jay ask, "How many paintings do you have here, Nick?"

"Thirty-three," Nick answered.

"They represent a lot of years in Ernie's life," Rose added. "He was dabbling around with paints when I was just a kid. He was still fishing for a living then, and he never had much to work with. But people knew he liked to paint, so after the accident, when he was still in the hospital, a bunch of his friends got together and bought him a big case full of paints, an easel and a lot of brushes. Guess they considered it would be therapy for Ernie."

"Yeah," Nick agreed ruefully. "I guess that's what we thought, too. Sure, we all thought he did nice pictures but nothing great. Funny thing is," he admitted, "now that other people are interested in them, they keep looking better and better to Rose and me.''

Hilary smiled at this confession. What Nick was saying was true of just about everything . . . and everybody.

Throughout the afternoon, she kept waiting for Jay to say something about Roy and the copies. When he didn't, she wasn't sure whether to be glad or sorry. It was a temporary respite, and sooner or later the truth would have to come out.

Hilary was very tired—physically, mentally and emotionally—as she and Jay started back to Devon. They drove through a raging thunder and lightning storm and were turning into the entrance to Sand Terraces before she realized what he was doing. Still, she wasn't about to protest.

Once in the apartment, he said firmly, ''You go wash your face, brush your hair and stretch out on the couch. I'm going to fix you a drink. Then I'm going to broil steaks and toss a salad for our dinner. After that, I'm going to tuck you into bed.''

There was a hint of Jay's usual devilry in his dark eyes as he added, ''But tonight, *cara*, I'm not going to bed with you. For once, you need your rest even more than you need me!''

Chapter Fifteen

Roy LeClair called Hilary from Boston a week after her viewing of the Arruda paintings. He sounded like his usual, insouciant self as he told her he was heading back to the Cape that afternoon, and asked if she'd have dinner with him if he stopped off in Devon en route to Provincetown.

His invitation put Hilary in a quandary. The last thing she wanted was to go out to dinner with Roy. She couldn't imagine them in a tête-à-tête situation, especially under the present circumstances. On the other hand, because of those same circumstances, she hated to refuse him.

She pleaded that she was dealing with a special customer and asked Roy to call her back in half an hour. Then she quickly dialed the bank and, when Eleanor Roberts told her Jay was in conference, made it clear that she needed to speak to him as immediately as possible.

Jay called back five minutes later. By then, Hilary had fled upstairs to her bedroom so she would have privacy when she took his call.

"What'll I do?" she moaned, after telling him about Roy's invitation.

"I think you have to go for it," Jay admitted reluctantly.

"Jay...there's just no way I can sit through a whole dinner with Roy."

"I'm very glad to hear that, *cara*. Look..."

"Yes?"

"Well, do you think this is a purely social invitation? Or do you think it's tied in with the paintings?"

"I don't know," Hilary confessed. "I suppose that depends on whether or not Roy's been in touch with Garry Hinfield since he left the Cape. Somehow...well, somehow I doubt he has. He sounded as self-confident as ever. If he's at all itchy about the paintings, I didn't get any vibes over the phone."

"Could you tell him you have a yen for Italian food, say, at the Gondola?" Jay asked.

"I suppose so."

"Try to set it for the early side," Jay advised. "They probably won't get crowded till later in the evening, even this time of year. Tell him you have to get back to the shop to do some accounting...or whatever. Aim for a quarter of six, okay?"

"I'll try," Hilary agreed doubtfully.

"I'll be at the bar when you get there," Jay promised. "I'll stroll over casually to say hello. You can introduce me as your friendly neighborhood banker. I can behave like enough of a clod to ask if the two of you mind if I join you. You'll quickly say 'No, of course not,' and I'll take it from there."

"Are you sure?"

"Yes, I'm sure. Also, ask for a booth, okay? They're big enough to accommodate four people. I'll slide in next to Roy. That should annoy him."

"I take it you want to annoy Roy?"

"I'd love to annoy Roy. But I have an ace up my sleeve, *cara*. Just trust me, okay?"

It wasn't a question of trusting Jay. It was a question of trying to keep her feelings under wraps, Hilary thought miserably, as she worked her way through the rest of the afternoon with frequent, apprehensive glances at the wall clock in the shop.

Roy agreed to the early dinner hour. He estimated his time of arrival at five-thirty. When he walked into Treasures & Tea at five o'clock sharp, Hilary angrily realized she should have known not to take his word.

She also sensed that Roy had decided he'd use this element of surprise to his advantage. He strutted into the shop, bestowing wide smiles on everyone.

Olivia had been about to lock the front door so no more people could get in. There were a few customers still browsing around—invariably, they lingered when the shop was about to close—and Hilary had yet to think of a polite way to oust them.

Thelma and Amy were straightening up the merchandise so that everything would be in order for tomorrow. They bestowed their usual appreciative glances on Roy, and Hilary felt like taking them aside and lecturing them about not judging books by their covers.

Roy was sauntering around the shop as if he owned it, and that further aroused her resentment. She saw him scan the paintings with their Sold signs. Then he came across to her, beaming.

"I told you, Hil," he said triumphantly. "You and I have a good thing going here."

Hilary nearly choked. She yearned to fling the truth right in his handsome face, but logic surfaced, and she managed a weak smile.

"Well," Roy said briskly, "I guess we have a little financial transacting to do, don't we?"

It dawned on Hilary that he was expecting her to dole out seventy percent of the prices she supposedly had sold the paintings for. She nearly choked all over again, but somehow managed to say, rather stiffly, "I'll write you a check, if you like."

"No hurry," Roy assured her breezily. "I'll bring the rest of the paintings down from P-town tomorrow or the next day, and we can settle then."

"The rest of the paintings?" Hilary echoed faintly.

"Right," he said, and frowned slightly. "I gather you have the other three under wraps?"

"Yes."

"And you've sold four, for a total of seven," Roy explained patiently, as if he were teaching a child elementary arithmetic. "I have three more finished canvases out in my studio," he reminded her, "and two others that are almost done."

"Oh."

He smiled complacently. "Believe me, Hil, this'll make me put my nose to the good old grindstone," he assured her. "You're going to find me painting day and night, from here on in."

I'll just bet, Hilary thought grimly.

She realized she was developing a splitting headache, a valid enough headache to call off her dinner engagement with Roy. Even he, she thought, should see that she was suffering. But Jay would be waiting, Jay had something up his sleeve and the inevitable couldn't be put off forever.

"Excuse me for a few minutes, will you, Roy?" she asked hastily. "I'll be right back."

Before he could comment, she fled up the stairs. Once in her room, she closed the door behind her and leaned against it, breathing heavily. She felt trapped and totally on edge. Hilary didn't see how she could last from the shop to the Italian restaurant without saying something to Roy about the paintings.

One thing she'd learned about herself through all of this—duplicity was totally foreign to her nature. She hated it!

She changed from the slacks and blouse she'd been wearing into a sheer summer dress, did her hair up in a quick version of a twist, added some fun white jewelry and swallowed two aspirin. But she felt as harried as ever as she went back downstairs. And her head was still throbbing.

She soon discovered that she didn't have to worry about what she might say to Roy because Roy was perfectly content to do all the talking.

"I have to tell you, Hil," he announced seriously, following her directions to the Gondola, "I'm not sure I can continue to give you an exclusive on my paintings."

"Oh?" Hilary queried.

"I took the photos to Boston with me and showed them around at a few places," Roy told her. "Everyone up there wants to see the real thing."

Dog! Hilary hissed the word silently, then made silent apologies to all the dogs in the world.

"Why don't we say I'll stick with your shop through the first twenty sales," Roy suggested amiably. "After that, you and I can reassess the situation, okay?"

She mumbled a reply.

He went on about a "humdinger" of a scene he'd started painting before he left for Boston and couldn't wait to get back to. He glowingly described a vista of the Outer Cape's rolling moors with a lighthouse in the distance. Hilary recognized the picture immediately. She'd seen the original in Rose and Nick's attic.

If she'd needed anything to convince her of Roy's chicanery, that was it. She shot him a glance of pure disgust. Fortunately, his eyes were on the road, and his mind was on himself.

As luck would have it, the booths at the Gondola were already full. When the hostess mentioned, though, that one couple looked as if they were about to leave, Hilary quickly told her they'd wait.

"Wouldn't a table do just as well?" Roy asked, looking around the restaurant. There were plenty of empty tables.

"I'd really rather have a booth," Hilary said.

He looked pleased. "Well," he admitted, "they are more intimate."

She shuddered, wishing she could fast-forward the sixty minutes in the next hour.

The wait for the booth was longer than the hostess had predicted. Roy, growing impatient, made it plain that he was willing to settle for a table, intimacy or no intimacy. Hilary murmured that the man in the booth they were waiting for had just taken out his wallet and was paying his bill. A few minutes later the couple left.

Hilary's knees were trembling as she slid into her seat. The waitress asked if they wanted anything from the bar. Roy promptly ordered a Scotch sour, and Hilary asked for a soda water. She didn't want to touch even a drop of alcohol until this present ordeal was over.

It seemed forever until she heard a familiar voice drawl, "Well, hello there."

She looked up into Jay Mahoney's dark eyes, and her heart flipped over. She wanted to fling herself into Jay's arms and beg him to take her away from all this. She was amazed that she controlled her voice, managing to sound suitably surprised when she said, "Why, Jay!"

Roy looked up, then turned his attention back to his menu, evidently not expecting anything further from this encounter.

Hilary said sweetly, "Roy, I'd like you to meet Jay Mahoney. Jay's the manager of our local bank."

"One of our local banks," Jay corrected pointedly, reminding Hilary that the Hyannis bank where she'd established her line of credit also had a Devon branch.

She gritted her teeth and said, "Jay, this is my friend Roy LeClair from Boston."

"Glad to meet you," Jay said politely, then added, "I'd just stopped by for a drink at the bar, but now that I've found friends, I wonder if I may join you?"

"Of course," Hilary said, before Roy could say anything.

Roy's lips tightened, and his smile was so phony Hilary nearly laughed. "Of course," he agreed.

Roy moved over, and Jay smoothly slid in beside him. There was plenty of room for two people, but Roy scrunched up against the wall as if he were being crowded.

The waitress appeared, and Jay ordered a martini. "That's what I started out with," he admitted cheerfully. "It's wise to stick with the same poison, don't you think?"

He made the cliché sound even worse than it was, and Hilary winced. She reminded herself that Jay had a fair share of acting ability. He'd certainly been acting when she'd encountered Madame Zola in the fortune-teller's tent, so she warned herself not to be surprised by anything he might come up with now.

They sipped their drinks and ordered a second round. This time, Hilary relented and agreed to have a glass of Chablis. It was amazing how much more *secure* she felt with Jay close at hand.

After they'd savored some buttery garlic bread, the waitress took their dinner orders and gathered up the menus.

Then, without warning, Jay pulled a folded brochure out of his pocket and handed it across to Hilary.

"Thought you might want to see this," he observed casually. "There's a rather interesting exhibition coming up in Provincetown. A one-man show of the works of an old Portuguese fisherman named Ernesto Arruda. He did some fantastic seascapes...see, there are a couple of photos in the brochure. Anyway, he died ten years ago, as an unknown talent. But my bet is that his stuff will be discovered fast, once the exhibit opens. I was thinking maybe you might want to acquire some of his paintings for your shop before the prices go sky-high."

Hilary tried to look at the brochure Jay had given her, but suddenly her hands were shaking so much the words and photos became blurred. She dared to glance up at Roy—and saw that he'd gone white as the tablecloth!

"May I see that please?" he asked politely, his voice betraying nothing at all.

Hilary was glad to hand the brochure over to him. She watched as he perused it and saw the muscle in his cheek twitch violently. But he only commented, "Interesting. I don't believe I've ever heard of this man."

"Not many people have," Jay put in. "As it happens, I knew Ernie Arruda when I was growing up in Provincetown. He was a close friend of my uncle's, and I saw some of his paintings years ago. Just recently, as I understand it, a niece of his discovered a whole collection of his work stashed away in her attic. Then, some man who has connections in art circles in New York heard about them, went to have a look and that started the ball rolling...."

Roy looked sick.

"One thing led to another," Jay continued urbanely, "and now it looks as if Ernie will finally get the attention he deserves."

Roy glanced at the brochure. "The show begins next week," he managed levelly.

Jay nodded. "That's right."

With a swift gesture, Roy slipped the brochure into his coat pocket. "I'll have to remember that," he decided. Watching him, Hilary realized that only someone who knew him as well as she did would know he was upset. Very upset. He swallowed hard, then said, "Dammit, where is that waitress? Our orders are taking forever."

"Roy, we just placed our orders," Hilary reminded him patiently.

"Well, it seems like forever. Do you eat here very often?" he asked, turning to Jay.

"Now and then," Jay murmured.

"I guess I'm used to the kind of service you get in a city," Roy mumbled.

Hilary smiled. "So is Jay," she said innocently. "He spends a fair bit of time in Boston, don't you, Jay?"

"A fair bit," Jay agreed. "Perhaps you'd like another drink, Mr. LeClair?"

"Thanks, I don't think so." Roy glanced at his watch. "Damn," he complained. "I'd completely forgotten this, but . . . I have an urgent appointment in Provincetown this evening. Hilary, I'm sorry. I wouldn't have suggested we dine tonight if I'd remembered."

"You're not going to leave without having your dinner, are you?" she asked.

"No, of course not. I just wish that girl would get a move on, that's all."

The waitress appeared with their dinners a couple of minutes later. Roy attacked his food as if he hadn't had a meal in weeks, polishing off everything on his plate before Hilary had even finished her salad.

Noting this, Jay said smoothly, "Look, Mr. LeClair, if you have an important date to make, I wouldn't mind seeing Hilary home for you."

"No, no, I wouldn't want to ask that," Roy protested swiftly.

"No problem," Jay said. "It's not out of my way."

"If you're sure..."

Roy, at that moment, looked like a drowning man who'd been tossed a life preserver. "Hilary, I hate to do this...."

"Perfectly all right, Roy," she assured him.

Jay stood. Roy wriggled out of the booth, got to his feet, then paused by Hilary's side. "I'll call you in the morning, darling," he told her, and had the added gall to bend down and kiss her cheek.

Hilary counted to ten. When she was reasonably sure Roy had left the restaurant, she exploded with a wrathful, "I don't believe him!"

Jay laughed. "I rather admire his cool," he admitted.

"You call that cool?"

"Well, I'd say he handled the situation a lot better than most people would. Perhaps he's not as new at this as we thought. I mean, I wonder how many of his paintings are really originals?"

"All the bad ones," Hilary stated dourly.

Jay chuckled. "You should have seen your face when he agreed to let me take you home!"

"Well, he might have flattered me just a little...."

"Are you saying you wanted him to take you home?"

"You know better than that."

Jay's eyes were pure jet. He said softly, "I'm so sorry about this, *cara*."

"About what, Jay?"

"Well, it must be very disillusioning."

"I was disillusioned about Roy a long time ago," Hilary conceded. "I just wasn't facing up to it, that's all."

"Well . . . I'm thankful," Jay said.

"Thankful?"

"Thankful that the experience with Roy didn't turn you off men," he told her.

"Oh, it did," she assured him. "Believe me, I had no intention of getting involved with another man for a long, long time, if ever. Then one night I walked into this phony blue tent and there was this ridiculous fortune-teller . . ."

"Ridiculous, eh?"

"Wonderfully so," Hilary said, letting her love for Jay shine through.

He got the message and asked huskily, "Do you want any dessert?"

"No."

"Okay, I'll get the check." He grinned. "I wonder if your friend Roy will remember he didn't pay his bill," he mused.

"Jay, I'll get it," Hilary said quickly.

"Don't be silly. It was worth twice the tariff to get rid of him," Jay told her. "You know, *cara* . . ."

"Yes?"

"I don't think I've ever wanted quite so much to be alone with you."

Hilary stayed with Jay at his condo that night. He took her home very early in the morning—after presenting her with coffee in bed—and it wasn't until she was in her own house, the day's first sun rays streaking through the windows, that reality struck fully.

She'd escaped with Jay, last night, and then she'd fallen asleep in his arms. This morning, there really hadn't been time to get into anything concerning Roy or what they were going to do about the paintings. Jay promised to call her during the day, and they planned to see each other that night. For the moment, Hilary had to be satisfied with that.

She crept slowly up the stairs. She had the better part of two hours before she had to open the shop and thought about snoozing for one of them. But she was too geared up, too nervous, to relax.

She walked toward her bedroom but stopped on the threshold to take a good look at her present living quarters. Something had to be done about them. Maybe it was the contrast between Jay's place and hers, but she needed something better than this to live in.

During the morning, Hilary called the plumber, the carpenter and the electrician who'd worked on the shop. They agreed to stop by before the end of the day and give her estimates about converting the second floor into a comfortable apartment, as Betty Daniels had originally suggested.

When she reported this to Betty, Betty smiled. "Chalk that up as a couple of personal victories for you, Hilary," she said. "Those men must have liked working for you or they wouldn't be coming around for more at this time of year."

Hilary knew that was true. Still, she didn't feel like chalking up any victories about anything. The whole situation with Roy and the paintings was too much of a blot on her horizon.

It was late afternoon when the electrician, the plumber and then the carpenter appeared. They evaluated the work that needed to be done and gave their estimates. The three men even agreed to synchronize their work, and Hilary decided, on the spot, to give them the go-ahead. She had her line of credit to draw on, so cash wasn't a problem.

Jay called and suggested they drive over to the Beach Shack in Orleans for fried clams, onion rings and a walk by the ocean. By the time they'd finished eating, the beach was surprisingly deserted. Hilary lifted her face to the strong breeze, loving the feel of the sea air on her face and the tangy taste of salt on her lips.

She felt refreshed as she and Jay started back to her house. Refreshed, and ready at last to get into a discussion of what to do about Roy and the paintings. She led Jay out onto the veranda—the tearoom had long since closed for the day—and sat with him sipping chilled lemonade, as dusk gave way to darkness.

"Are you sure about the number of paintings Roy has duplicated?" Jay asked.

"Yes, I doubt if he's hedged about that," she answered. "He was very anxious to sell them all and then start on more. He warned me, though, that he couldn't give me an exclusive after I'd sold the first twenty. He's generated some interest in Boston, evidently."

"The guy's incredible," Jay conceded. "Too bad all that energy and talent can't be channeled in a different way."

Hilary tried not to scoff.

"Look," Jay continued, "I hate to put this to you. But you've got to get him to bring you all the copies he's done of Ernie's work."

She strained to see Jay's face through the darkness and asked, "You're kidding, right?"

"No, I'm not. We need them all before we'll really have the upper hand with Roy. At that point, I doubt we'll have any problem getting him to cease and desist, as far as copying original artwork goes. He'll have the sense to know he's getting off very lightly."

"You mean, we should let him go scot-free?"

"Is there a choice?" Jay asked. "It would really be up to Nick and Rose to prosecute when you get down to it. I don't think you'd have much of a case. You accepted his paintings, after all. He could always claim you were in on the whole thing from the beginning."

"Jay!"

"*Cara*, stop scorching me with your indignation! I know better, but I'd swear to you that's what Roy's testimony

would be in a court of law. Unless Nick and Rose prefer
charges against him, I think it would be difficult to get a jury
to convict him. It would be a long, costly, emotionally
wearing process for everyone."

"Yes, that's true."

"As it is," Jay continued, "the exhibition is slated for
next week. Rose wants to donate half of the proceeds to a
fund that will be set up in Ernie Arruda's name. Nick suggested it be used for the benefit of Cape fishermen who can
no longer work. My idea," Jay proposed, more carefully,
"is to get Roy LeClair to pledge—in a written statement,
which will be duly notarized—that for the next five years he
will donate to this fund twenty-five percent of the money he
makes from his own painting. That should morally even the
score, don't you think?"

Hilary nodded uncertainly, though the thought was appealing.

"He does sell a painting of his own now and then, doesn't
he?"

"Yes," Hilary admitted grudgingly, "he does. He has a
couple of patrons on Beacon Hill." She paused, then added,
"I'm sure this is the first time he's ever copied anything.
Everything else I've seen is . . . well, it's Roy, all right."

After a silent moment, she asked, "What do you think
should be done with the copies?"

"We'll destroy them," Jay retorted promptly. "In fact,
just to make sure, we'll let Roy help us."

"Are you serious?"

"I've never been more serious in my life."

"He'll never go for that!"

"Let's wait and see," Jay cautioned.

Hilary found it difficult to be content with that, but she
couldn't offer any viable alternatives.

They hit the first snag in Jay's plan when Roy refused, the
next morning, to bring in any more of the paintings. Hilary

reached him at Garry Hinfield's apartment on the third try, but Roy sounded breathless as he answered the phone. Nor was he especially pleased to hear her voice.

"What is it, Hil?" he asked sharply.

She'd not only invented a story, she'd rehearsed it to herself several times. She said, "Roy, there's been quite a lot of interest in your paintings today. The ones that have been sold, that is," she fibbed. "You're going to bring down the others, aren't you?"

"No, Hil," Roy told her, his voice catching. "I—I've changed my mind."

"But they'd sell so quickly if you did," she protested.

"I've decided to take my stuff straight to Boston," Roy countered. "Matter of fact, I'd like to take the ones you have, as well. You'll have to refund the money to the customers, of course."

"I can't do that."

"Why not? You still have the paintings in your shop, don't you?"

Hilary caught the anxiety in his voice and realized she should have fibbed again and told him the paintings had already been taken away. Unfortunately, she'd never been very good at dissembling.

"Right," Roy said, noting her silence. "I'll be by later," he promised, and rang off.

Hilary was on edge all day, waiting for him to appear. By five o'clock he still hadn't shown up. She reluctantly waited an extra fifteen minutes, then closed the shop. Jay, she knew, was going to a meeting of the Cape Codders Club. She tried to reach him at the bank, hoping he was working late, but got no answer. Then she let his home phone ring ten times before she finally hung up the receiver.

The old Forsythe homestead suddenly seemed huge, dark and full of shadows. Having made no plans for dinner, Hilary suddenly decided to go out. She had no desire to stay here alone and forage among the tearoom's leftovers for something to eat. Nor did she want to go to any of the restaurants she'd been to with Jay. She'd miss him too much.

She wished she'd called George Delacorte for company, but George and Betty were increasingly a twosome these days, sometimes joining Ed and Helen Bentley for double dates. Hilary thought ruefully that with those four she would, indeed, feel like a fifth wheel.

She settled for picking up a cheeseburger and a milk shake at a local fast-food place and took her supper over to a beach on the bay. Then she sat in her car, watched the glorious sunset and missed Jay terribly.

It was nearly nine o'clock when she got home. She was fumbling in her handbag for her house key when she heard her name called, and swung around so sharply she dropped the key into the grass.

Roy made no secret of his annoyance. "Where the hell have you been?" he demanded roughly.

"Out," Hilary stated coldly.

"You knew I'd be coming by."

"I waited all day for you, Roy," she snapped, refusing to be intimidated. "I thought that was enough."

"Okay, I couldn't make it any sooner. Look, I'm heading up to Boston, and I need to get on the road. Let me in so I can pick up the paintings, will you?"

"I just dropped my keys," Hilary informed him.

Roy swore briefly. Then he said, "I have a flashlight in my car. Wait here while I get it."

Hilary didn't like taking orders from Roy—about anything! She stared after him resentfully, noting that he'd parked his car well down the street. She wondered why he hadn't chosen a closer spot and concluded that he hadn't wanted to be that visible.

A faint sense of alarm stirred her. Still, whatever Roy might be, he wasn't dangerous. He'd certainly never hurt her.

Would he?

Chapter Sixteen

Roy's flashlight needed a new battery. He shone its pale beam around the base of the front steps, but the light was too weak to penetrate very far. "Is there another way to get in?" he asked.

Hilary was scrambling around on her hands and knees, peering through the thick clumps of grass around the base of the steps.

"No, there isn't," she said, getting to her feet. "Everything's locked up tight, and the security system's on."

"Security system?" Roy asked suspiciously.

"That's right. I have too many valuable things on consignment that belong to other people," Hilary informed him. She was tempted to add, "Like your paintings," but she bit back the words. "I had a security system put in not long after I opened the shop," she said instead.

"Damn!" Roy muttered.

Hilary thought she saw a glint in the grass, but decided to overlook it. She suddenly had no desire to find herself alone inside the Forsythe homestead with Roy.

"Look," she suggested. "I could drive uptown and try to get a locksmith to come down here."

"At this hour?" Roy exploded. "That could take all night!"

"If we break a window," she warned, "the alarm will go off and the police will arrive in very short order." At least, Hilary hoped that was true.

Roy muttered something considerably stronger than "damn," while Hilary brushed off her coat. She said firmly, "I'm going to try to find a locksmith."

"Wait a minute," Roy urged. "Look, doesn't anyone else have a key?"

Hilary was tempted to laugh, because Jay had a key. They'd had duplicate keys to their respective dwellings made only yesterday and had exchanged sets. Betty Daniels also had a key, as did Olivia Harris. But Hilary preferred to go with Jay.

"Come to think of it," she said, pretending to remember this, "Jay Mahoney has a key."

"Jay Mahoney, the banker?"

"That's right."

Roy towered over her, his voice dark with anger, and demanded, "Why the hell would Mahoney have a key to your house?"

There was a proprietary note in Roy's tone, which, under other circumstances, Hilary might have found amusing. As it was, she simply said, "I gave him a key, Roy."

"Why, for God's sake?"

"Because I wanted to," she retorted.

"I knew it!" Roy exclaimed, with bitter triumph. "I knew there was something going on between the two of you when we met up with him in that Italian place the other night.

That bit of business when he showed you the brochure about the Arruda exhibition...it was all prearranged, wasn't it?''

Hilary couldn't find words to deny the accusation.

"You know!" Roy snarled. "Damn it all, the two of you knew the other night!"

"Yes, we knew," Hilary admitted. Almost sadly, she added, "Why, Roy? Why did you do it?"

To her surprise, Roy was silent. Then he expelled a deep breath and sat down heavily on the steps. The moon was keeping to itself tonight, but Hilary could see that he was running his hands through his hair. A long moment passed, before he mumbled, "Believe me, I wish I'd never seen the Arruda paintings! The whole damned thing was Hinfield's idea."

"Your friend Garry?"

"Yeah...my *friend* Garry." Roy shook his head, then said bluntly, "Look, those paintings had been stuck away in that attic for years. There was no reason to believe that the Cordeiros would ever do anything with them."

"On the contrary," Hilary pointed out, "the very fact that the Cordeiros were looking around to see if they might sell some of the paintings should have cued you that they weren't going to stay in the attic much longer."

Roy pounded his fist on the step. "Don't you see, Hil?" he demanded. "Garry and I were going to buy the originals."

"You were going to *buy* the Arruda paintings?"

"That's right. We planned to give it a month, to let the Cordeiros think I was talking to people in New York. Then Garry was going to tell them I couldn't strike interest...that the art critics I talked to in New York said the paintings didn't have any real value but were only the work of a fairly competent local artist."

"That's pretty low, Roy."

"Whatever," Roy allowed grudgingly. "What we didn't figure on," he continued, "was that the Cordeiros would get so itchy they'd give up on us and go elsewhere. We thought we were playing it smart by letting them cool their heels for a month."

"It was more like three months," Hilary pointed out levelly.

"I realize that!" Roy moaned. "I still can't believe how this thing has . . . mushroomed, thanks to your friend Mahoney!"

"Jay really didn't have much to do with it," Hilary said quickly. "Rose Cordeiro knew a woman connected with the Provincetown Art Association. She went to her, just as Nick had gone to your friend Garry. Except the response was quite different."

"Tell me about it!"

Hilary gathered courage and asked carefully, "You took photos of all the Arruda paintings, didn't you?"

"Yeah," Roy admitted dully, "all thirty-three of them. Why?"

"How did you manage to do your copies so quickly?"

"Garry happens to have a darkroom," Roy told her. "He enlarged the photographs so that they were practically life-size. All I had to do was sketch them out and mix the right colors. . . ."

"You make it sound so easy," Hilary muttered sarcastically.

"Well, it demanded *some* skill," Roy shot back defensively. "I mean, only another artist could get down the nuances of color and texture. Matter of fact, Garry said he tried and couldn't do it. That's why he took me in on the scheme."

"I see."

Roy stood up so abruptly it startled Hilary. "Oh, what the hell!" he finished. "Where do we go from here, Hil?"

She stiffened. "*We* don't go anywhere, Roy," she said levelly.

"You don't think so, huh?" Roy scoffed. "I can tell you right now that if you blow the whistle about this, whatever happens to me will happen to you. Remember, Hil, you have those paintings for sale in your shop. You've even sold four of them...."

"Wrong," she cut in, shaking her head.

"What do you mean, wrong?"

"I put Sold signs on them because Jay warned me I might be in for some real trouble if they left the shop," Hilary reported.

"But you offered me a check."

"I know."

"I wish I'd taken it," Roy said grimly. "That would have proved complicity."

"You know damn well there isn't any complicity!" Hilary snapped. "Anyway, it appears you're going to get away with your fraud, except you're not going to benefit from it."

"What's that supposed to mean?"

"That you're going to pay, Roy. You're going to help me destroy all your paintings, plus the photographs of the originals."

Hilary felt his eyes burn into her through the darkness. "Like hell I will!" he thundered nastily.

"Ah, but you will," Jay corrected, deadly serious, as he emerged from the deep shadows behind Hilary.

Without taking his eyes off Hilary, Roy muttered, "So, you set me up again, Hil. You, of all people."

"She didn't set you up, LeClair, if you're talking about my suddenly appearing on the scene," Jay said. "My uncle's been keeping a watch on things out in Provincetown. He had a feeling you might head for Devon tonight, so he gave me a call."

Jay started up the steps, and Hilary saw the glint of a key in his hand. Over his shoulder, he said, "My uncle called your studio a while ago, and your friend Hinfield said you'd left for Boston. Phil doubted you'd pass through Devon without stopping by to harass Hilary," Jay concluded, then pushed open the front door. "Got any more questions?"

He flipped off the security system and began switching on lights, making an illuminated path into the house for both Hilary and Roy. Then he marched directly into the shop and over to the wall where the four paintings marked Sold still hung.

"I think we'd better begin here," he announced.

Hilary glanced at Roy. He was ash-white, and his eyes burned like coals. He began furiously, "If you think you're going to do one damned thing to those paintings, Mahoney..."

Jay smiled coldly. "I'm in the mood for a bonfire," he said.

"You think you're going to burn up my paintings?"

"All seven of them, LeClair. There's an empty dumpster out back. It shouldn't take too long, especially since you're going to help me," he ordered, a dangerous edge to his voice.

He reached up and removed the first painting just as Roy lunged. Then, like a matador in a bullfight, Jay neatly stepped back, holding the painting out like a torero's cape. When Roy lunged again, he tossed the painting aside and moved so quickly that Hilary wasn't exactly sure what had happened. She only knew that one moment Roy looked like a menacing wild beast, but the next he was sprawled on the floor!

Jay picked up the discarded painting and said, in an almost conversational tone, "Let's start with this one."

Hilary was watching Roy. He was, figuratively speaking, licking his wounds. Then he slowly struggled to his feet.

"Got a little kerosene stashed someplace, by any chance?" Jay asked Hilary. "It would expedite things."

As it happened, she did. There'd been a small kerosene heater in the kitchen before the remodeling, and Hilary'd stored a leftover can of fuel in the garage. She hurried out to get it for Jay, but her heart was heavy. Regardless of the fact that Roy had forged the Arruda paintings, the copies—while not nearly so beautiful as the originals—were still very lovely. It was a shame they had to be destroyed.

She thought Roy was going to be sick as he watched his paintings burn. As the last one was going up in smoke, Jay said suddenly, "I'll be glad to meet you out in Provincetown tomorrow, LeClair."

"What for?" Roy demanded sullenly.

"To finish the job. My uncle got a permit from the town hall this afternoon to do a little trash burning. Provided there's not too much wind, we shouldn't have any problems."

It was very difficult for Hilary to keep her mind on business the next morning. As she worked in the shop, she had constant visions of what must be going on out in Provincetown between Jay, Phil, Roy and Garry.

Jay had promised to call her as soon as he was back in Devon. Instead, he stopped by Treasures & Tea shortly after noon.

He surprised Hilary from behind and asked, "Could we go upstairs for a few minutes?"

She shook her head. "The workmen are upstairs," she said. "They started this morning. Everything's cleared out of my bedroom. That's where they're beginning."

"And where will you sleep tonight, fair lady?"

"I doubt I'll get any sleep."

"We'll see about that!" Jay quipped. Then, eyeing Hilary closely, he gently observed, "You're very upset about all of this, aren't you?"

"Yes."

"*Cara*, let's get out of here for a few minutes and take a ride over to the harbor. Olivia can look after the shop for a little while, can't she?"

"I suppose so."

"You sound totally dejected," Jay commented once they were in his car.

"It's too bad you had to destroy the paintings."

"I was thinking of Ernie Arruda," Jay said patiently. "I mean, would you have let Roy keep his forgeries?"

"Of course not! I just wish he'd never painted them, that's all."

"So does he."

Hilary looked across at Jay, perplexed.

"It seems Roy has been living on a scale that far exceeds his income," he explained. "He saw a chance to make a small killing with the Arruda paintings and grabbed it. Now he knows he's going to have to cut down considerably on his life-style, especially since he'll be paying twenty-five percent of whatever he makes painting into the Arruda fund for the next five years. If you ask me, I think it'll make a better man out of him."

"I didn't ask you," Hilary stated tartly, "and I wish you wouldn't sound so damned smug!"

Jay stared at her. "Me, smug?"

"Rather like the cat that swallowed the canary," she accused.

"I did what had to be done," Jay stated. "For your information, both Roy and Garry Hinfield were meek as lambs out in Provincetown. Everything has been taken care of. No more forgeries, no more photos. We even shook hands when we parted. Could you ask for more?"

"Yes," Hilary sputtered. "It would be nice if you weren't practically gloating over the way you handled it. My God, Jay...you have it over Roy in every way. Last night, you just about beat him up in my shop...."

"In self-defense," Jay agreed.

"Call it whatever you want," Hilary told him unhappily. "All I know is, you floored him. That surprised me."

"Oh, I see. You expected him to mop up the floor with me, is that it?"

"I don't know what I expected."

"I'm not sure I like that," Jay mused, his brow knitting into a frown. "Just so you'll know, swimming wasn't my only sports activity in college. I also learned judo. In fact, I'm a brown belt."

She glared at him. "What else don't I know about you, Joaquim Mahoney?" she demanded.

Jay grinned approvingly and said, "Nice pronunciation. Maria must be giving you Portuguese lessons."

"That's not funny!"

"*Cara*, don't look so threatening. You know I'll never be able to defend myself against you."

"Dammit, Jay!"

"Hilary, can't you tell yourself that this unhappy episode we've just been through is closed and let it go at that? Everyone's satisfied...even Roy, I think. I honestly don't believe he enjoyed doing the forgeries. He's not that bad a guy."

"My, aren't you charitable," she muttered.

"Sometimes," he allowed, with an infuriating smile.

They reached the harbor, and Jay parked near the breakwater. For a few minutes they sat in silence, just taking in the beauty of Cape Cod Bay. Then Jay said seriously, "Look, Hilary, there's something else I need to discuss with you."

She studied his face. "About the bank?" she guessed.

"Yes."

"Jay," she said, "my going to another bank for a line of credit didn't really have a bad effect on your career, did it?"

He smiled wryly. "No, just on my ego. Actually, it would appear my career is blossoming, *cara*. They want me in two places—Springfield and Boston. Either slot would mean a promotion to vice-president...."

"Well, that sounds pretty impressive," Hilary managed, trying to camouflage the sinking feeling that threatened to engulf her.

"A bank as big as Commonwealth has lots of vice-presidents," Jay told her, passing this off. "Still, it's nice to know that the top hierarchy is giving me opportunities for advancement. I like banking, and I like dealing with people. I like being their friendly neighborhood banker. Fortunately, not too many walk out on me and go elsewhere."

She grinned. "You'll never let me forget that, will you?"

"Probably not," Jay teased, chuckling. "I like having something to hold over your head. Such a lovely head, too..."

"Jay?"

"Ummmm?"

"What are you going to do?"

He swung around and faced Hilary directly, his midnight eyes intense. "What would you have me do, *cara*?"

"Don't you think that's your decision?"

"I'd like to think it's our decision."

Suddenly, Hilary felt at a loss. She stared at Jay, not knowing how to answer him. She knew the bottom of her world would fall out if he moved even as far as Boston, let alone across the state to Springfield. Neither city was really that far away. But she had the awful feeling that if Jay left Devon, it would put more than a geographical distance between them.

He asked gently, "Is my question that hard for you to answer?"

"Yes," she said honestly. "This is your career we're dealing with. I know how hard you've worked and how much this means to you."

His eyebrows arched. "Go on," he invited.

"I suppose what I'm trying to say is . . . I think the decision is one you have to make for yourself, not for me."

Jay leaned back and closed his eyes wearily. Then he asked, "Am I just a summer love for you, Hilary?"

"What?" she answered weakly.

"Summer affairs do happen," Jay ventured, his tone subdued. "Especially in resort areas like Cape Cod. People come together more easily in a vacation setting. They know that when the summer is over they'll go their separate ways, so they're a little less cautious than they might be ordinarily."

Hilary stared at him, stung. "How can you say that to me?" she demanded shakily.

"There's always a chance that Treasures & Tea is just a summer playhouse for you," Jay pointed out. "Come Labor Day, or certainly by Columbus Day, you might decide you've had enough of business for now and prefer to take up residence in Boston. . . ."

"The dossier again?" she asked nastily.

Jay smiled. "The files do show that you'll inherit your uncle's town house in the Back Bay. By this fall his estate should be settled, and you'll be quite a wealthy young woman. You'll have more money than I could ever hope to have. That's something I've considered," he finished.

Hilary flinched. "I don't believe you, Jay."

"Don't you? I for one am fully aware of the differences in our backgrounds. Add to that a considerable difference in bank accounts and a few gaps could loom up, wouldn't you say?"

"No, I wouldn't say."

Jay shook his head. He said, "It occurred to me that if you do intend to move back to Boston in the fall maybe I should take the job in Springfield."

Hilary felt sick. Inside, she began to crumble. "If that's the way you want it," she said coldly, instinctively dodging behind her ice-maiden facade.

Jay watched her for a long moment without saying anything. Then, suddenly, he grinned. "So!" he exulted triumphantly. "You really do want me around, don't you?"

The ice began to melt. "Am I so transparent?"

"Only to me, I hope," Jay murmured. He reached over and touched Hilary's hair. "*Cara*," he said gently, "I had to say these things to you. I wasn't trying to hurt you. Anyway, I've already decided what I'm going to do, and I'm meeting with Bert Doane in Boston tomorrow afternoon to give him my decision."

Jay felt Hilary stiffen and saw the mute plea in her clear blue eyes. "I'm going to stay in Devon," he told her.

"*What?*"

"I'm going to stay in Devon."

"Do you really mean that?"

"Absolutely, Hilary. The Cape has been growing for some time now, and—for better or worse—it's bound to continue. There's a lot to be done with Commonwealth's Devon branch. Horace Mayo was an excellent manager. I'm not faulting him. But I don't think the bank's entirely kept up with the times. So I've worked up a portfolio of ideas to present to Mr. Doane tomorrow. I'm reasonably certain that he'll agree with everything I've suggested, including leaving me in Devon to oversee our operations on the Cape."

Jay paused, then admitted, "I still hope to take them up on that offer of a vice-presidency I told you about, but not for a while. It would mean moving to Boston, and I'm not ready for that, yet. Perhaps in a year or two, when your business here will be established to the point that you can hire a manager to run it . . ."

Hilary smiled. "You do think ahead, don't you?"

"Where you're concerned, yes."

"Don't you know," she queried softly, "that I'd follow you anywhere, Joaquim Alvaro Mahoney? Don't you know that nothing much matters to me except being with you? Don't you know that I'd go to Boston, or Springfield, or to the ends of the earth with you?"

"How about all the way to the stars?" Jay asked huskily.

"Yes, all the way to the stars."

Returning to work that afternoon was a terrible letdown. By the time Hilary closed the shop, she felt grumpy and out of sorts. She couldn't wait to get upstairs and take a bubble bath.

The workmen had left earlier, happy to report that her bathroom was finished—it had only needed scraping and painting. In a day or two, she was told, she'd be able to move back into her bedroom. Meanwhile, she'd set up a cot in the corner in one of her storage rooms, where she planned to spend the night. It was hardly luxurious, but Hilary was so tired she could have fallen asleep right on the floor.

Just as she was closing the last window in the shop, Betty Daniels appeared.

"How about a cup of tea?" Betty invited cheerily.

The two women seldom had the chance to get together, and Hilary hated to turn Betty down. "Okay," she agreed, hiding her reluctance.

They took their tea out on the veranda and sat down.

"Phew!" Betty exclaimed. "It feels great to get off my feet."

"I'll second that," Hilary managed.

Betty still had energy, though, and Hilary couldn't remember her ever being so voluble. She rattled on and on about a variety of things, until it was all Hilary could do not to get up and excuse herself.

Suddenly, Betty glanced at her wristwatch and smiled. "Well," she said, "I'd better be going."

Betty'd literally been in the middle of a sentence and had shut herself up so abruptly that Hilary was nonplussed. Still, Hilary was grateful to start up the stairs, her concentration solely on the long, steamy bubble bath she was planning to take.

When she reached the top of the stairs, she saw that the shades on the hall windows had been pulled. The hallway was in semidarkness, and there was a weird, bluish light emanating from her bedroom.

One of the painters, or maybe the electrician, must have forgotten to turn something off, Hilary reasoned, as she neared the room. Then, reaching the threshold, she gasped aloud.

Several lamps with blue light bulbs had been placed around the empty room. In the center was a round table with a fringed red cloth that touched the floor. Dominating the table top were a crystal ball, behind which sat Madame Zola in purple robes, a gold turban and a lacy black face veil.

"Ah!" Hilary was greeted. "Come right in, *cherie*."

Wavering between laughter and tears of joy, Hilary advanced through the musky aroma of incense and took the chair Madame Zola indicated. She stretched out her right hand even before she was asked to. Immediately, it was enveloped by a much larger hand encased in an absurd pink glove.

"You have come back to me," Madame Zola murmured in dulcet tones heightened by a wonderfully phony accent, "so that I can finish the fortune I began for you. Am I right?"

"Yes," Hilary whispered, smiling to herself. Now she could understand why Betty had delayed her. Betty and Jay had been in cahoots!

Eyes black as midnight surveyed her. "A tall, dark man has invaded your life, has he not?"

Hilary nodded dutifully.

"And you have promised to seek the stars with him?"

"I hope so."

"Soon," Madame Zola intoned, peering intently into the crystal ball, "you will marry him. I see...three children, and a lifetime of blissful happiness. Meanwhile, you are to wear this, to keep you aware of his love for you and secure in it forever."

Hilary saw the shimmer of gold in Madame Zola's hands and recognized the medallion Ernie Arruda had given Jay a long time ago. A lump filled her throat, because she knew how much this gift meant to Jay.

"Bend forward," she was commanded.

She did so, and Madame Zola carefully fastened the medallion around her neck.

"You will marry your star seeker, will you not?" she was asked. Madame Zola's voice had suddenly grown husky.

"I will marry him."

"And you will stay with him forever?"

"Yes."

Madame Zola exhaled a deep breath, seemingly relieved. "In the future," she advised, "you might share a few more confidences with this man...like the fact that your birthday is the day after tomorrow!"

Hilary had completely forgotten about her birthday. Staring at the familiar eyes across from her, she demanded, "How did you know?" Then, remembering, she answered her own question. "That damned dossier! It must even have my birth date on it!"

"Indeed it does," she was informed.

"And you looked it up!"

Madame Zola chuckled. "The star seeker did not need to look it up. He recalled seeing it once before...."

Hilary felt love infuse her, watching this wonderful man she'd just promised to marry. "How am I going to live with your memory?" she teased.

Jay pulled off his turban and face veil, and flashed Hilary his most devastating smile. "Learn to appreciate it, *cara*," he suggested simply.

Coming around the table to embrace him, Hilary did exactly that.

Silhouette Special Edition

COMING NEXT MONTH

#385 FORBIDDEN FRUIT—Brooke Hastings
Noble Lady Georgina felt obliged to marry her social equal. But
when her grandmother hired macho, working-class Mike Napoli to
chaperone Georgina, attraction soon outranked obligation!

#386 MANDREGO—Tracy Sinclair
Elissa had vowed to avenge her father's ruin. Her plot led her to
an island paradise—and into the arms of her enemy's bodyguard,
dangerously attractive Troy Benedict. Could revenge possibly be so
sweet?

#387 THE MIDNIGHT HOUR—Jude O'Neill
Sassy Cleo and wise-cracking Gus were once partners in mystery
writing and marriage, but their famed collaboration had led to
calamity. If they reunited, would they be crafty enough to write
themselves a happy ending?

#388 THE BABY TRAP—Carole Halston
Ginny Sutherland wanted a baby—without the complication of
remarrying. Still, she'd need a male temporarily, and virile Ed
Granger might just be the man for the job....

#389 THE SUN ALWAYS RISES—Judith Daniels
Restaurateur Catherine Harrington didn't want to love and lose
again, but wandering, "no-commitments" Nick O'Donovan was
convincing her to take the risk....

#390 THE FAIRY TALE GIRL—Ann Major
When her fairy tale marriage failed, Amber Johnson left the
Bahamas with her illusions destroyed. So how could she believe
rancher Jake Kassidy's promise that with him she'd live happily
ever after?

AVAILABLE THIS MONTH:

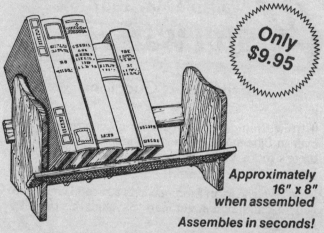

Available May 1987

Still Waters

by
Leslie Davis Guccione

If Drew Branigan's six feet of Irish charm won you over in *Bittersweet Harvest*, Silhouette Desire #311, there's more where he came from—meet his hoodlum-turned-cop younger brother, Ryan.

In *Still Waters*, Ryan Branigan gets a second chance to win his childhood sweetheart, Sky, and this time it's for keeps.

Then look for *Something in Common*, coming in September, 1987, and watch the oldest Branigan find the lady of his dreams.

After raising his five younger brothers, confirmed bachelor Kevin Branigan had finally found some peace. He certainly didn't expect vibrant Erin O'Connor to turn his world upside down!

D353-1